OLD HOUSE OF FEAR

OLD HOUSE
OF FEAR

Russell Kirk

WILLIAM B. EERDMANS PUBLISHING COMPANY
GRAND RAPIDS, MICHIGAN / CAMBRIDGE, U.K.

© 1961 by Fleet Publishing Corporation

This edition published 2007 by
Wm. B. Eerdmans Publishing Co.
2140 Oak Industrial Drive N.E., Grand Rapids, Michigan 49505 /
P.O. Box 163, Cambridge CB3 9PU U.K.

Printed in the United States of America

11 10 09 08 07   7 6 5 4 3 2 1

Library of Congress Cataloging-in-Publication Data

Kirk, Russell.
Old house of fear / Russell Kirk.
p.   cm.
ISBN 978-0-8028-1762-4 (pbk.: alk. paper)
1. Americans — Scotland — Fiction.   I Title.

PS3521.I665O43   2004
813'.54 — dc22
                                          2006103519

www.eerdmans.com

Contents

OLD HOUSE OF FEAR

CHAPTER 1

On this shrouded night, five men tossed in a boat off the island of Carnglass, where the sea never is smooth. So thick about them hung the fog that they could not see the great cliffs. Knowing, though, every rock and reef, they sensed where the island lay.

Of a sudden, a tall flame shot up from Carnglass, fierce and unnatural. Across the swell there came to the men in the boat the crash of some explosion. Clinging to their oars, they stared silent toward the land; the oldest man crossed himself. The flame, surging and waving for some minutes, soon sank lower. In a little while they heard faint distant sounds, several of them, like gunshots. The younger men looked to the old helmsman, who pulled hesitantly at his white beard.

Then he signed to them to put the boat about. Glancing fearfully at the distant flame as they heaved, two men hauled at the sail. In a minute they had changed course, and the fire in the night glowed at their backs as they pulled away from the uneasy neighborhood of silent and invisible Carnglass.

Three thousand miles away, two men sat in a handsome office. "That's our island," Duncan MacAskival said: "Carnglass."

Across the Ordnance Survey map his thick forefinger moved to a ragged and twisted little outline, away at the verge of the Hebrides, which even upon the linen of the map seemed to recoil from the Atlantic combers. "The tattered top of a drowned mountain. And that's the castle, by the bay to the West, Hugh: Old House of Fear. I like the names. You're to buy Carnglass for me, cliffs and clachans and deer-forest and Old House and all; and price is no object."

Hugh Logan smiled at the heavy old man in the swivel chair. "Why send me to the Western Isles to haggle for a speck of rock I know nothing about, Mr. MacAskival? Why do you need Carnglass? And why not have a Glasgow solicitor do the business for you? I'd enjoy the trip, right enough, but I don't need to tell you that my time costs you bona fide money. Any junior clerk could buy an island for you."

"Look out there, Hugh." MacAskival swung round his chair to the big window at the back of his teak-panelled office. Far below, stretching eastward for a quarter of a mile along the river, the stacks and coke-ovens and corrugated-iron roofs of MacAskival Iron Works sent up to heaven their smoke and flame and thunder. "Look at it all. I made it. And what has it given me? Two coronary fits. I'm told to rest. But where could a man like me fade decently? I'm not made for quiet desperation. There's just one place, Hugh, where I might lie quiet; and that's Carnglass."

MacAskival peered at his map. "I haven't seen Carnglass," he went on, "except in pictures, and no more did my father, or his father. But the MacAskivals came out of Carnglass to Nova Scotia in 1780, and they didn't forget the little croft below Cailleach — that's the sharp hill north of the Old House, Hugh. Their Nova Scotia farm was sand and stumps, and yet not so barren as that Carnglass croft. Still, they'd have traded ten farms in Nova Scotia for that wet little plot in Carnglass. And after two strokes, I think I'd give the mills and all for that croft — with the island thrown in."

Logan had walked to the window, and now stood looking toward the glare of the coke-ovens; the flames went up hotly into the Michigan twilight, that April evening, and the incandescent masses of coal fell roaring. "Why, I think we might make a better bargain than that, Mr. MacAskival. Peat bogs and tumbledown castles go cheap nowadays. But why do you mean to send a man like me to buy you a few square miles of dripping misery?"

"Cigar, Hugh?" MacAskival pushed a box toward him. "The doctor says I can have just one of these a day. Well, I'm not so crazy as I seem, and you know it. Under your veneer, you're like me — sentimental as a sick old ironmaster. Don't tell me you've never thought of having an island all to yourself. So I'd like to see you hunt this dream of mine; you work too hard for your age. 'Getting and spending, we lay waste our powers.' I don't plan to bare my bosom to the moon in Carnglass, but it should do you good to play at being a pagan suckled in a creed outworn — for a few days, anyhow."

Old Duncan MacAskival was a trifle vain of his quotations and allusions, Logan thought. But Logan liked MacAskival, a self-made man, a good deal better than the average product of the big business-administration schools. It came to Logan that he, Hugh Logan, rapidly was growing into an old man's young man. It had been more than a dozen years since he had led a battalion in Okinawa. He knew much of Scotland, born in Edinburgh as he had been, though his parents had taken him to America when he was nine; and he had gone back to take a degree at Edinburgh University. A slackening of pace, for a week or two, might do no mischief. All his life he had hurried: schools, the university, the war, and the firm: in too much of a hurry, either side of the water, to laugh, to marry, or even to dream. "No Mr. MacAskival," Logan said, "I'm not the man to laugh at you. But you're a canny Scot, though five generations removed. Do you need to pay my price just to draw up a deed to an island?"

"You're more of a Scot than I am, Hugh, though you look American enough nowadays." MacAskival leant back in his heavy chair. "Well, yes, you'll be worth your price in this business. You know something of Scots law and tenures. And you can wheedle odd customers; Lady MacAskival is one of that breed, they tell me. Here, look at yourself in that mirror." MacAskival nodded toward the baroque glass against the teak panelling.

Logan saw reflected a mild-seeming, amiable face — or so most people would call it, probably — almost unlined; still a young man's face. Sometimes, when he had been a major of infantry, that face had tended to mislead people, and then Logan had to rectify impressions. He had a spare body. "Do I look like a fool?" he asked MacAskival.

"Not exactly a fool, boy, but close enough. You're innocent: that's the word, Hugh. What a face to set before a jury — or a crazy old creature like Lady MacAskival! Anyone signing a contract with you assumes that he's had the better of the bargain. Now I've tried before this to buy

Carnglass; I've been at it more than three years. I've tried those Glasgow solicitors. They're too sharp: what we need with Lady MacAskival is babyish innocence."

"Can't you find any intermediary but a Glasgow solicitor?"

"Why, Hugh, somehow I got in touch with a retired major or captain — Indian Army, I think — who wrote that he might do my business for me. He seemed to want his palm greased. His name was George Hare, or George Mare, or something of that sort."

Logan rubbed his chin. "In Glasgow? There was a criminal case, if I'm not mistaken — something to do with state secrets, or vexing little girls, or some nasty affair — in Scotland, a year or two ago, with the defendant a cashiered Indian Army officer — and that sort of name. I may have a clipping about it in my files. I'm not sure, though, that the name was either Hare or Mare. A captain, I think."

"For all I know, Hugh, this may be your man: anyway, though I greased his palm in moderation, I've never had a line from him since. He said he knew Lady MacAskival. So that's a bribe down the drain. Now will you take my shilling?"

"All right: I'll take my innocence to Carnglass." Smiling, Logan turned back to the map on the big desk. "There still are MacAskivals in the island, then? And what sort of cousin of yours is this Lady MacAskival?"

"Call me Duncan, Hugh," MacAskival said, "if you'll really take up the business for me. No, there's not a real MacAskival left in Carnglass, so far as I can learn. Lady MacAskival was born Miss Ann Robertson; her family owned distilleries, money-makers. It was a queer match when she married Colonel Sir Alastair MacAskival, Indian Army, who was old enough to be her father, or more. Sir Alastair had scars and medals, but nothing besides. Though he was chief of the MacAskivals — and there's precious few of that little clan left — he was born in a but-and-ben in North Uist. I get all this from an Edinburgh genealogist. Sir Alastair's great-grandfather ran through his property so as to keep up a fine show in London. The Great Clearance of Carnglass was in 1780 — that's when my people were booted out, you remember — and it was the work of that old reprobate Donald MacAskival, our Sir Alastair's great-grandfather: he turned the whole island into two big farms and a sheepwalk, on the chance of squeezing more money from the rents, and told all the crofting MacAskivals to go to Hell or Glasgow. A few had the money for steerage passage to Nova Scotia, which eventually made me president of MacAskival Iron Works. My father was a pushing Scot, and so am I — and you, too, Hugh."

"So Ann Robertson brought money back to the MacAskivals more than a hundred years after the Clearance?"

"Not simply money, Hugh, but Carnglass itself. What little extra Donald MacAskival contrived to wring out of the rents after the Great Clearance did him no good. He died bankrupt; and the creditors took Carnglass. His son sank down to being the factor for a small laird in North Uist, and there the family lived on, hand to mouth, until young Alastair went out to India and got some reputation for himself along the Northwest Frontier. When he was past forty, he sailed home to Edinburgh on leave. There he met Ann Robertson, and married her, and they bought back Carnglass with Robertson money, and restored Old House of Fear."

Logan bent over the map to find the tiny square that marked the Old House. "That's an uneasy name, Duncan, for an ironmaster who wants peace and quiet."

"But it's a brave old house, Hugh. And the name is Gaelic, not English: 'fear' is spelled 'fir' or 'fhir,' sometimes, and it means 'man.' Old House of Fear is Old House of Man. Old! Why, the foundations of the oldest tower go back to Viking times. The Norsemen took Carnglass in 799 or thereabouts. But there was some sort of chief's house — Picts or whatever they were — before then. There's a tale in the island that Carnglass was Eden: man started there, and woman too, I suppose. But Carnglass hasn't many living souls today. Old Donald MacAskival swept off five hundred people — MacAskivals and MacLeods and MacDonalds — in the Great Clearance, which left only thirty or forty souls, all named MacAskival, in the whole island. There still were twenty or thirty of their descendants living in Carnglass when Alastair and Ann bought it back. But Ann, Lady MacAskival, isn't much of a hand for company, it seems; because when Sir Alastair died, in 1914, she got rid of what MacAskival crofters were left. Off they went to a smaller island, Daldour, three miles south across the Sound of Carnglass, one soaking peat bog: if Carnglass was Eden, Daldour was Hell. And there they are still, for all I know, if they haven't starved. Our Lady MacAskival, who's over eighty now, lives alone at the Old House with only a handful of Lowland and English servants, according to what I could learn from Ed-

inburgh. She never leaves Carnglass. And she doesn't often answer letters."

"Then she's not even a cousin of sorts to you?"

"Not she. The chiefs of MacAskival were of Norse stock — the
name's Norse, at least. And she's from the Lowlands. Sir Alastair and she
never had children — I gather, besides, there wasn't much love lost between them — and she has no heirs, so far as I can find. And anyway,
Hugh, the odds are that I'm a Pict or a Scot, not a Viking. The island people generally took the chief's name for a surname, though they might
have no blood connection, I don't mean to set up for chief of Clan
MacAskival: my people were fishermen or crofters who got themselves
killed, now and then, in MacAskival's feuds. Old Donald MacAskival's
father was out for the Pretender in '45, which is one reason why Donald
went so deep in debt and made the Clearance. No, all I want is to live in
the Old House and look across the Sound of Carnglass, Hugh. That's the
dream that I want you to buy for me."

"The Old House is liveable, then, Duncan?"

"Sound enough, they say, though hardly anyone but Lady
MacAskival and her servants has seen the inside of it since 1914. That
Edinburgh man couldn't find any photographs for me later than 1914."
MacAskival pulled open a drawer. "There they are: not very good pic-
tures, taken the year Sir Alastair died. It seems to have been foggy that
day."

"I presume it usually is foggy in your tight little island, Duncan," Logan said as he took up the half-dozen old prints. "There's no inhabited
island further out into the Atlantic." Foggy, yes; and yet the great bulk of
Old House of Fear loomed distinctly enough in the middle ground of the
photograph. Carnglass meant "gray stone," and the whole stern mass of
masonry was of a gray that blended into the outcrop of living rock upon
which the Old House was built. But the castle was not of a single period.
The first photograph showed, on the left, an enormous square tower of
rubble, capped by a high-pitched roof apparently sheathed with stone
slabs. At one corner of this tower, a little turret stood up, perhaps covering the top of a stair in the thickness of the wall; Logan knew something
about Scottish medieval architecture. To this great tower was joined a
range of domestic buildings, three stories high, with dormers and
crowstepped gables, also built of gray rubble: early seventeenth-century
work, Logan thought. A smaller square tower closed the range. And

then, abruptly tacked upon the right side of the smaller tower, commenced a mansion-house of ashlar, with small barred windows on the ground floor but very large windows of plate glass above; this was in the Scottish "baronial" style of Victorian times, yet carried out with some taste and not altogether disharmonious with the medieval and seventeenth-century buildings. A large door in the middle of this latter-day façade seemed wide enough for a carriage to pass through; perhaps it led to an interior courtyard. "All this on the right is Sir Alastair's addition?" Logan asked.

"Yes," said MacAskival, "and the place is bigger even than it looks: there's a courtyard behind, with buildings all round. The Robertson distilleries paid for it. When Sir Alastair and his wife bought back the island, the original castle hadn't been lived in for seventy years or more, and the roof was collapsing but they put everything in shape and made the place twice as big. I suppose old Lady MacAskival rattles about in it now. Even though she's one of the richest old women in Britain, income tax and surtax won't let her keep much more than five thousand pounds' income, and that probably only pays the servants she has left, and for her food. She has trouble finding help, by the way, I hear. It's not everyone who wants to scrub floors in Old House of Fear."

"And you want a white mastodon?"

"Only to die in," MacAskival told him, cheerfully. "Every man to his own humor, Hugh. I have the money to keep the place as long as I live; and if I stay there only from time to time, I can keep clear of British income tax. I may as well spend a few million, because the Treasury and that foundation you set up for me will take all that's left when I die, anyway. I might leave you the Old House, though: it shouldn't take you long to acquire a taste for that style of living."

Hugh was turning over the other photographs. "One of the clachans: one of the two villages in Carnglass. These are what they call black houses, because the peat smoke just goes out of a hole in the roof, after circulating round the room — but I suppose you know all this, Hugh. Snug, anyway. And I don't suppose any one of these is lived in now, except possibly by a gamekeeper or two. Now have a look at this other picture. What do you make of it?"

In the foreground, Hugh saw a desolate graveyard, a low drystone wall enclosing it; some tall white monuments showed above the wall, and in the center stood, at a perilous angle, an immense Celtic cross. Beyond the monuments was what seemed to be an ancient chapel with a modern roof. And away in the background there hulked, dimly, a tall circular building, rather like a vast beehive.

"It all looks like something from before the Flood," Logan murmured.

"Well, much of it is nearly as old as anything in Iona," MacAskival observed. "That's the chapel of St. Merin. She was stoned to death, I think, in the days of St. Columba. Sir Alastair restored the chapel as the family burial-vault. And that's the famous Cross of Carnglass, tenth-century; or it would be famous, if Lady MacAskival ever let archeologists ashore. I don't know what the thing beyond can be. Do you feel more like becoming Laird of Carnglass?"

"It's a strange island," Logan said, unsmiling.

"Yet it can't be so strange as the rumors make it." MacAskival was pleased, clearly, at having shaken Logan out of his commonsensical ways. "Except for a few friends from London, the old lady's let nobody poke about since her own little clearance of 1914. They say that boats trying to put into the harbor have been shot at. And they say there are more bogles stalking through the heather than there are live folk. And servants who've left the Old House have told people in Oban and Glasgow that some of the London visitors are worse than the bogles."

"Scotland has no law of trespass — only acts of interdict after damage has been done to property."

"You can tell that to our old lady, Hugh. If we do get Carnglass, I'll let the archeologists and the naturalists browse. I'm told there are rare plants and birds, and a few fallow deer still. Nearly the whole island has become deer forest. One of the farms — the one closer to the old house — seems to be kept in fair order; they have Highland cattle. I learned that from Lagg, the factor, a Galloway man."

"You've corresponded with him, Duncan?"

"In a unilateral way. First, three years ago, I wrote to Lady MacAskival herself: no answer. Then I found out the names of her London solicitors. I sent them an offer, and they wrote that they'd refer it to Lady MacAskival. Then silence. I wrote again. The solicitors answered that Lady MacAskival would give me a reply after reflection. More silence. I wrote to the solicitors a third time, a year ago yesterday, and got a letter back promptly: Lady MacAskival no longer did business with them, they said, and I should write to her factor in Carnglass, Thomas

Lagg. I did. Ten months ago, Lagg replied that Lady MacAskival was in-disposed, but would communicate with me after some interval. She never has said no — mind that, Hugh. Then still more silence. I wrote to Lagg three times; no reply. But yesterday this letter came." From under his blotter MacAskival drew a sheet of cheap notepaper, which curled up as he tried to lay it before Logan.

"I told you she was odd," MacAskival said, as Logan smoothed the sheet. "The envelope was curled, too, and only partly straightened by having been in a mail-bag." Also the paper seemed water-stained, and the writing in one corner had run badly. Though it was in a clear femi-nine hand, it appeared to have been written very hastily:

"*3rd March*

"*Duncan MacAskival, Esq.*

"*Sir:*

Lady MacAskival desires to discuss with you at once the pro-posal which you have set forth. She requests that you come in person to Carnglass without delay, or send confidential agents. Immediate action is imperative."

There was no signature. "Lady MacAskival's own hand?" Logan in-quired.

"Presumably," MacAskival said. "The doctor tells me that I'm not quite fit for ocean cruises just now. So Hugh Logan, Esquire, is my confi-dential agent. Do you think you can act properly conspiratorial? I saw you as Cassius in the Players' Club performance of *Julius Caesar* last month, you remember, Hugh; and you were the best man in the cast. You'd have done as well as a professional actor as you have with the law. Well, I've cabled both the old lady and Lagg. I've told them that you'll ar-rive this week."

"This week, Duncan? Next month, at the soonest."

MacAskival's thick eyebrows lowered. "Hugh Logan, I've given you a boost for your firm, now and then. I'm not a man who enjoys being crossed — you know that. Now this business is something that matters to me. Who knows how much longer the old lady will live? I don't in-tend to miss this chance, after three years of trying. If you think any-thing of me, you'll fly to Prestwick tomorrow; and it will do you good,

Hugh: an easy bit of work in a charming quiet place. We can't delay. Notice the date of that letter. It's been stuck somewhere en route; and it
came by ordinary surface mail, which took a week or more. I don't want
the old lady to change her mind. In my cables, I asked to have Lady
MacAskival's yacht — I suppose she must own something of the sort —
put into Glasgow or Greenock for you. You've a room reserved at Todd's
Hotel, Glasgow, and Lady MacAskival's people should get in touch with
you there. Will you go, or do I have to send some fool? I want to use
your innocence-mask, Hugh."

"Needs must when the devil drives," Logan said in his easy way.
"Give me those plane tickets. I usually humor madmen. Besides, I mean
to find out what that beehive building is."

"Then it's my Carnglass." Duncan MacAskival slapped his hand
against the desk. "Here" — he fetched out a manila envelope — "here's
my correspondence with the old lady's people. And here's some estimate of what the island ought to cost, kit and kaboodle, that I got from
solicitors in London and Glasgow. And this, too — this will interest you,
Hugh."

It was a slim old pamphlet, the covers nearly ripped away. "It's rare,
Hugh. Thin's of Edinburgh found a copy for me. Take it along to read on
your plane." MacAskival opened to the title page: "A Summary History
of the Islands of Carnglass and Daldour, in the Western Isles of Scotland; with some Account of the Traditionary Tales of those Parts. By the
Reverend Samuel Balmullo, sometime minister of the Parish of
Carnglass and Daldour. 1818." MacAskival was something of a book-
collector. "I know you're wanting dinner, Hugh," MacAskival said, "and
I'll take you to the club in a minute or two, but let me read you a bit of
this:

"'Among the surviving peasantry of Dalcruach village, on the eastern strand of Carnglass, superstition exerts an influence as powerful as
it is debasing. In this clachan are said to reside four or five Sgeulaiche,
or narrators of traditional tales of an extravagant character, many of
which antedate the arrival of Christian evangels from Ireland in the
sixth century. These relations often reflect, and endeavor to excuse, the
lingering of heathen and impious practices among this ignorant folk.
They speak, for example, of a "Third Eye," said to appear afresh, from
generation to generation, among the inhabitants of Carnglass, whether
native-born or newcomers; and such a spot upon the forehead is said to

confer amatory powers, and is regarded by these children of the twilight with a respect not far removed from veneration. To labor among parishioners possessed by such delusions is weary work; it has been said that to preach the Gospels among the Pequots or Narragansetts is a facile undertaking by the side of any endeavor to redeem from heathen error these denizens of the furthermost Hebrides.'"

MacAskival turned the page. "The Reverend Samuel Balmullo — he was from the Lowlands, Hugh — tends to be longwinded, but rewarding. Balmullo seems to have been a sour old fellow. He was interested in the MacAskivals, though — give me a moment more." Duncan MacAskival leafed through the pamphlet.

"'Indubitably,'" he read, "'a family of the first antiquity in the Isles, the chiefs of MacAskival, though at present reduced to mean estate, are said to be a sept of the MacDonalds, Lords of the Isles, early parted from their headship by internecine conflicts. These MacAskival chiefs themselves maintain, however — and with some show of reason — that they descend from a stock older still. As their ancestor and the founder of their fortunes, they claim a certain Sigurd Askival, a Viking adventurer, who espoused the Pictish heiress of Carnglass, one Mary or Merin. This noble lady of Carnglass was a woman of remarkable beauty, despite her flowing mane of red hair, which the refined taste of modern days would disapprove. In passing, it is necessary to notice a tale, germane to the genealogical claims of MacAskival, that one Mary or Merin, saint and princess, at a remote period was redeemed from captivity to a bestial creature, described as the Gabharfear, Firgower, or man-goat; and that her rescuer was Sigurd Askival, a Norse freebooter.

"'One single substantial proof of the venerable lineage of MacAskival is reputed to have survived well into the last century: a set of chessmen carven from a blue stone, the "Table-Men of Askival," exhibiting the weird handiwork of a ferocious epoch, which objects long continued the proudest possession of the chieftain of MacAskival. These, however, no longer are to be found in the Old House of Fear, their asserted repository; nor have they been transferred to the elegant New House by the quay, although the present proprietor made close search for the pieces. According to one fabrication of the aged men of Carnglass, these "Table-Men" were immured in a tomb by the last chieftain, to propitiate the Fiend. Once more the author apologizes to his gentle readers for this trespass upon their hours of serious reflection.'"

"Old Mr. Balmullo," Logan broke in, "seems to have taken a fearful joy in recording superstitions. He protests too much."

"Yes, I think Carnglass bewitched Samuel Balmullo, Hugh. 'Glamour' is an old Scots word, you know. Watch out, boy, that some Hebridean Witch doesn't catch you: three days in Carnglass might turn the trick."

"Never fear, Duncan," Logan told him, with his slow smile. "The Harding case comes up next month, and I'll be back for it."

"Fear? Why, there's no danger of any sort in Carnglass, I suppose." MacAskival turned again to the window overlooking the plant. Now it was dark, and the coke-ovens glowed against the night like the flaming City of Dis. "Danger? Probably Carnglass is one of the few tolerably secure places on earth. Sometimes I think we'll turn the world into one final hell of a coke-oven, Hugh. There may be some islands, though, left in that fire. And Carnglass, where man began, ought to endure when man has put an end to himself. I hope you can put this MacAskival back into his island, Hugh."

"You're really going to give me dinner at your club, Duncan?"

Nodding, MacAskival reached for their coats. As they went out of the office, he turned quizzically toward the younger man. "Speaking of witches and bogles and man-goats, Hugh, why hasn't any woman ever captured you?"

"Probably because there's no romance in me," Logan murmured, straightfaced.

"Why, there's a good deal in you, Hugh. You're canny, but have a certain way with you."

"Don't forget this, though, Duncan —

"'You can grave it on his tombstone, you can cut it on his card:
A young man married is a young man marred.'"

"Well! Hugh, you're full of surprises. I thought only aged creatures like me still read Kipling. I can match you —

"'Down to Gehenna or up to the Throne,
He travels fastest who travels alone.'

Which way are you travelling, Hugh, with that innocent face of yours?"

"Judging by what you tell me of the warlocks of Carnglass, down to Gehenna, Duncan." Then the elevator came, and the club, and the dinner, and the brandy. That night Logan dreamed of a Carnglass Cutty Sark capering round Carnglass Cross. And the next night he was aboard the plane to Prestwick.

Chapter 2

On a wet and windy morning, Logan descended from the plane at Prestwick. Once past the immigration officers, he took a taxi across the moors to Glasgow. Now and then they sped past rows of white-harled Scots cottages, some empty and far gone in decay. The heather and gorse by the roadside called to Hugh Logan. He had walked the Pentland Hills, and the Lammermuirs, in his Edinburgh years — sleeping in the open, sometimes, when he had been a university student. The law-office and the courtroom seemed remote in time and space, as he sat in this speeding Rolls; and he indulged the fancy that perhaps he ought never to have taken the bar-examination.

In some ways, those savage months of pushing northward in Okinawa had been the best of his life. The law was safe, and might make him famous; yet there came hours, now and again, when Logan thought he ought to have settled for a life of risk, a life lived as if every moment might be the last.

The cab-driver was saying something. "A foul day, sir. There'll be a storm out tae sea, sir. Spring's late to Scotland this year." The driver never had heard of Carnglass, Logan found. Now they were coming into the ugly sprawl of outlying Glasgow council-houses. And then the great grimy city closed upon them, and soon Logan was getting out before Todd's Hotel in India Street, a building of blackened white granite.

At Todd's Hotel, the taffy-haired little receptionist in the tight black dress never had heard of Carnglass. Having left his suitcase in his room,

Logan came down again to inquire of the manager. That civil gentle-man, indeed, had heard of Carnglass; but he never had known anyone to go there. And no messages from Lady MacAskival or Mr. Lagg were awaiting Logan. He was not altogether surprised: eccentricity and delay were to be expected in that quarter; he suspected that he might have to make his way independently to the island.

He might telephone or telegraph, though, to learn whether the yacht or launch had been sent for him, and whether he would be welcome at the Old House. It was no use, he soon discovered: the information opera-tor on the telephone, after lengthy consultation with someone at the Glasgow central exchange, informed Logan that there was no cable laid to Carnglass, and that no way of sending messages to the island was known, there being no wireless recorded in the exchange's books, except by post. Logan called the central post office. Letters and parcels for Carnglass, it appeared, and Daldour too, were sent by MacBrayne's steamer to Loch Boisdale, in Smith Uist, where they were called for as anyone from those islands, or their agents, might happen to put into Loch Boisdale. How long would an express letter take? It was impossible to say: it might not reach Carnglass for some days, depending upon whether any boat should happen to call at Loch Boisdale. Also, however, letters for those islands sometimes were left with an agent of the Carnglass factor, here in Glasgow, depending upon instructions from Carnglass. Who was this agent of the factor? That information the postal authorities were not authorized to give out.

But Logan was a patient man. After lunch, he returned to his room and dressed in a heavy suit that had been made for him during his uni-versity years: of indestructible Harris tweed, the suit still fitted tolerably well. Rain was coming down heavily now, so this suit was made for the climate. He had with him a thorn stick, a memento also of Edinburgh days; it might be useful for hill-walking in Carnglass, should there be time for that. The little receptionist, who smiled fondly upon Logan, rec-ommended a travel-agent in Argyle Street; so Logan took a cab there.

Before entering the door of Moore Brothers, Travel Agents, Ltd., Founded 1887, he stopped at a shop adjacent and bought an oilskin cape, which probably would be the thing to wear in Carnglass; he had it sent to Todd's Hotel. Then he went up to the counter in Moore's, where an eager youth — with a manner the British call "smarmy" — proceeded to set his hand on a pile of tour-folders.

But the eager youth had no notion of how a gentleman might find his way to Carnglass. He had special de luxe tours to Iona and Skye to offer; these were much better-known islands than Carnglass, he told the gentleman. No one ever went to Carnglass. Logan asked for the manager.

This old man with steel spectacles at the end of his nose could suggest only that the gentleman take MacBrayne's steamer to Loch Boisdale. From South Uist, drifters and trawlers sometimes coasted off Daldour; there was no harbor in Daldour, but he had heard that the islanders — "verra queer folk, sir" — sometimes launched a boat and came alongside a drifter. He did not know how anyone contrived to live in Daldour, it was Ultima Thule. As for Carnglass, he had been told landing never was permitted. Oh, the gentleman was invited? An American? Then no doubt it would be possible. Perhaps the people in Daldour could take him across the sound in their boat. The manager would be glad to sell the American gentleman a first-class steamer ticket to Loch Boisdale, but he could do no more. And a first-class railway ticket from Glasgow to Oban: that was where one boarded MacBrayne's steamers. This month, ordinarily, there were plane flights three times a week to South Uist; but the weather had been so wretched for the past week that flights had been cancelled, and it might be two or three or four days before they could resume.

Logan bought his railway and steamer tickets. As he turned to go, the manager had an afterthought. "One moment, sir. Meg, d'ye mind the card that man left? The man that spoke with me concerning Carnglass?" Aye, Meg — a stocky red-faced lass in her teens — minded it; she put it bashfully into the young American gentleman's hand. "Aye, sir, I had near forgot," the manager said, "but this man came in a month gone and said that should any gentleman inquire after Carnglass, he might put him in the way of a passage."

It was a soiled card with crumpled corners, cheaply printed, and it read, "James Dowie, Commission Agent. 5 Mutto's Wynd, Gallowgate."

"How far is Gallowgate?" Logan asked.

The old manager drew in his lower lip and then protruded it meditatively. "Why, sir, the Gallowgate's far above the Tron. And it's late in the day. Would tomorrow do as well, sir?"

"No," said Logan, "I'm usually in a hurry. Surely a taxi could take me there in ten minutes?"

The manager fumbled with his spectacles. "Between ourselves, now, sir, the Gallowgate's not the place for an American gentleman by himself, with the night coming on. Mind ye, sir, I've had no trouble of my own in the Gallowgate. But this Mutto's Wynd will be some wee vennel or passage, and dark. Ye've heard tell of Teddy Boys and such? Aye. Well, if ye must go, take a cab, sir; and make the driver wait for ye. The man that left this card — he would be a bookie, I think. Nothing against him, sir, nothing whatsoever. And the chief constable has done fine work in the Gallowgate and the Gorbals, verra gude work. They were worse when I was a lad. But were I yourself, sir, I wouldna stop in a pub there. In the Gallowgate, the folk think all Americans are millionaires. Would it were true, sir? Ha, ha. Aye, would it were true."

Going into the washroom at the travel-agency, Logan took out of his pockets his passport, his traveller's checks, and most of the pound notes he had got at the hotel desk. He put them into the leather money-belt he wore beneath his shirt. Logan had been around, though most people wouldn't credit it, apparently, when they looked at his face; and he had the thorn stick with him. Then he took a cab to Mutto's Wynd, in the Gallowgate.

Mutto's Wynd turning out too narrow for any motorcar, the driver parked the cab at the mouth of the entry. In Mutto's Wynd, most of the buildings were derelict, and some unroofed, since the Scots pay no taxes on roofless buildings. Even for smoke-grimed Glasgow, Mutto's Wynd was very black. The dreary little building that was No. 5 stood near the mouth of the vennel, and the cab would be almost within call.

Although the windows of No. 5 seemed not to have been washed in this decade, a freshly-painted sign nailed above the door read "J. Dowie, Commission Agent." Logan gave the driver a pound note. "Keep the change," Logan said, "but wait for me." The driver sighed, looking uneasily down the wynd. Three doors beyond, there projected the sign of a public house, the Dun Stirk. "But stay near the cab."

"O aye," the driver grunted, "ye needna teach this auld dog new tricks." Logan rapped at the battered door of No. 5.

Quite promptly, a heavy-jowled little man in a sagging business-suit and a soiled old cap opened that door. "Come in, mon," he said. "Ye'll be thinkin' o' the pool?" The little low room — this building, elderly for rebuilt Glasgow, seemed once to have been a stable — contained a decrepit desk and three straight chairs; the walls, long ago, had been painted cream-color. The little man spoke the thickest Glasgow speech, with its clipped words and rolled r's.

"Mr. Dowie?" Aye, he was Mr. Dowie. "Mr. Dowie, I've been told you might know of a way to get to Carnglass."

Dowie, sucking in his fat cheeks, looked long and slyly at Logan. "Tak' a chair, mon. Ye'll no be frae these parts?"

Logan sat. "I'm an American, Mr. Dowie, with business in Carnglass."

Dowie leaned against the desk. "An' what wud that business be?"

"I'm representing my principal."

"Weel, then, Mr. American, ye'll no object if I draw the curtains." Dowie pulled heavy blanket-drapes across the filthy glass; he bolted the door. Logan sat easily on the rickety chair. "If it be Carnglass," said Dowie, "that ye mean tae see, then ye'll ken Tam Lagg?"

"The factor. Yes, we've corresponded with him."

"Aye, just so. And ye'll ken Dr. Jackman?" Here Dowie, stooping slightly, looked Logan in the eyes.

"No, Mr. Dowie, I don't know any Dr. Jackman."

"Ye dinna ken Jackman? Noo think o' this, Mr. American: I'm official agent o' Tam Lagg. Ye've no need to keep matters frae me. What might your name be?"

"Hugh Logan. I'm to see Lady MacAskival."

"O aye. Lady MacAskival. She's no keepin' verra weel, ye ken."

"So I understand."

"No weel enough for chit-chat, Mr. Logan." Dowie nodded mournfully. "And noo ye're in auld Scotland, ye'll tak' a trip to Rabbie Burns' country?"

"I've only time for a Carnglass trip."

"Rabbie Burns' country is Alloway and Ayr, ye ken, Mr. Logan. A braw poet, Rabbie Burns. 'A mon's a mon for a' that' — eh, Mr. Logan?" An unconvincing smile came suddenly over Dowie's sodden face, and he clapped a dirty hand on Logan's shoulder, in token of comradeship. Logan did not move or smile.

"I suppose what Burns meant, Mr. Dowie, is that worth and genius matter more than rank — or as much, anyway. I don't know that he had Glasgow bookies in mind."

"O aye," Dowie muttered, removing his hand. He scowled uneasily, and then brightened artificially again. "O aye. I see ye're a card, Mr. Logan. Aye, a poet o' the first water, Rabbie Burns. But ye've fine writers in the States, too. Political writers. Ye'll ken ane or twa o' them?"

Logan shook his head. "I don't know a single political writer, Mr. Dowie."

"And ye'll no ken Dr. Jackman?"

"This literary conversation is very pleasant, Mr. Dowie," Logan said. "But do you know of a ship or a launch that will take me to Carnglass?"

Dowie sat down at the desk and pulled open a drawer. "Noo your principal, Mr. Logan — he'll be Mr. Duncan MacAskival?"

Over the edge of the open drawer, a cablegram form was just visible. "Then you're the agent for forwarding the post to Carnglass, Mr. Dowie."

"Wha' loon told ye that?"

"Has Lady MacAskival received our cables?"

"Wud I be a miracle-man, Mr. Logan? I canna send word tae Carnglass by Tellie — by TV, ye Yanks say. And wha' wi' the high seas, there's no boat that wud put oot for Daldour nor Carnglass these three days syne."

"Then I suppose Lady MacAskival's not expecting me?"

"Ye can suppose wha' ye like, Mr. Logan."

"When can I get passage from Glasgow to Carnglass?"

"Na, na, mon, I'm thinkin' there'll be no boat for Carnglass." Dowie rested his chin in his pudgy hand. His eyes swept over Logan with that look of low cunning Logan had seen, so often, in malingering or thieving soldiers. "But bide a wee, Mr. Logan: we'll fetch a cup o' tea for ye while ye're here. Jeanie! Jeanie!" He shouted toward a back room. "Dinna fret, Mr. Logan: Jeanie's my auld wifie. Jeanie! A cup o' tea for a Yank gentleman!"

Around a door-jamb peered a worn face. Logan rose. "Na, na, Mr. Logan, sit ye doon: it's but Jeanie. Jeanie, chat wi' the Yank gentleman while I see wha' can be done to obleege him." Dowie slipped into the back room at the moment Jeanie entered. Taking a chair, she sat staring dully at the grimy floor, quite silent.

"Rather a clammy day, Mrs. Dowie." Mrs. Dowie, who had a scarf tied round her head, said nothing at all. Dowie seemed to be telephoning from the back room; and Logan, an old hand at snapping up scraps of whispered evidence, contrived to make out a few words:

"Aye, Jock, a Yank, but no in Yank's clothes. Quick, noo." The phone was hung up, and Dowie returned, that fixed smile across his face. "Jeanie! Hae ye no been entertainin' the gentleman? Fetch the tea, lass."

Jeanie went. "Well, now, Mr. Dowie," Logan said, "have you found something for me?"

"Ye wudna wish to go where they'll no be expectin'ye, wud ye, sir? And Lady MacAskival's ower auld for company. Tak' the plane home, Mr. Logan. Ye'll do no business in Carnglass."

"If you'll do nothing for me, Dowie, I'll go elsewhere. It's getting late."

The look of triumphant cunning was back in Dowie's eyes. "Aye, but the tea, Mr. Logan; bide for the tea." Jeanie returned with a wooden tray, a teapot under a cozy, and three cups. Logan stood up.

"I'm always in a hurry, Dowie. Thank you, Mrs. Dowie, but I haven't time for tea." There seemed to be voices raised outside in the wynd, now, and a heavy thud, rather as if someone had kicked the side of an automobile. "Good day to you."

"But first, man," said Dowie, sidling between Logan and the street door, "we'll shake hands a' roun', should auld acquaintance be forgot." Logan briefly took Dowie's hand, and then Jeanie's. "And ye'll confess, Mr. Logan, that ye came here o' your ain free will, an' no invitation." Logan agreed. "Ye heard, Jeanie," Dowie muttered. "Ye're a witness." In the street beyond the mouth of the wynd, a motor started, and Logan thought he heard a car drive away.

"That may be my taxi leaving," Logan said. He had his stick in his hand.

"Weel, noo, Mr. American," Dowie told him, with what possibly was intended for a convivial smile, "I'm sorry I couldna serve ye. Cheerio the noo. I'll open the door for ye." He did. And the second Logan stepped out, the door was slammed behind him and bolted.

Mutto's Wynd was shadowy. Yes, the taxi had gone; and lounging against the wall of No. 5 were four men. Logan faced them. They were very young roughs, three of them, with the greasy sideburns and the pimpled faces that went, in their sort, with a diet of fish and chips. The fourth man, a big lank fellow, older, wore a wide leather belt round his waist, and he had a very nasty smirk. By way of obstacle, the lank man thrust out a long leg.

"Hello, Yank," the lank man said. The other three came slowly round Logan.

"Good evening, friend," Logan answered. No one else was in the wynd.

"This is the auld Gallowgate, Yank," the lank man went on. "This was where they hangit the gallows-craws. We're gallows-craws, Yank." He gave a short, harsh whiskey-laugh, and the three young roughs cackled in echo. "Ye'll stand us a dram at the Dun Stirk, Yank?"

"I'm sorry, friend, but I'm in a hurry." It was quiet and dark in Mutto's Wynd.

The lank man smirked. "Damn ye, Yank, ye'll no be in sic a hurry noo!" He flung himself toward Logan, one foot going out to trip him.

Logan was ready. He thrust the point of the thorn stick into the lank man's belly, and the lank man screamed and stumbled back. But one of the greasy youngsters had his arm round Logan's throat, from behind. Taking the boy's fingers, Logan bent them backward: the rough yelled and let go. And now they were on him, all four.

Someone had a long razor. Logan caught the wrist that held it, striking with the point of his stick at the face behind; the razor dropped to the cobblestones, but someone else got Logan's legs out from under him. He fell heavily on the wet stones, and took a kick in the ribs. Another razor flashed. Someone had a hand inside Logan's coat. The mackintosh he wore hampered him. There came a kick at his head, though a glancing blow. He had hold at last of someone's thighs, and was struggling upward. A kick in the back; and a razor slashed one sleeve of the mackintosh. All that saved him for the second, Logan knew, was that they were so close about him as to get in one another's way.

This was no simple robbery: they meant to slash or cripple him, or something worse. Another fierce kick in his ribs. The man he had got by the thighs slipped and fell upon him. And as Logan fought clear, he heard steel-plated heels running over the cobbles. Someone was helping him up: a tall policeman. Another policeman was chasing four dim figures down the wynd.

The policeman who had lifted Logan had a bruise over one eye. "That was Jock Anderson's lads, Donald," he panted to the other policeman, returned from the unsuccessful chase. "Jock gie me the bash over the eye." Logan was getting his breath back. "If ye'll prefer charges, sir," the policeman said to him, "we'll have warrants out for these chaps; we know them."

"There's small harm done, constable, and I'm leaving Glasgow tomorrow."

"Did they not take your money, sir?"

Logan felt inside his coat and discovered no billfold. "Yes, but I hadn't much with me."

If the gentleman would come to the station and swear to a complaint, the second constable told him, they might not have to trouble him further. "Your cabbie found us, sir; they forced him awa'." Logan left a five-pound note with the policeman for the driver. "Were ye in No. 5 yonder, sir?"

Though the constable named Donald knocked hard at the door of No. 5, no one answered, and the building showed no light. "By this time," Donald said, "Jim Dowie's flitted, and his wife Jeanie with him. And I dinna think we could charge them. But we're keepin' watch on Dowie, sir: a slippery one."

Then, in the Gallowgate, they found him another taxi to take him back to the hotel. And in India Street, Logan washed the grime of Mutto's Wynd from himself. Stiff and bruised: but no ribs broken, and the razor had slashed only the mackintosh. There still was time to go down to dinner. Afterward, Logan had promised, he would go round to the station and swear to a statement.

In his hot tub, Logan tried to make sense of what had happened. The policemen took it for a simple case of pocket-picking, perhaps abetted by Jim Dowie, Commission Agent. But Logan thought that Dowie had meant to keep him out of Carnglass — possibly. Who was this Jackman that Dowie had mentioned? Lady MacAskival's private physician, or merely some crony or invention of Dowie's? And what interest had Dowie, or anyone else, in keeping him out of Carnglass? And why should Thomas Lagg the factor have a friend, and mail-forwarder, like J. Dowie? Logan felt full of fight. He would take the morning train to Oban, and there, no matter what the price, he'd find passage to Carnglass.

On going down to dinner, Logan stopped at the reception-desk to see if there might be a message from Carnglass. There was none. Presumably Dowie really had Duncan MacAskival's cables in his desk. But also it was likely that Dowie, during this weather, had no way of getting word to Carnglass. If so, Logan would be quite unexpected when he landed. That might be just as well, supposing that Lagg had some connection with the queer business in Mutto's Wynd.

As he turned away from the reception-counter, Logan felt himself being watched. Or were his nerves on edge? He glanced to the right, and a man's eyes met his, but dropped away hastily. It was like looking into the eyes of a bird: little black eyes, darting and quick to flee. The man, he thought, had been looking at the top leaf of the open hotel register. As Logan went into the dining room, he looked back: the man was going out into the street. But he had a good view of him.

Birdlike? The man's body was anything but birdlike, unless one thought of a stork. Tall, with shoulders thrown back; a heavy, rather clumsy torso, protruding in front; but the legs extremely thin. The man wore a bowler and a good worsted town-suit, dark gray; he was getting into a raincoat as he passed out of Logan's sight into India Street. He carried a long malacca stick. Even in these brief glimpses, Logan had the impression that this fellow meant to be taken for a country gentleman or a retired officer. Yet somehow the effect did not quite come off. Logan told himself not to be edgy: it wouldn't do to suspect every hotel-guest of dark designs. Perhaps the man had only been glancing at a raw spot on Logan's cheek, where Jock Anderson's boot had scraped.

Yet after dinner, and just before he took a cab to the police station, the receptionist with the taffy hair spoke to Logan. "Did the gentleman find you, sir?"

"What gentleman?"

"He didn't leave his name, sir; he only asked after you — if you were staying in the hotel — and waited a moment by the counter. I thought he would have seen you when you went into dinner. A military gentleman, perhaps."

Yes, that would have been the man with the bird's eyes: a military, or pseudo-military, gentleman. Logan made up his mind to remember that gentleman.

Of that gentleman, and of his business in Carnglass, however, Logan said nothing to the Glasgow police, who took his deposition and promised action. Already they had been looking for Jock and his lads, but with no luck. It was odd, the constable named Donald said: to get out of town, or to find some snug hidie-hole, Jock and his gang would have required more money than they took from the gentleman. Yet somehow they had gone to earth, and so had Dowie.

Logan told the sergeant that he was touring Scotland, and would be in Oban a few days, at the Station Hotel. "Never place money with lads like Jim Dowie," they told him.

An hour later, in bed at Todd's Hotel, and tired though he was, Logan took up "A Summary History of Carnglass and Daldour." Balmullo, the old minister, might have been a bigot; yet he had a keen eye and ear. There was a page of description of the New House of Fear, built down by the harbor by Donald MacAskival — one of the extravagances that had ruined him — in 1777.

"It had been the MacAskivals' design," Balmullo wrote, "to have demolished *in toto* the Old House. But the chieftain's means did not permit of this undertaking. Accordingly, — and to the chagrin of every connoisseur of the arts who sets foot upon the mole of Askival harbour, — the rude Gothic construction has been permitted to loom intact upon its ruder eminence, denuded of its plenishing save for the gigantic carven chimney pieces. There remains also, above the principal entrance to the Old House, a tremendous escutcheon, its bearings in some part defaced, but yet displaying the graceless figure of a Wild Man, armed with a dirk, which Wild Man the vulgar name Askival, the reputed founder of the fortress; and beside the Wild Man a female figure in a state of undress, whom, with still less authority, the folk of the island call Marin or Merin. Below these sculptures, in the letters of a later period, is inscribed the legend, 'They have said and they will saye. Let them be saying.'

"Of baseless rumor and frantic conjecture, the island of Carnglass has no stint. In contempt, I must record that the natives of this island, blind to the perfections of the New House, continue to allege that Donald MacAskival built afresh not out of an elevated taste, but rather because, in the Old House, he had dwelt in dread of the wraiths of his fathers, said to have waxed wroth with their descendant for his prudent decision to expel from Carnglass the superfluous population. A gaunt and bearded spectre, to which is given the appellation of Old Askival, is reputed to stalk the empty corridors and chambers, in particular the subterranean portions of the oldest tower. An obscure tradition asseverates that a hidden passage leads from these cellars to a recess, and thence to the outer world. Yet the Old House having been builded upon the living rock, as has been observed elsewhere in these pages, this supposition can have no more substance than the Kingdom of the Fairies."

Here Logan turned out the light. For all his aches and pains, he never had slept sounder in his life.

On his second Scottish morning, Hugh Logan took the train for Oban. The wind had gone down somewhat, and the rain was over, though grim gray clouds still lay to the west. Through Larbert and Stirling, past the Castle high on, its rock, the train puffed up to Callender. Logan sat in a compartment where two old ladies dozed over their knitting. Half the time he looked at the hills and villages, and half the time he read in Balmullo's "Summary History." And so the train swept into the West Highlands.

As they approached Loch Awe, someone paused outside the glass door of Logan's compartment. Looking up, Logan saw the man clear: the man in the bowler, the "military gentleman" with the little black bird-eyes. That military gentleman was observing him; but the furtive look moved on to the two somnolent old ladies opposite. For a moment, Logan thought the man was about to pull back the door and enter. Yet the face turned away, and the military gentleman was gone from the corridor. Logan had enjoyed a thorough look at his face: the swollen long nose; the red and purple veins that bulged against the coarse skin; and those tiny, frightened, frightening black eyes, sunk into the skull. About fifty years old, Logan estimated, though seeming older. And a cashiered British officer, some intuition suggested.

Cashiered, yes. Logan made almost a hobby of collecting clippings from newspapers about curious cases of criminal law, strange points of evidence, failures to convict despite strong testimony. It was power of memory, as much as anything else, that had brought Logan success at the bar while he still was young. Now he tried to dredge up from memory that repugnant face of the military gentleman. Cashiered, cashiered. Hadn't he read of a captain or major cashiered in India, and subsequently tried by a criminal court for some separate, though related, offense — and got off by a very clever barrister? A barrister with somewhat unsavory politics connections? The case had been nasty, remarkably nasty — and the officer's acts nastier still. Hadn't some London friend, years ago, sent Logan the penny-press clippings about the case, with a picture or two of the accused? What had the fellow's name been? Something short? Gale, or Hare? No, even Logan's trained memory could not recall the details. Yet the face of the military gentleman at the hotel and in the corridor, Logan felt, was curiously like the nasty face he half-recollected from the smudgy newspaper photograph. Had there been espionage hinted at the military hearings? The man had been a bad lot in many ways. But Logan couldn't feel quite sure he had not fancied the resemblance.

By Ben Cruachan, through the Pass of Brander; across the river at Bridge of Awe; then Connel Ferry. The mountains loomed nobly as the train approached the coast. The military gentleman did not return. A few minutes more, and the train swung into the resort and fishing-port of Oban, on the Firth of Lorn. Now the Western Isles were in plain sight — Kerrera, at least, right opposite Oban. Logan could see its treeless bulk from the window of his hotel. Of the military gentleman, no trace. Logan looked for him in the railway station, but he must have got off hurriedly from a forward coach and have gone into the town. Not that Logan much desired to see the military gentleman again.

CHAPTER 3

"You might inquire at the North Pier, Mr. Logan," said the Reverend Andrew Crawford, "but I do not believe any fisherman will undertake to set you ashore in Carnglass. All the boats will be gone from the harbor until sunset: the storm kept them in port for three days, and they won't wish to waste another day in carrying a passenger to Carnglass."

The Reverend Andrew Crawford, minister of St. Ninian's Church, was a knowledgeable man. The people at the Station Hotel had sent Logan to him, not knowing themselves how he might get to Carnglass. Mr. Crawford had set foot in most of the Outer Isles that still were inhabited. Now he and Logan stood at the door of the manse, looking down the hill to Oban town and the piers, with the dim gray Hebrides far beyond the blue sea.

"I'd pay whatever they might ask," Logan told him.

"It's not wholly a matter of *l.s.d.*, Mr. Logan. The swell round Carnglass and Daldour always is heavy. I had difficulty in getting ashore in Daldour, the day I visited, and I never have seen Carnglass, except from Daldour or a boat. Lady MacAskival does not let even the minister or the priest ashore. She has her own style of religion. And these trawlers from the mainland aren't popular with the island folk. Once the keepers fired at an Oban boat that tried to put into Askival harbor; nor are the men in Daldour much more hospitable. No, I think you'd best take MacBrayne's steamer to Loch Boisdale: the South Uist fishermen know the Carnglass waters. The reefs off Carnglass are murderous."

"Who lives in Daldour, Mr. Crawford?"

"There is but one name in Daldour — MacAskival. An inbred folk. In Daldour there is a little machair — that's the sandy land of the Island — and the island people fertilize it with seaweed, and grow potatoes. Also they gather seaweed and sell it; in the season, a drifter puts close into shore, and the Daldour men bring out the seaweed in their lobster-boats and load it aboard, and it is sold on the mainland. On the day I visited Daldour, all the folk were at the beach with their carts, running straight into the surf to gather the tangle. Theirs is a poor life. The Daldour women weave a few decent rugs and sweaters. They speak a strange Gaelic, with some Norse words in it. For a month, one of our missionaries lived in Daldour, but he was half daft when he left. 'Mr. Crawford, I have served my time among the Mau Mau,' he said to me. And that though he was a Highlander and a Gaelic speaker."

"Can you tell me anything about Lady MacAskival, Mr. Crawford?" Logan asked. But — after a slight discreet pause — Mr. Crawford could not. Logan, leaving him, went down to the North Pier to make inquiries after any boat that might carry him to Carnglass.

He had no luck. It would have to be MacBrayne's steamer to Loch Boisdale in the morning, he thought, for already it was late afternoon. If the sea should be calm tomorrow, even a big motor-launch ought to be able to carry him from South Uist to Carnglass. After a stroll along the esplanade to the cathedral, Logan went back to his hotel at the other end of the town and had dinner. The trawlers were in the harbor now, unloading their catch upon the quay. But the fishermen were too busy to be bothered with eccentric Americans that wanted passage to Ultima Thule, Logan suspected. A light rain was coming down. Despite that, after dinner Logan put his oilskin cape over his shoulders, took up his stock, and — for lack of anything better to do — climbed the hill behind the town.

At the summit there was a strange building, Logan had noticed as soon as he had come out of Oban railway station: a circular roofless affair, like a ruined temple. This, according to the hotel people, was called McCaig's Folly, and had been built long ago as an observation-tower, but never finished. Now, in the gloaming, Logan found himself close beside the Folly. The season being too early for tourists at Oban, the area round the Folly was deserted, so that Logan walked alone in the drizzle, thinking idly of the Old House of Fear and old Duncan MacAskival and his own solitary and work-laden life. A scrap from Scott came into his head:

"Sound, sound the clarion, fill the fife!
    To all the sensual world proclaim
One crowded hour of glorious life
    Is worth an age without a name."

Was that the way it went? Even leading his battalion, Logan never had known that crowded hour. And as he thought of how some men are drunken with drink, and others drunken with work, he heard steps in the darkness behind him.

Looking over his shoulder, Logan made out a familiar figure, a few paces distant: the military gentleman. When Logan slackened pace, the military gentleman hesitated for a moment, and then strode on toward him. "Captain Gare!" the military gentleman called out, by way of introduction.

"Good evening, sir," Logan said. Captain Gare, coming very close up to him with a swagger of sorts, looked down from his stork-height upon Logan. Flickering from side to side, the disconcertingly mobile little black bird-eyes never paused for more than a fraction of a second to meet Logan's stare. The man struck his long stick against his own trousers-leg. He opened his mouth, paused, gripped his stick more firmly, and then spoke in a reedy educated voice.

"Look here," said Captain Gare. "I say — I . . . That is, cigarettes — yes, cigarettes . . ." There was an aroma of whiskey about Captain Gare, but Logan did not think he was drunk. Certainly Gare was exceedingly nervous, and he seemed disposed toward bullying.

"I'm sorry," Logan told him mildly, "but I don't have any cigarettes about me."

"No, no." Captain Gare, scowling, paused afresh, perhaps trying to take a new tack. "No, I don't require cigarettes, not really. I don't smoke — nor drink, either. I say: you're an American, are you not?"

"Why should you think so, sir?"

"Don't take offense," said Captain Gare. "Are you ashamed of being an American? I'm not a chap people can take liberties with. You're an American chap, I know. Your name is Logan."

"I saw you at Todd's Hotel," Logan observed.

"Did you? Did you really? I travel a great deal, Mr. Logan: private means, you know. Yes, that's it: I saw your name in the hotel register, and thought we might have something in common."

"What might we have in common, Captain Gare?" Logan spoke evenly. Captain Gare swept his bird-eyes across Logan's face again, seeming to gain heart. He slapped the stick against his leg, below the short mackintosh he wore.

"I say — don't know India, I suppose? Never tried pig-sticking? No, I suppose not; not you American chaps. True sport, you know. I was rather good." He towered belligerently above Logan. "There's nothing like steel. See here." Captain Gare tugged at the head of his stick, and it came way from the wood. It was a sword-stick, two or three inches of blade showing above the cane. Logan had an amusing momentary vision of a fencing-match there in the rain, complete with cries of "touché!" Captain Gare, glowering upon him, rammed the blade back into its stick-scabbard.

"I take it that you know the world, Captain Gare," Logan said, smiling slightly.

"Rather better than you do, I fancy, Logan." It was clear that Captain Gare now felt himself master of the situation. "I say, we needn't beat about the bush, eh? I'm told you've been at the pier inquiring after passage to Carnglass."

"You're an astute man, Captain Gare."

"That's as it may be." Captain Gare's swollen features bent toward Logan. "Look here: it's quite pointless for you to go to Carnglass, you know — quite. I suppose you're a solicitor-chap, are you not?"

"That's as it may be," said Logan. "My father and grandfather were Writers to the Signet. You have an interest in Carnglass, Mr. — that is, Captain — Gare?"

"One of my friends has an interest there, sir. He knows Lady MacAskival very well. Handles her affairs, as a matter of fact. Saves her annoyance. She never welcomes callers, you understand."

"I'm afraid my business is with Lady MacAskival herself."

Captain Gare edged still closer. "Lady MacAskival is not competent to transact business, Mr. Logan. I mean to say that she's infirm. Quite old, you know. No taste for American trippers."

"She has been in correspondence with my principal."

"Nonsense!" Captain Gare brandished his stick. "Mean to say, that's rubbish, you know. Lady MacAskival never writes. Infirm, a very elderly party. Come, now, Logan: I dare say you've gone to moderate expense in this fool's errand. You'll never see Carnglass. My friend is a liberal man, and very close to Lady MacAskival. Money's little object to him or her. Suppose, now, on their behalf, I give you three hundred pounds, if you like? Simply by way of reimbursement, we may put it, Logan. Fair enough, eh? And then back to Brooklyn with you, eh?"

"You have the money in your pocket?" Logan inquired.

"Of course not." Captain Gare gave him a supercilious smile. "A man doesn't carry such sums on his person, you know. Come back into town with me, like a good chap, and I'll write a cheque in your favor."

"I do happen to carry such sums on my person, Captain Gare," Logan told him.

The military gentleman's little eyes widened and flickered. His left hand stole nervously along the sword-stick. "Not really? Hundreds of pounds in notes in your pocket? I say . . ."

"Not in notes, Captain Gare: in traveller's cheques." Here Captain Gare sighed slightly, and his grip on the stick slackened. "Now could you be interested, Captain Gare, in some such sum as six hundred pounds?"

"Six hundred pounds?" Captain Gare drew a sudden breath. "Really, my dear fellow, are you suggesting that you might pay me six hundred pounds? Whatever for?"

"For certain information."

"What manner of information, my dear sir?" Captain Gare turned slightly, there in the dark, as if to make sure no one was at hand.

"For instance," Logan said, "detailed information concerning the past, present, and future of Jackman."

That bow, drawn at a venture, sent its arrow home. On Gare's unpleasant face the mottled veins seemed to swell; the man stepped back. "Who the devil are you?" cried Captain Gare, with a quaver in the reedy voice.

"I take it that you know now what I am," said Logan, still quietly. "Whatever made you think I might accept money?"

"I beg your pardon, sir; really, I . . ." Captain Gare was stumbling over his words. "That is, you did not seem precisely an American. All a pose, eh? I say, you don't mean that you're . . . that I'm . . ."

"If you tell me about Jackman," Logan went on, "we need say no more of all this, so far as you are concerned. We already know a great deal about Dr. Jackman, of course, but conceivably you might add something or other. You're the fellow who was cashiered, I take it. We know enough about you."

"I swear it was a miscarriage of justice, Mr. Logan — or whatever your name is, sir. I mean that affair in Madras." Gare was almost panting. "But Jackman — no, really, I can't say anything, not for six thousand pounds. My life wouldn't — but you know that quite as well as I do."

The swollen face had gone deathly pale. Even had he been able to probe deeper without giving away his game, Logan reflected, this man would have been too frightened to be of any real help. It had been a good random thrust, that mention of Jackman, whoever Jackman might be.

"Very well, Gare," Logan said. "If you don't choose to clear yourself, that's not my concern. Very likely you'd be of no use to us. We'll have Dowie and Anderson any hour now." Gare shivered. That shot, too, had gone home. "As for you, Gare, you understand that if you don't sever all connection with this business, we'll see that you're taken into custody? Perhaps the Continent would be a safer place for you at present. And throw away that silly sword-stick: you couldn't frighten babies with it." Logan snatched the thing from Gare's hand and flung it toward the lip of the hill; the steel flashed in the moonlight, and then blade and stick were lost in the gorse. "Be off, now; I've tired of you."

Gare, backing further away, muttered pitifully, "Then you're . . . Then I'm not under . . . ?" Logan gestured impatiently toward the town below.

"You can go to the devil, Gare."

Captain Gare turned with clumsy haste, all his swagger gone, and scuttled heavily down the path toward town; after he had gone a few paces in the dark, Logan thought he heard him break into a run. Yes, it had been a thoroughly satisfying random shot. He did not think he would see Captain Gare again.

Yet whoever thought it worthwhile to offer Logan three hundred pounds to steer clear of Carnglass? Gare had bungled the business badly; he must have been acting without instruction from his principal, Logan thought — whoever that principal might be. Dowie? Or Lagg? Or this fellow Jackman? There were depths in this business, surely, unplumbed by old Duncan MacAskival. Trying to piece the thing together, Logan walked slowly back to the Station Hotel. There the night porter gave him tea and biscuits, and afterwards Logan went up to his rather chilly high-ceilinged room, and stared at the plaster cornice for half an hour before he went to sleep. But he could form no clear picture of what he had begun to call to himself the Carnglass Case.

As he dressed, next morning, Logan saw from his window the steamer "Lochness" at the pier: it would take him to Loch Boisdale, and he hurried into his clothes and gulped down tea at 5:45. This was Wednesday, his third morning in Scotland. Thus far, only frustration: and yet the sort of frustration which roused Logan's energies. To judge from the impromptu and ineffectual measures that Dowie and Gare had adopted, he was dealing only with an ill-organized and eccentric opposition — though with adversaries sufficiently unscrupulous. And it seemed to be an ill-informed opposition. Either that, or else Dowie and Gare were out of touch with the real intelligence at work, for some reason, supposing that they *had* principals for whom they were acting. Certainly neither of those two had seemed quite the man to concoct a scheme to keep an American from his prospective purchase of Carnglass. If there were a principal, would he be in the island? Lagg, the factor? The storm of two days ago might have kept the people in Carnglass from communicating with the mainland; but presumably messages now could be sent and received by boat. Whatever messages might be sent, it scarcely was possible that he should receive in Carnglass the sort of rude welcome he had got in Mutto's Wynd. Even if Carnglass was Ultima Thule, still it was part of Britain, the most law-abiding of nations; and, there would be Lady MacAskival for surety.

At six o'clock the "Lochness" steamed away from the pier toward the Sound of Mull. They crossed the Firth of Lorne; and then, to the south, they skirted the great rocky mass of Mull, while the wild shores of Morven frowned upon them from the north. Several islanders were among the passengers, and for the first time in years Logan heard the Gaelic spoken naturally, that beautiful singing Gaelic of the Hebrides. It went with the cliffs, the sea-rocks, the ruined strongholds of Mull and Morven, the damp air, the whitewashed lonely cottages by the deep and smoothly sinister sea.

As the hours passed, the steamer put into Tobermory, and later touched at the flat islands of Col and Tiree. It crossed the broad rough waters of the Little Minch, with the romantic line of the Outer Isles before them, and the round bulk of Barra drawing closer. After Castlebay, in Barra, the "Lochness" steamed north past Eriskay, and into the splendid dark anchorage of Loch Boisdale, in South Uist, that sprawling low island of peat.

It was nearly midnight now. Going ashore, Logan got himself a room at the homely, cordial inn above the harbor. There was a schoolmaster in Loch Boisdale village, the hotelkeeper said, who might know of a drifter that could put Logan ashore in Carnglass.

Once more alone in a rented room with only conjectures for company, Hugh Logan settled himself in bed and took up that battered pamphlet by the Reverend Samuel Balmullo. Mr. Balmullo's taste certainly had run to old bones. Here was a tidbit:

"Even in the fierce chronicles of the Western Isles, the chieftains of MacAskival are distinguished by a repute for deeds of blood and passion exceedingly disproportionate to the wealth and power of their sept. In the last century, upon the removal of the plenishing of the Old House to the New House of Fear, there were discovered in a curious pit or oubliette in the crypts the skeletal remains of a human being, still bearing the marks of violence. This pit long had been put to the office of a brinetub, and it is supposed, accordingly, that the bones had lain hid at the bottom for a great while, perhaps some centuries. By any person inured to the sorry superstitions of the people of Carnglass, it might have been anticipated — as, indeed, it befell — that the vulgar peasantry, upon the exhibition of these sad relics of mortality, would allege the bones — some of which were curiously injured or deformed — to be those of a Firgower, or Man-Goat. A legend less incredible, however, relates that the skeleton is that of an illicit lover of a lady of MacAskival, seized by stealth at his abode in North Uist, transported to Carnglass, subjected to indescribable torments, and at length drowned in the brine of the oubliette. What the Duke of Clarence suffered in a butt of Malmsey, some obscure chieftain of the barbarous Hebrides, about the same period of antiquity, may have endured in a darksome pit filled to its brink with pickled herring."

At the close of this charming paragraph, Logan settled himself to sleep.

In the morning, on his way to seek out the schoolmaster who might help him to a passage to Carnglass, Logan was surprised to find Loch Boisdale and its neighborhood bursting with activity. Navvies were unloading enormous crates from a freighter; two new bulldozers rumbled down the road toward the interior of the island; recently-built huts of corrugated iron, an age away from the primitive thatched Uist cottages of field-stone that stood scattered over the oozy plain, shouldered one another near the pier. The hotelkeeper had said briefly that something important, in a military way, was in progress in the heart of South Uist. A range for guided missiles, perhaps; and perhaps something even newer. Idle policemen, the hotelkeeper had said, lounged about the approaches to the construction-area. He did not like it. It would spoil the snipe-shooting, and also evict honest families from their crofts. "Those men in London are spoiling the best places and the best people."

About the middle of the morning, Logan plodded up the soggy road to the schoolhouse. The sky was very gray again, and a fairly heavy rain was falling; but even the guidebook confessed that the climate of South Uist was the worst in Britain. MacLean, the rawboned schoolmaster, would do what he could to assist the gentleman. Leaving the schoolroom in charge of a senior boy, he went back with Logan toward the harbor. Yes, Mr. MacLean knew the master of a drifter, now in Loch Boisdale, who might conceivably engage to land Mr. Logan in Carnglass. This fisherman, though akin to the schoolmaster, was a very remote cousin, mind, and in need of money, to pay a fine. A fine for what? For poaching. Logan wanted to know what sort of poaching — fishing in forbidden waters?

"No," said MacLean, shortly, "sheep. Judge not that ye be not judged. My cousin Colin knows all the shore of all the lonely islands, and on some of the islands there are sheep, and deer. Whatever Colin is or is not, there is no better pilot in all the Outer Isles."

Although Colin's boat was in the harbor, the man himself was not in sight when the schoolmaster and Logan got down to the pier. "He will be drinking somewhere," the schoolmaster said. "But here are some people to interest you: people from Daldour."

Seated on the clammy pier, eating bread and butter in the drizzle, were three men in rough island dress and rubber boots — or, rather, two men and a bright-eyed boy. All three had about them a twilight look. Their bodies were lean, their cheeks were hollow, their teeth protruded slightly; a Lowlander might have said that they were not canny.

They seemed so much alike that, but for differences in age, they might have been triplets. "MacAskivals," the schoolmaster murmured. "A dying breed. In Daldour, now, most are old bachelors and old maids; they have seen too much of one another, and will not marry. The last of an old song. That big lobster boat by the pier is theirs; the MacAskivals have but a naked beach at Daldour. I will speak the Gaelic to them, for they will speak no English, although this boy knows the English well enough. Among themselves, Mr. Logan, they speak a dialect as strange to me as the Gaelic is to you."

Except for the boy's bright glance, the three MacAskivals had given no sign of recognition as the schoolmaster and Logan approached. Now, as Mr. MacLean spoke to the three in Gaelic, there came very faint shy smiles to all three narrow faces; the two men nodded, and the boy replied in the slow flowing Gaelic. Presently, in a cautious tone, the schoolmaster seemed to say something significant. The boy turned to the elder of the two men, who spoke curtly, and the boy translated for him to the schoolmaster. As he finished speaking, over the boy's eyes came a kind of glaze, and the two men turned again to munching bread and butter, as if they had forgotten the existence of everyone else.

"I asked them," the schoolmaster told Logan, "whether they would take you with them to Daldour, and then to Carnglass. They are in Loch Boisdale for this day only, to buy what few things they do buy, from month to month. They said they would not take you to Carnglass; it is not a good place for a man to go."

"Not for fifty pounds?" Logan asked.

"For no price, I believe. But if money speaks, my cousin Colin is the man for you. And here he comes." A squat man was sauntering along the pier. "Colin is not overly civil, and he is fond of the drink; but he knows the waters and the coasts." They turned away from the three silent MacAskivals and walked to meet the fisherman-poacher.

What is uncommon among the people of the Isles, Colin MacLean seemed surly. He did not acknowledge the schoolmaster's introduction of Logan. "Colin," said the schoolmaster, "Mr. Logan asks you to set him ashore in Carnglass. I will leave you to make your bargain." Logan shook his hand, and the schoolmaster strode up the hill.

Colin MacLean gave Logan a long hard look from under the brim of his sou'wester. "Carnglass, is it?" The only polish about Colin was his careful English speech, no doubt learned from the British Broadcasting Company, and uttered with a musical Gaelic intonation. Colin MacLean spat upon the pier. "Carnglass: and so Lagg and his keepers would shoot holes in my boat. You may go to hell, Mr. Logan."

Logan drew from his billfold ten big colorful notes of the Royal Bank of Scotland: five-pound notes. "This is yours, Mr. MacLean," he said, "if you'll set me ashore anywhere in Carnglass. It needn't be Askival harbor. Is there no other spot where a boat might put in?"

Colin stared at the notes. "There is a place, Dalcruach, in the east, where at high tide a boat — a small boat — can pass over the reefs, if the sea is calm. All the rest is cliff. But I would not risk my drifter among the rocks. You would need to row over the reefs alone. Here: I have an old dinghy. For twenty pounds more, I would sell it to you. I would bring you as close to Dalcruach as I could, and then you would take the dinghy and fend for yourself, Mr. Logan. Are you a seaman?"

"I've rowed before," Logan said. "Here's another twenty pounds for the dinghy."

"The swell about Carnglass is a fearful thing," Colin went on, shaking his heavy head in doubt, "and the reefs are like knives. Now would you sign a paper to say that Colin MacLean would be in no way responsible for the possible drowning of Mr. Hugh Logan?"

"I would," Logan answered. "Take me aboard your drifter, and I'll write it now."

Colin tucked the five-pound notes into his pocket. "Midnight, Mr. Logan: come aboard at midnight, and we will make for Carnglass. It is not good to be seen landing in Carnglass; there might be a keeper with a rifle, even at Dalcruach. I will land you at Dalcruach early in the morning, with the tide in flood, the weather permitting. And then I wash my hands of it."

That afternoon, Logan borrowed from the hotelkeeper an old knapsack, into which he put some socks and underclothing, a shirt, sandwiches and chocolate, and a thermos of coffee. He would leave his suitcase at the hotel. He put on heavy waterproof boots and an old cap, and wore his oilskin and carried his stick. And he was ready long before midnight.

Colin MacLean, with two less dour South Uist men who made up his crew, received him solemnly aboard the drifter. They puffed out of Loch Boisdale into the sea, with only two lights showing; and after that, for hours, Logan could perceive nothing but the obscurity of the night sky, clouds shutting out moon and stars. Before dawn, they stopped the engine, and Logan thought he could make out, vaguely, an enormous land-mass to the south. The drifter rolled heavily in a menacing swell; and there came the noise of that swell breaking upon rocks. "I will give you back your money for this dinghy," said Colin, with a sour grin, "if you have changed your mind."

"Let me into the dinghy," Logan told him, "and I'll cast off."

"The more fool you," Colin growled. They picked their way over the uneasy little deck to the stern, where the dinghy was in tow. MacLean let down a rope ladder into the little boat; he held an electric torch to light Logan's descent. "Here," said Colin, in a last-minute access of charity, "I will make you a present of the torch, Mr. Logan. And here is something else for you." Colin took a bottle of whiskey from a jacket-pocket and thrust it into Logan's canvas pack. "You will be wetted in beaching the boat, and the sea is cold. Row straight for the cliff ahead. The tide will carry you over the reef, but you must watch sharp for the needle-rocks. At Dalcruach clachan there is a keeper's cottage, and perhaps you can dry yourself there." Under his breath, Colin muttered something like "God help you."

Then Logan cast off and took the dinghy's oars. The drifter receded into the night.

For a moment, breaking through the pall of cloud, the moon showed him the cliff-head above Dalcruach. What with oars, tide, and a slight breeze, Logan swept in toward Carnglass, the Heap of Gray Stones.

CHAPTER 4

At Logan's back, as he rode the crest of that grim darkling swell, the forlorn hope of sunrise was fighting upward in the sky. By that pallid light, diffused through a gray mist, he saw that he was in perilous waters. Had the breeze been higher, he could have had no hope for making the shore, amateur oarsman that he was. Sweeping round the reefs toward the sheer cliffs just visible in the west, a current tugged in ugly mood at the oars; and he pulled hard against this current, for it would have hurried him against that fearsome wall. Still coming in toward shore, the tide helped him against the current. And now he was among rocks.

From the white heave of the water, he perceived that he was passing over skerries which would be dry at low tide. What was worse to the eye, here and there stuck up sharp rocks like swords menacing the sky, the "needles" of which Colin had spoken. Had it not been dawn, surely he would have run straight upon one. All about them — they lay too close, and suddenly he was passing some by — were wicked immense swirls and eddies, enough to bring a man's heart into his mouth. And Logan's heart did come into his mouth.

Once only, in all his life before, had he been so frightened; and that had been in a place very different, though equally eerie — a broken tomb in Okinawa, where he had crouched with two other cut-off soldiers while the Japanese scouts shuffled and whispered in the dark all about. This fearsome coast was worse than the tomb had been, for here he was utterly alone, in a hostile element. The mind-picture of the Okinawan tomb, hurrying through his brain in this horrid wet moment, vanished when the dinghy swung toward one of the smaller needles as if drawn by a magnet. Logan thrust the tip of an oar hard against the rock, and the boat slipped past. A wild scraping sound and a trembling assailed him then: the dinghy hesitated, in the flood of the tide, right upon a reef barely submerged. Yet her bottom held; and next she was off that rasping bed and hurtling on toward the dim line of the beach.

Logan was nearly powerless. What a fool he had been! This one crowded hour of glorious life he would have exchanged, gladly, for a life-time of servitude in the law-office. Yet there seemed to be sand dead ahead; and if he could pull hard enough against the weakened current, he might yet get ashore.

In the growing light, the island of Carnglass loomed like one tre-mendous barrier of naked and sheer precipice, except for a kind of fis-sure or den which was his goal, vague beyond the whitecaps. The nee-dles were gone now; the swell was full and heavy, as if the skerries were past; and he could make out the waves flinging themselves upon a dark beach, fighting high toward some grass and stunted trees, and then re-treating to the terror of the abyss. Two minutes more, and the dinghy was tossed by those waves right upon the sand.

Leaping out, Logan tugged with all his remaining strength at a line attached to the bow, to draw the boat as high upon the shore as he might, the water swirling about his waist. Back came the surf, flinging the dinghy higher yet, and blinding and drenching Logan, almost taking his feet from under him. Yet, persisting, he dragged the little boat over the sand with a power he had not known was in him; and when he thought she might be safe, he reached over the gunwale, grasped the heavy chunk of rusted iron that was her anchor, and flung it into the oozing sand. More he could not do; if the waves swept her out again, that was beyond his power to remedy. He staggered from the boat to-ward the tide-line and the grass beyond. When the sand grew firm un-der his feet, he fell nerveless to the beach, a spent man. And there he lay perhaps five or ten minutes, like a stranded jellyfish.

It was done. The thing was done. He was ashore in Carnglass, and a whole man, though shivering and shaking with the reaction from his fright among the needles. Perhaps the game, after all, might be worth the candle.

As some strength returned to him, his first thought was for the dinghy, in which his knapsack lay. Her anchor having held, the little boat rested askew upon the sand; he must have come in at the very flood of the tide, for already the combers broke further out, and the dinghy's bows were altogether out of the water. Reeling to the boat's side, Logan hauled out the knapsack and then plodded up the beach to the place where the heather and the gorse began to grow. He was in a kind of cove or pocket between thousand-foot cliffs, a triangle of land sloping steeply upward toward a third range of cliff at the back; and upon the face of that rearward cliff, not so beetling as its sea-neighbors, he thought he could make out the faint line of an ancient path.

Something more welcome, however, now huddled close before him: a line of low rubble walls, the work of man. These were primitive cottages, no doubt the clachan of Dalcruach. They were larochs, roofless ruins, deserted these many years.

All but one. Toward the end of the row of forlorn dwellings, a single thatched roof remained, kept secure against the Hebridean gales by a wide-meshed net spread over the rough thatch and anchored by big stones lashed to the net-ends. The hut had no chimney, but only a hole in the middle of the thatch; it had no windows, and a single door; this must be the "black house" of the Isles, one of those Viking-age cottages still inhabited, squat, thick-walled, snug, out of the childhood of the race. People dwelt in them still, Logan had been told, here and there in Uist and Barra. And this one might be the cottage of the keeper or gillie that Colin MacLean had mentioned. Incautious in his weariness, Logan limped to the heavy door and pounded. No one answered: the hut seemed to be as empty as its roofless neighbors. And then Logan observed that the door had been secured by a padlock and hasp, but the hasp had been tipped away from the door-frame, the screws hanging impotent in their holes. Lifting the latch, Logan entered.

Yes, it was a black house. Lacking proper fireplace or chimney, the peat smoke had eddied round the single room for centuries, perhaps, turning stone walls and beams and thatch to ebony. But it was dry, and it was furnished. There were a table and shelves, and a chair or two, and a heap of dry peats by the rough hearth below the gap in the thatch. And in a corner stood that rare object, the old-fashioned cotter's closet-bed, built of boards up to the roof to keep off the draughts, with only a wide hole for the occupant to crawl in upon his mattress, and a curtain over that aperture. Logan pulled back the curtain. There was no one inside, but there were decent blankets upon the bed. Feeling like Goldilocks in the house of the Three Bears, Logan flung down his pack.

Some dry bits of driftwood lay by the peats. Logan tested the cigar-lighter he had kept in an inner pocket of his jacket, to see if it would work; it still would. Making a little heap of kindling upon the hearth, he banked peats about it, and lit a fire; in three or four minutes, some of the brown and springy squares of peat had begun to smoulder, and Logan piled more peat upon them to keep the fire going while he slept. Only then did he throw off his drenched clothes, laying them upon a chair near the fire, and drag himself naked into the venerable bed, rolling deep into its blankets. Swiftly Logan sank into unconsciousness.

~~~~~

The sea-water having affected his watch, Logan could not tell what time it was, precisely, when at length he woke; but surely it was well into the afternoon. Some vigor had returned to his body. The slow-burning peats still glowed upon the hearth; the house was warm, and thick with the sweet smoke; daylight — the sun must be free of the clouds for a time — came through the smoke-gap in the thatch. There was no sound but the unending wash of the sea upon the beach, deadened here by the thickness of the walls of rubble. His clothes, still very damp but wear-able, lay faintly steaming on the chair by the fire. This was the loneliest spot Logan ever had known.

Having dressed, Logan turned out the contents of his knapsack, which had not suffered badly from the sea. A pair of binoculars he had bought before leaving America was intact, and he had his shaving-things, and the ordnance-map and old Balmullo's pamphlet, and what mattered most to him, the thermos of coffee, Colin's bottle of whiskey, and the big parcel of sandwiches from the hotel. Of those sandwiches, he promptly ate all but a reserve of two. Pouring the coffee into a pan he found upon the shelves, he set it to warm by the peats. Life was liveable again. And opening the door with the broken hasp, Logan went out into the Carnglass afternoon.

The ghostly clachan of Dalcruach lay silent in a cul-de-sac formed by the sea, the two sea-cliffs, and the inland cliff. Just now the sun was peeping through the gray blanket above. Everywhere water was running: little torrents foamed from the lip of the cliffs, and springs sent tiny streams down to the rocky bay, through gorse and heather and bracken. Between cliffs and tide, this bit of lowland must have been cultivated intensively for centuries, but now a towering forest of green bracken, high as Logan's head, came right down to the backs of the ruined cottages. Except for some gulls, the only animate thing which Logan could see was a shape high up the face of the landward cliff: a goat, or perhaps a deer. Primroses already flowered upon the cliff-face. Upon these scanty and isolated acres, a little village of MacAskivals had subsisted from time out of mind. But they were gone, and Logan stood in this wet green desolation as if he were the last man on earth.

He went down to the dinghy. The receding tide had left her high enough, but soon the sea would return; so he took off shoes and stockings and tried to drag her to a more sheltered place by a shelf of rock that ran up from the skerries into the silver sands of the beach. But though he bailed her out, she was too heavy for him; only the tide could budge her. Her oars he carried back to the black house. And now he would make his way across the island to the Old House, before evening came. The sun had withdrawn again, but surely he could find his way up the cliff, despite the mists, and so across brae and valley and hill to the Old House and Lady MacAskival. Already he had been nearly six days on the way.

Sitting on a boulder by the door of the black house, he examined the ordnance-survey map of Carnglass, Daldour, and the waters round about. Carnglass really was a peculiar island. A ring of tremendous cliffs seemed to guard her from the sea at all points, except here at Dalcruach and at Askival harbor, a larger opening at the opposite extremity of Carnglass, away to the southwest. To judge by the contour-lines, these sea-cliffs also had an inner face, standing some five hundred feet high above a kind of central valley or moor. Halfway between Dalcruach and the Old House by Askival harbor, this valley was interrupted by a tall, sharp hill, ridges from which extended across the valley to the cliffs on either side of the island, a sort of watershed.

As the gull flies, it could not be more than three miles from Dalcruach to the Old House. But there was the hard climb of the landward cliff behind Dalcruach; then the valley or moor would be boggy; and the ridge in the middle of the island must be surmounted; and between that ridge and the Old House were some markings which Logan took to indicate a bad bog. The trip would require some hours, and he had best set off. The dotted line of a minor path, on the map, suggested that some track ran across the island, but surely nothing like a road. Then Logan took up his thorn stick and began the ascent of the landward cliff.

Up this dim path, surely little but sheep, goats, and deer had gone for many years. Here and there a hazel bush clung to the cliff's edge. Though the day was cool, that sharp climb made Logan pant. After half an hour, he was at the summit, and much of Carnglass spread out before him — or would have been visible, had not the mist been growing thicker. He could make out the big hill — on the map it was called Mucaird — in the middle of the island, but the ridge and hill would have shut off Old House and New House, even had the day been clear. As a gust of wind in this high place dissolved the fog for a few moments, he glimpsed a derelict farm or sheep-steading nestled against Mucaird. And the valley between him and the high hill was not an even plateau, but rugged and broken with spurs of rock, though the bracken waved over the higher parts of it. He turned his glasses toward the south. There, across the deep blue of the Sound of Carnglass, lay the low isle of Daldour.

Now he would have to descend the inner face of a cliff, perhaps four hundred feet high, to the green valley: a descent more precarious than the climb from Dalcruach, for boulders lay tumbled upon the inner face, as if ready to fall to the valley floor, and their shapes were hidden by a dense growth of fern. He must step with care. Down he started.

But about three boulders down, he halted again. The mist — here it hung cloud-like — lay just over his head, the sunlight coming through in a dim religious way. At the moment, the valley beneath him, nevertheless, was quite clear of fog. And almost straight down, in the part of the valley at the foot of his cliff, men were moving. Logan turned his binoculars upon them.

Away to his left, a small puppet that must be a very big man was running frantically across the valley floor, just here rocky and bare. Some two hundred yards behind him, three other men trotted. These were armed men: it was rifles they seemed to be carrying. None of them were looking upward toward Logan. One of the three halted, knelt, brought his gun to his shoulder, and fired. The report echoed uncannily from the cliffs. He had shot at the big man leaping toward the further rocks: there could be no doubt of it.

But the big man was not hit. He had reached some boulders near the southern cliff, and now crouched behind one of them, drawing something from the long cloak or coat he wore. As his three pursuers came on — the man must have been hidden from their view, Logan thought — a report came from behind the cluster of boulders: the big man had a pistol. Immediately after firing, the man in the coat darted on to the next clump of boulders, and waited there. Stooping and taking what cover they could in the bracken, his three adversaries cautiously pushed forward, about ten yards from one another. The big man held the advantage of higher ground. As the three neared the rocks he had just left, and so came within range of his pistol, the big man fired a second time. Now the three pursuers fell flat on their faces, for the bullet seemed to have ricocheted against a boulder perilously close to the foremost rifleman. And taking advantage of their discomfiture, the big man scrambled on toward the mouth of a small ravine that appeared to twist into the southern cliff.

Swinging his glasses toward the three riflemen, Logan thought he caught some movement to *their* rear. He focused the binoculars. Though he could not be sure, it seemed to him that someone or something was stealthily drawing closer, through bracken and gorse, to the three men. Whatever it might be — and if it was not an optical illusion — it kept hid in the green stuff; no head ever showed. If there, it must be moving on all fours, beast-like; what one detected was not a form, but a trail of movement through the dense bracken, to be discerned only by an observer who, like Logan, was perched high above.

Logan looked back toward the big man, who was just disappearing into the gully or den at the southern cliff. Two of the pursuers, who now had got to their feet, fired at him as they stood. The big man stumbled, recovered, and was gone into the recess. And the riflemen resumed, at a walk, their tracking. Then the bank of mist settled over Logan's head and lower into the valley, cutting Logan off from sight of whatever was happening below. He heard two more shots, though; and then silence followed. Through all this, no human voice had drifted up to him.

Logan clung astonished to his perch. Here in Carnglass were wheels within wheels. He had suspected something was amiss in the island: but to discover, as if he were an Olympian looking down upon the follies of humankind, this curious sport of island man-hunting was bewildering even to Hugh Logan, who had been around. This, after all, was a small corner of Great Britain, in the year of Our Lord one thousand nine hundred and sixty. In Mutto's Wynd, his own struggle with Jock Anderson's gang conceivably might have been only a chance encounter; and even if it had been part of someone's design, no more had been meant, perhaps, than a brutal robbery. The sinister-ludicrous figure of Captain Gare had come to him at Oban through no chance encounter, but that insubstantial personality had vanished before a little chaffing. This affair in the valley of Carnglass was deadly serious — this stalking of a man as if he were a rabbit. And Logan had not the faintest notion of what pursuers and pursued might be.

So what should he do now? The mist, reinforced by a light rain, had become so dense below him that the remaining descent of the cliff, in these conditions, would be almost foolhardy until some sunlight worked its way through. In any event, what with this delay, it seemed improbable that he could make his way to the Old House before sunset. And, judging from the silent hunters far below, to knock at the gate of the Old House after sunset might be highly imprudent. Logan did not relish the thought of being taken for the big man with the pistol, supposing that person still to be in the land of the living. Besides, the quarry might be doubling back across the valley by this time, and for Logan to descend unknown into that scene from the Inferno, with bullets flying, wasn't the best policy for a rising man of law. Everything considered, he had better creep back along the dim path to Dalcruach, and there spend another night in the black house, even though this must mean he had taken a full week to reach Lady MacAskival. He could make a safer start early in the morning; perhaps Lady MacAskival's demoniac gillies did not hunt before breakfast. And there was a queasy feeling at the pit of his stomach. It was thoroughly improbable that any man would try to make his way over the cliff to Dalcruach this evening, what with fog, wind, and the clammy emptiness of the dead clachan in the cul-de-sac.

So Logan, still marvelling, shuffled carefully back toward Dalcruach, where he could enjoy the peat fire, and eat his remaining sandwiches, and write some memoir of this past week to post to Duncan MacAskival when the business was accomplished. He had found a kerosene lamp on one of the shelves, with fuel still in it. He might even read a bit in old Balmullo, for the sake of settling his nerves. Though the hasp was torn loose, the heavy door could be barred from within by a balk of sea-worn timber that fitted into holes on either side of the door-frame; and Logan did bar it. Now no one could get at him suddenly except through the thatch of the roof. And if folk outside did not know Logan to be unarmed, they would think twice about bursting blindly through the roof. Lighting the lamp, Logan took some sheets of paper — somewhat blurred and dampened by water — from a pad in his pack, settled himself at the table, and began to write with his ball-point pen.

He would save the sandwiches until he had finished writing. He was hungry, though; and despite the moist air, his throat felt dry. Logan put down his pen, threw his oilskin over his shoulders, and went out to the spring that bubbled only ten yards from the door. Coming back with a full pail, he drank deep and put the rest of the water — tasting faintly of peat — by the shelves. He drew up the chair and resumed his writing.

Then a deep voice spoke behind him. "Will you be a writer, or a philosophist?" the voice said.

Upsetting his chair, Logan sprang nimbly round to face the voice. He saw a very big man in a drenched ragged overcoat; and in the man's massive fist was a little old pistol, held steadily. The big man was bareheaded and baldheaded: a sloping dome of a head, with strong flattish features, battered and seared, and a broad, full-lipped mouth. Blood was caked all down one cheek of that hard face, and seemed still to be oozing from a gash high on the bald skull, where a little flap of skin fell away from the bone.

Logan's visitor stood gigantic in the shadows, close by the boxed bed; probably he had hidden there. "Don't move your hands," the deep voice said. "I'm Seamus Donley: so don't move your hands. I said to you, 'Will you be a writer, or a philosophist?' Or, now, will you be a police-detective?"

Immobile, Logan thought he detected some humor in that wide mouth. "Good evening, Mr. Donley," Logan said. "Put away that toy, and eat a sandwich with me."

"Turn round, Mr. Police-Detective," Donley told him, "and hold your hands high." There was nothing else Logan could do; besides, if the man had meant to shoot him in the back, he could have done that already. Donley's rough hands ran over and into Logan's pockets. "Now where might your gun be, Mr. Police-Detective? Your friend Seamus has looked in your rucksack and in the bed already." This was a wild Irishman: the brogue was pronounced, and possibly a little exaggerated, as if Donley strove for effect.

"I have no gun, Mr. Donley."

"Swing round again and let me look at you," Donley grunted. He had stepped back a pace, by way of precaution, but in the lamp-light Logan saw clearly enough the reckless, not ill-natured face of a man in late middle age; and below that face an immense barrel-chest and powerful arms. The gunman must stand nearly six feet six. "Faith," Donley went on, "I come near to believing you. You've the look of innocence. But whatever were they thinking of to send an acolyte of a police-detective after Jackman's fellows? Now listen to me, Mr. Police-Detective: if you've a gun about you, fetch it out, for you need it as much as yours truly, Seamus Donley. Would the lads in the Republican Army ever have believed that Old Seamus should be asking a police-detective to help him? Sure, it's your life, man, as much as mine. We can't tell but Jackman's chaps might be at the door this living minute."

"I don't understand you, Mr. Donley, and I didn't bring a gun."

Donley scowled. "Saints in heaven! Now's no time for playing little games, Mr. Police-Detective. This is not London. Those fellows would put you over the cliff as quick as myself. That's what they did with Lagg; but you can't know that. You know me: any police-detective knows Seamus Donley, that lay in Derry gaol four hard years, breaking out last Christmas. Do you think it's myself would be telling you my own name, and showing you my own face, if we'd no need for standing back to back? A fine young police-detective you are! Here, now: I'll send Meg to bed." He thrust the gun back inside his coat. "There, I'm trusting you, Mr. Police-Detective, and you must be after trusting me. We'll put out the light, for 'tis a standing invite to Jackman and his bully boys." Donley blew out the wick. "And we'll trample the turfs." Donley crushed under his boots most of the peats, and tossed ashes over the rest of the fire, leaving only a faint glow. "These three days gone, Mr. Police-Detective, Jackman's gang have let me be after dark, but they might change; and there's others might come."

Logan groped about the table in the dark. "I'm afraid I can't offer you much refreshment, Seamus Donley, but there are two sandwiches left, and most of a bottle of whiskey. Why do you take me for a detective?"

"I'd have eaten and drunk your victuals before now, Mr. Police-Detective, but you gave me no time. I'd but a moment to slip through your door and into your bed while you were at the well. A fine young police-detective you are! But Donley's not the man to let his host go hungry." He handed back half a sandwich to Logan, wolfing the others. "And the poteen: that's the medicine for myself when I've been three days and nights in caves and bogs. One morning I caught a rabbit and ate it raw, and another time I cut a sheep's throat and had a supper of the bloody ribs; but for the rest, it was birds' eggs got on the cliffs and sucked on the run, and a few shellfish I pulled from the rocks on this very beach."

Logan — his eyes had adjusted fairly well to the dark now — brought two tumblers from the shelves and filled them with whiskey. "Your health, Mr. Seamus Donley."

The Irishman chuckled. "There's this to be said, young fellow my lad: you're a cool police-detective. And how do I know you're a police-detective? Why, what else might you be? It's not an Englishman that you are, though — there's that for you. I'm thinking you'll be an Edinburgh man."

He might get more information out of Donley, Logan reflected, if he did not try to dispel this illusion. "More whiskey, Mr. Donley? Of course. And what is it I can do for you?"

Donley drained at a gulp his second tumbler of whiskey. He had taken a chair opposite Logan, and sat relaxed, though watchful: a hardened customer. "Why, just this, Mr. Police-Detective: first we'll take those oars of yours out of this hovel, and then we'll launch that boat of yours between the two of us, with myself inside, and then it's Seamus for Scotland and Mr. Police-Detective back to his but-and-ben in Carnglass — back to Hell, that is."

Upon the thatch the rain fell heavily now, and the wind has risen. "You have turned daft, Seamus Donley," Logan said. "Listen to that wind. You'd never get over the skerries in that little old boat this night, let alone row to the mainland. Daldour would be the best you might hope for."

"Daldour?" Donley snorted. "And land among the heathens? Why not the Cannibal Isles? Besides, there I would rot in Daldour till you, Mr. Police-Detective, might choose to come for me in the police-launch. No, it's not Derry gaol for Seamus. It's a Kerry man I am, and as good a boatman as any in these islands — born by Bantry Bay. No, I'll be hid in Glasgow or Birmingham or Liverpool before you report to the Chief Constable, my boy — supposing that ever you get clear from Carnglass, which I do very much misdoubt."

"If you must be fool enough to go boating this night, Mr. Donley, then wait an hour on the chance of the wind falling. The boat's light enough for you and me to get her afloat, even so: the tide must be up beyond her now. The risk of this wind is greater than the risk of low water on the skerries."

Bending forward, Donley gave Logan a light approving tap on the shoulder. "For a police-detective, you're a decent sort. What would your name be?"

Logan told him.

"See here, Mr. Detective Logan: I'll wait that hour, but no more. Never would I have guessed a police-detective would have a regard for Seamus Donley's skin. And see here: you'd best come with me. If you'll give myself your word of honor bright — you're no Englishman, that I'll say — to grant myself twelve hours pursuit-free once we set foot ashore, then it's Seamus who'll set you in Scotland safe, Mr. Scots Detective, and shake your hand at parting."

"No, thank you, Seamus Donley," Logan answered, "but I've business in Carnglass. Lady MacAskival will see that I get to Oban or Glasgow, when the business is done."

"Lady MacAskival! Do you think they'd let you see her, or that the Old One gives orders today? And even were they all saints in Carnglass they've no boat to put at the service of one Mr. Logan, Police-Detective, with a face like the cherubim. Was it not my fire that fetched you here?"

"What fire?"

A note of pique came into Donley's voice. "Then you will have known of Jackman's doings earlier, and I've had half my labor in vain. I might have told Jackman that what with his crew, the police were sure to find him out. 'Tis this: I burnt the yacht and wrecked the launch three nights gone. That was for spiting and hindering Jackman. And I had hopes of folk spying the fire and sending word to shore."

"Then they've had no communication with the mainland for three days?" This, Logan thought, could explain the confusion of Dowie and Gare.

"Three days? What with the storm, Jackman's sent no messages, nor got any, all this week. The wireless is a wreck. Jackman will be raging like an imp from the Pit, that oily limb of Satan. Oh, he'll be cursing the day he crossed Seamus Donley."

He might worm the whole story gradually out of Donley, Logan hoped: it was clear enough that Donley assumed he already knew a good deal of it. "Tell me this, Mr. Donley, while we're waiting here: what state are matters in at the Old House?"

"Do you take me for an informer?" The heavy voice, there in the smoky darkness, took on an ominous tone. It never would do to forget that Donley must be a thoroughly dangerous man.

"I take you for a man who's been tricked, Mr. Seamus Donley, and who needs what aid he can find. While we're on that topic, I'll do what I can for that bloody spot on your head. Did a bullet come close to finishing you?" A little light shone from the peats, and by it Logan set to washing the wound and bandaging it with two clean handkerchiefs from his knapsack. Donley, gritting his teeth, seemed to trust Logan sufficiently to let him do the job, though he kept one hand upon the pistol within his coat. Logan put back the flap of skin upon the skull and improvised a kind of scarf-bandage that probably would not endure long; he washed the caked blood from Donley's lined face.

"No, that was a damned fall this afternoon, when Ferd was shooting at me, Mr. Detective Logan. In all my years with the I.R.A., I never came so close to my end. But I'll even scores, trust Seamus for that."

The man had not winced much during the bandaging. "Keep your hand in, my boy, and in no time you'll be as fine a doctor as any at Dublin, or as Jackman himself. Jackman will be no true physician, but I'll not need to be telling you that, Mr. Police-Detective. 'Tis a doctor of philosophy he'll be, University of Leningrad, or Moscow. Yet I'm not the man to be stinting anyone of his praise: Jackman's clever with splints and medicines, and all else under the sun. A clever child, Edmund Jackman. Jackman it was that drew me out of Derry gaol, he having use for me. Jackman it was, sure, but not for Seamus' sake. For doing the Devil's work, there'll be none better than Jackman."

"And what," Logan continued as he adjusted the clumsy bandage, "is life like at the Old House?"

"Well, now, Mr. Detective Logan, do you mind that bit in Dante's Inferno where old Dante and Vergil observe the stewing of the frauds in the chasms? That'll be your reception at the Old House, and if you've a brain in your skull, Mr. Logan, you'll be jumping into the little boat with Seamus and making for your headquarters. You'll require a dozen constables with rifles, or more, to take Jackman's gang."

Despite his brogue — which, Logan suspected, was in part the affectation of a virulent Irish nationalist, or of whimsy — Donley had not spoken like an unschooled man; and this literary allusion confirmed Logan's surmise. "I think you're what you Irish call a 'spiled praist,' Seamus Donley."

"Sure, never a praist," Donley answered, grinning, "not myself. Yet I had some inclination after being a monk, and a lay-brother I was for nine praying months, in Sligo, till the love of the drink and the love of the girls undid me. Jackman was after calling me 'Father Seamus': he's eyes in his head, more eyes by one than most men. His boy Ferd was for giving me a third eye for myself." Here the gunman gingerly touched his bandaged forehead. "Ferd will be the deadliest of Jackman's imps, as you'll find to your sorrow; do you watch sharp for him. 'Tis the Maltese Cat I call him. Swift with a gun, and swift with a knife. And Jackman sent him to the Old One for a cook at the Old House! Ferd has virtue as a cook, no denying: the father of him keeps a little eating-house in Soho. But Ferd's better at murthering than cooking."

"How many others are in the Old House?"

Again Donley filled his tumbler of whiskey. "Jackman himself, and that walking cadaver Royall, that he calls his secretary — the only other political man in the lot. Then there will be five manservants, or a set of cutthroats that Jackman pawned off on the Old One for servants: butler, footman, gardener, gardener's boy (a broth of a boy!) and a fellow that passes for stableman or cowman. I was the keeper or gillie. Then there are three men for the yacht and the launch, all Jackman's pick: I singed the whiskers of one of them, Harry Till, a Liverpool longshoreman, and he may be at death's door, praise be to the saints. Because Jackman told them so, the Old One and the Young One turned off all the old servants, even the laborers at the farm; Lagg sent his wife back to Galloway, and at the end, he was living in a room or two by himself at the New House. Except for the Old One and the Young One, there's but one woman in Carnglass, and that's a poor shawlie, old Agnes with the arthritis, fit for no better than scrubbing floors and carrying trays to the Old One. So the odds will be ten or eleven to one against Mr. Police-Detective, as they've been against myself these three days past. Come away, Mr. Detective Logan: yourself would last two days less than Seamus has."

"Do you mean that Lagg is dead?"

Donley shifted uneasily. "Mind this, Mr. Logan: 'tis no doing of mine. What could be done to help Lagg, the old toad, I did. Nor did I see him die. They took him beyond the Chapel, to the highest of the cliffs, and they did not bring him back. 'Twas Seamus was meant to do the job, but I was one too many for even Dr. Edmund Jackman. Should ever there be a trial, and should yourself and myself come alive out of this, Mr. Logan, you'll bear that in memory."

"If I'm to bear witness for you, Seamus, perhaps you'll tell me the details of your part in the business."

Donley sighed. "Never did I think myself would turn informer, but that comes of the keeping of ill company. Not that Jackman and Royall will be common criminals: they're uncommon enough. The rest will not be politicals, only hard cases that Jackman has some clutch upon. As for myself, Mr. Detective Logan, I never took a penny that was not mine, unless on Army orders."

Getting up abruptly, Donley went to the door and put his ear against it. "The wind is high still," he said, "and sure they never will come to us in such dark as this — not Jackman's town crew. But 'tis my nerves that are on edge, Mr. Logan: three days with next to nothing in my belly, mind, so that there have been times when I thought more people than Jackman's were walking in Carnglass. A damned island. Well, then, my autobiography, or a bit of it, Mr. Police-Detective. Much good may the telling of it do you, or myself." Thrusting his chair toward the smouldering fire, Donley warmed his boots. What little light there was played upon his scarred face. And Hugh Logan listened.

Chapter 5

"Belfast it was where I met with Davie Anderson," Donley began, "a Glasgow razor-slasher of blasphemous conversation. Taking up with him was folly, Mr. Logan, but I'd small choice. The Republican Army — mollycoddles they are these days, to a man — would do nothing for me but hide me a week or two, and that with ill grace.

"'You're impulsive, Donley,' said they to me. I do believe they wished me back in Derry gaol. And who was it that blew the bridge ten years past? And who was it that was at the lighting of the fires in Belfast, to show the Luftwaffe where to drop their bombs? Why, Seamus Donley, none other. The Germans were nothing to myself, nor Jackman and his politics, neither; but it was enough for me that the English would catch it.

"No, the I.R.A. never sent the files that took me out of Derry gaol, nor the money, nor the motorcar, though at the time I took it for their work. Jackman it was: Jackman knew Seamus Donley for a man to handle the explosives." He poured more whiskey.

"When Davie Anderson came to me, I said I would do Jackman's work for Jackman's pay. A month ago it was that they brought me to Carnglass, and made me gamekeeper, and showed me the explosives, and told me the work I was to do, when the time came. Davie Anderson! Davie Anderson! Once let me come in reach of you, Davie Anderson, and you'll seduce no more honest rebels."

"Does Davie Anderson have a brother Jock, in the Gallowgate of Glasgow?" Logan put in.

"That has he, Mr. Detective Logan. I perceive you're not so innocent as you seem, not by half. A bad case, either Davie or Jock, like all Jackman's lot. Nine tenths criminals, and but one-tenth politicals. And that political tenth not my patriotic politics. 'Tis a rough life I've led, Mr. Logan, and I'm no man for small scruples. But needless murthering, unpolitical murthering, never suited my fancy. And in the murthering of women I will have no part, not even the murthering of old witches. And Jackman's plan it was, or I'm a Black and Tan, to lay the slaughter to Seamus Donley's account."

"What good would killing women be to Jackman?" Logan asked.

"There's no need for you to play the cherub with me, Mr. Police-Detective. 'Twas the money, of course: all that money. 'Tis not for his own self's sake Jackman seeks the money, but to ingratiate himself again with his party. Sure, and didn't they cast him out for a premature deviationist, and for the wild things he'd done? But the money, and the spying about the islands, and the explosives under the new installations — faith, if that thing might be done, the party would take him back, soon enough. A risky work it is, but if Jackman does it well, all's kisses. And the party is all Jackman's life, he being a political through and through: that I'll say for him. Jackman and his boys never told me, for never did they trust me, nor I them. But I've eyes in my head, Mr. Detective Logan, and a brain for right reasoning. When the time came, the women must die. And if ever it came to the prisoner in the box, who would they have for scapegoat? Why, old Seamus Donley, that's a fugitive from English justice."

"And did Lagg know of this?"

"Tam Lagg took Jackman's money two years and more. Yet the murthering never came into Lagg's thick wits, I do believe, until a month ago. To help Jackman to bully the Old One into making him her heir was one thing; to plot murther was another. And treason, too. Lagg's was no stomach for such tactics. But where could Tam Lagg turn? He could not get ashore, nor even post a letter, without Jackman's leave. When Lagg saw what I had seen, and thought the thoughts I had thought — concerning the plot for murther, I mean — he took fright. Jackman sees through a man as if flesh were glass, and Jackman will have known this month past that Lagg could be trusted no more.

"Then Jackman was the cat, and Lagg the mouse. And Jackman and his boys watched Lagg by day and by night. When they caught Lagg lighting the fire behind the hill, they made an end of him."

"What sort of fire, Donley?"

"Why, the fire that might have been seen by folk in Daldour, to bring them over from curiosity; but it never came to a blaze. That afternoon I sat by my cottage at the New House, mending rabbit-snares — for they had lodged me in the keeper's cottage, as if they feared to have me much about the Old House, near the gelignite — when Jackman came striding up, and with him Royall and Davie Anderson and Rab, that holy terror of a boy. Three days ago it was, but for old Seamus it seems like three years, what with the hiding and the running and the starving since.

"'Donley,' Jackman says to me, in his quiet wicked way, 'come along. We're hunting today.'

"'Then I'll be wanting my shotgun, Dr. Jackman,' I say to him. But he shakes his misbegotten head.

"'No, Donley, you old ruffian,' says he, 'we've guns enough for this hunting of ours.' And I see that Rab and Davie have rifles slung over their shoulders. Jackman himself carries no weapon ever, they say; and sure I've not seen him with any. 'Tis terror that he carries.

"So up I get, as you see me now, bareheaded and in my coat, and tramp round with Jackman and his boys to the shoulder of the hill they call Mucaird, and over the shoulder till we come close up to the broken farmhouse there. And from within the house, smoke is beginning to rise.

"'Hush, gentlemen,' whispers Jackman. 'We must not disturb the factor at his little games.' In through the empty doorway we creep; and there crouches that fat toad Lagg, his back to us, feeding a fire in a corner, pouring petrol on a heap of trash, so as to set the whole ruin ablaze. A noble beacon it would have made.

"Jackman grins his devil-grin. 'Good day, Mr. Lagg,' says he. 'You're a warm friend, Mr. Lagg.'

"Tam Lagg squeals like a pig when you come with the butchering-knife, and jumps round: a gross ugly man in corduroys, his face red and puffy always, but now white as a cadaver's. 'Dr. Jackman!' he squeals. 'Dr. Jackman!' And he can say no more, for there is no more to be said.

"'Yes, your old patron, Dr. Jackman,' that Beelzebub tells him. 'I assume that you're weary of our company, Mr. Lagg.' Davie and Rab tramp out the fire in the damp roofless room, while Lagg crouches by the wall like a trapped hare.

"'Even the fondest of friends must part, Mr. Lagg,' says Jackman, cheery as a cat with a rotten mackerel, 'and you're come to the end of your tether, my good and faithful servant.' Then Davie and Rab take Lagg by the arms and fling him upon the rubbish, and Davie unslings his rifle.

"'For God's sake, Dr. Jackman,' says Lagg, puffing and weeping, 'I've an auld wifie in Galloway, by Gatehouse of Fleet, and four bairns. And this is a civilized land.'

"Why, Donley's compatriots have a phrase that fits your situation, Mr. Lagg,' smiles Jackman. '"What's all the world to a man," the Irish say, "when his wife's a widdy?" You'll never be missed, Lagg. You'll have been lost at sea, merrily fishing. These are wild waters round Carnglass. And as for civilized lands — why, "had ye been where I ha' been, and see wha' I ha' seen" — eh, Thomas Lagg? This is the end of an old refrain for you. I never took to your red face. And even if I wished to spare you, still there would be the problem of morale among my associates here, wouldn't there? There's nothing like an execution or two to encourage the others. And Lady MacAskival will be so obliging as to write to the police concerning your sad disappearance at sea.' He's in love with dying — other men's dying — is Jackman.

"It came to me then, Mr. Logan, that when my usefulness to Jackman was done, Jackman and his boys would crowd old Seamus into some such corner. There's no honor among the lot of them. Lagg and Seamus were outsiders. And that man Lagg did cry so, lying there in the smouldering rubbish. Davie pokes him with the muzzle of his rifle, and Jackman gloats, like a sloat down a rabbit's burrow. I was standing behind the crowd of them. 'Though the creature's a Presbyterian,' I say to Jackman, 'at the least you'll grant him a moment for his prayers.' And that said, I whisk out Meg here." Donley patted the revolver inside his coat. "Jackman's lot never had known I kept Meg under my arm.

"They all turn to face me, Davie with the rifle half raised. 'Davie Anderson,' say I, 'drop it!' And Davie lets the gun fall, for he knows the reputation of Seamus Donley. Rab's rifle is slung over his shoulder; Royall's pistol is in his pocket. Yet it is four to one. Jackman's devil-grin never changes.

"'Why, Father Seamus,' he says, genteel as Brian Boru, 'I presume you aspire to the role of confessor.'

"'No, I'm no priest, Jackman,' say I. 'Yet you'll have the grace to grant

Lagg a moment for repentance, or 'tis myself will have another English-man's life on my conscience.'

"'I'll humor your piety, Father Seamus,' Jackman says, though his black eyes are like hell-coals. 'Mr. Lagg, to your devotions.'

"Lagg grovels in the dirt, moaning; and if he prays, the words run all together; and as for myself, I am too bent on watching Jackman and the rest to listen to him. A long minute it was, Mr. Logan.

"Jackman looks at his wrist-watch. *'Pax vobiscum,'* says he, ever so sneering. 'And now, Father Seamus, seeing that you have your little gun conveniently in your Fenian paw, perhaps you will be so kind as to ad-minister the *coup de grace* to our old comrade here.' The eyes of those four murtherers are turned on myself like dogs round a badger.

"'Jackman,' I tell him, 'may I screech in Hell if I lift a finger in this bloody business.'

"'Perhaps, in any event, Mr. Lagg would prefer a cold plunge,' Jackman says, smoothly. Lagg does no more than look at me, gasping and choking, as if I were the king of glory. But the odds are four to one, Mr. Logan, and Seamus has himself to think of, and Lagg was a tricky old toad.

"'Being but one man, Jackman,' say I, 'I cannot hinder you. Yet you'll not harm the rascal in my sight.'

"'As you wish, Reverend Father.' And Jackman nods to Rab and Davie. They take Lagg by the arms, he screaming out my name the while, and drag him through the doorway; and Royall picks up Davie's rifle, though careful not to lift it high nor point it toward old Seamus. 'Donley,' Jackman murmurs, as he follows them out the door, 'go back to your cottage. You and I must have a serious conversation later.'

"And they lead Lagg along the hill toward St. Merin's Chapel and the cliffs, he weak as water, while I watch them from an empty window, be-ing cautious not to show much of myself, lest Rab or Davie be inclined toward a lucky shot. And soon the bracken swallows them. Seamus has given Tam Lagg his minute of grace, and now Lagg must give Seamus Donley his hour for action.

"Jackman is cunning, think I to myself; but this once he's reckoned without his man. There were two things that I might try: first, to get clean away from Carnglass, which would leave Jackman with no good hand for the explosives, and no scapegoat; or second, to send up a signal like the signal Lagg meant to make of that farmhouse to call heed to strange doings in Carnglass. Now being a runaway gaolbird, I preferred the first method, Mr. Logan; and besides, 'tis the surer method; and it might save the women, since what with Seamus gone to the mainland and talking with whom he might, sure Jackman would think twice before doing more murther.

"So soon, then, as Jackman and the rest were out of sight, I ran down the track toward the New House and Askival harbor — and the boats. Two craft there were in the harbor, both Lady MacAskival's, though she'd scant need of them for her own self: a sixty-foot sailing yacht, old but with an auxiliary engine, and a fast motor-launch, half decked. Could I but get aboard either, and take it out of harbor — the motor-launch would be the better — I might make land somewhere and be out of sight before either Jackman or you darling police might say Daniel O'Connell.

"But somewhere there would be seven more of Jackman's boys: Sam Tompkins, a Cockney, with the grand title of butler — though he's little better than a pickpocket, and not to be dreaded; Ferd, the Cat o' Malta; a tinker-like fellow called Niven, that they'd made gardener; a Lancashire rough, Simmons, the stableman. Then the three boatmen, all out of Liverpool: Jim Powert, Harry Till, and Bill Carruthers. If the gang should be at the Old House, all of them, well and good: I never would try for the Old House, that being a strong place with but one gate. And if there should be but a man or two at the harbor, my little Meg and myself, between the two of us, might do their business. Now I'd a shotgun at my cottage, and like enough Lagg had a gun or two in the New House, unless Jackman had taken precautions. A shotgun or a rifle in the hands of such a one as myself is worth half a dozen men, Mr. Detective Logan, as I fancy you've heard tell. So it was to my cottage that I ran first, not looking back toward St. Merin's Chapel, nor liking to think what might be done there on the cliffs.

"All the way, I met no man. And my cottage was empty; but the shotgun was gone. 'Oho,' say I to myself, 'then Jackman will have a suspicion of old Seamus, and will have left orders to keep a weather eye on him.' I stuffed my coat pockets with biscuits from a tin, for there was no saying when I might dine again; and then, very quiet, I had a look about the New House, which has a little fir-plantation between it and the gamekeeper's cottage.

"As bad cess would have it, three men — Ferd, and Niven, and

Simmons — came out of the back gate of the New House when I looked that way from the firs. They not spying me, I knelt there silent, and they walked on toward the Old House, having locked the door behind them. Simmons was carrying my own shotgun. These are dull dogs, Mr. Logan, with no talent for hide-and-seek — though Ferd is sharp enough, but being a Soho spiv, he's out of his element in Carnglass. Once they were gone, I trotted on to the harbor, just beyond the New House; they would have taken the guns from the New House, for Ferd and Niven, too, had been carrying weapons. Now it must be the boats for Seamus Donley, with no help but little Meg. The night was coming down, praise be, and I might creep along the quay safe enough, keeping behind a little low breakwater that has a walk between it and the outer edge of the quay.

"On the yacht a light was burning, and she lay hard up against the stone quay, with the launch moored just beyond her. Two men were on deck, worse luck, and there might be a third below; I thought I heard his voice. And one of the men — Powert, I thought — had a rifle across his knees as he sat there. 'Seamus,' say I in my head, 'this must be neatly done, if 'tis to be done at all.' So back along the quay to the harbor-head I make my way, like a mouse, and to the shed by the quayside. They had forgot to lock the door.

"Now if I might keep the men aboard the yacht with their hands full of work, I might hope to take the launch; or, failing that, I might burn both boats, making a beacon to be seen in Daldour or out to sea, and vexing Jackman's damned soul. In the shed, along with ropes and paints and such, I found what I had hoped for, a tin of petrol and a brace of empty bottles. And there were some oily bits of waste and rags on the floor. You'll have made a Molotov cocktail, Mr. Detective Logan? Now that would have been a fine present for Dr. Jackman, considering his political tastes; but I hadn't the proper ingredients. And the real explosives were tucked away at the Old House, beyond my reach. So the bottles filled with petrol, and the waste and rags stuffed into the mouths, would have to serve me. The matches I already had in my pocket.

"With the bottles in my coat, back I go along the quay, keeping out of sight. But close to the yacht, my foot strikes a stone, that tumbles into the harbor with a splash. Powert and Carruthers, sitting on deck, seem to be nervous as pregnant cats, for Powert springs up with his rifle and calls out, 'Who's there?' And he catches a glimpse of my bald head above the dyke. 'Donley,' he sings, 'if that's you, show yourself.'

"What with Powert's rifle in his hands, it was a risky stratagem. Yet I bob up from behind the dyke and lob the first burning bottle right for the open hatch, Powert firing at me on the moment. Powert misses, but the bottle sails true. Right down the companionway it falls, and in a second flames come bursting up. And up comes another thing: Till, who has been below decks. I see him as I toss the second bottle. His hair and shirt are all afire, and him screaming like a mad thing.

"The second bottle goes down the hatch, too, and more flames shoot up; and then Carruthers takes panic and dives over the side into the harbor, for I have lugged out Meg and sent a shot across the deck. Powert runs aft for a fire-extinguisher, while Till rolls screaming by the deckhouse; but I try another shot at Powert, and he follows Carruthers over the side, rifle and all, though I do not think I hit him. If those three had kept their heads about them, they could have put out the flames, but now it is too late. And now Seamus will have his try at the launch; for below decks in the yacht, the fire from the spattered petrol is gaining fine. Powert and Carruthers will have struck out for the far side of the harbor, not liking the bark of little old Meg in my paw.

"It was down the slimy old quayside steps and into the launch I went then. Ferd and the rest from the Old House would be upon me in a matter of minutes, seeing the fire from the yacht; and then, too, the yacht might explode, if there were fuel in her tanks, though she did not burn so hard and fast as I might have liked. The mist being heavy that night, it was odds against the fire being seen from land, unless from Daldour, for Askival harbor lies snug among the cliffs; and the weather was too much for any chance aircraft.

"I tried the engine of the launch, but she was as dead as Lagg must be. It may be they had taken the plug, or tampered with the wires, Jackman being a man of forethought. Be it whatever, Mr. Logan, I could do nothing with her. If there had been even oars, I would have put to sea with no motor; but the launch was too big for rowing. One thing I did find in the bows, for all that: a spanner. 'Well, Seamus,' I think, 'if you're not to have her, no more shall they.' And with that spanner I did abuse the engine so that no man might mend it, paying no heed to the noise I made.

"On the yacht's deck, Till had made an end of his moaning, and I could not see him; like enough he had fallen overboard, which he should have done the moment my bottle set him afire. But I could hear feet running and voices near the harbor-head.

"With the tide ebbing, it came to my mind that if I were to cast off, the current might carry the launch toward the harbor-mouth, perhaps close enough to the other side of the harbor that I might leap ashore dry. So I cut the painter with my clasp-knife, and no sooner than was needful. The tide began to take the launch the few rods between me and the harbor-mouth. But now four or five men were on the quay I had left, and two rifles were firing. They hit the launch sure enough, and put holes in her, like enough — but not in Seamus Donley. The blessed dark that preserved me! In no time at all the launch had drifted right up against the further quay, on her way to the harbor-mouth, and I had hold of an iron ladder that's fixed in the stones, and up I went.

"As for the launch, she will have drifted out with the tide, and sunk, what with the holes in her, for when I looked down toward the harbor from the cliffs the next morning, there was no trace of her. You can trust Seamus for a job of sabotage.

"But there was no time for self-congratulations, Mr. Logan. They would have seen me get ashore again, even in the fog, and would be at my heels. The best route for myself was the low ground between the Old House and the empty cottages at Duncambus, and then up to the caves in the cliffs. Oh, I knew the island of Carnglass, what with shooting rabbits and birds over the best part of it, while I played at keeper. There was but one hope for Seamus left, and that was the coming of some one in a boat, such as yourself.

"A man or two set out after me, I think, and there was shooting in the dark; but I showed them my heels, and made my way up the north cliffs; yet a climb it was that none but a drunken man, or a desperate one, would undertake. And before I had got to the foot of the cliffs, there came a great *boom!* behind me, and I looked round, and the yacht was blazing worse than ever, for her petrol-tanks had blown up. Yet they had been half drained earlier, so the explosion was not all I had hoped for. When I got to the cliff head, the fire in the yacht was out, so they must have got pumps to working on the quay; Jackman will have been back with his boys by that time, and what he told the boatmen could not have been fit for decent ears. At dawn, when I risked a look at the harbor, I could see the wreck of the yacht settled into the harbor mud, with the water up to her gunwales even at low tide; she must be all awash at high tide, and I doubt she'll ever sail again. Sure, Jackman can't repair her."

Logan had interrupted seldom; that seemed the best policy, when

Donley was full of whiskey. Now he asked, "Do you mean you've bottled up Jackman's people altogether, Mr. Donley?"

"And myself with them, Mr. Detective Logan. Even had Jackman means for sending messages to the mainland, he'd say nothing concerning the yacht and the launch, for fear of police coming to investigate. And he has no such means, public or private. There was a wireless in the yacht, but that's lost; and there was an old wireless in the Old House, but that's been broken for a fortnight, how no one knows.

"In a matter of days, sure, his agents in Glasgow will begin fretting after Jackman, what with no word from Carnglass, and will send out some boat with trusty men to see what's wrong. Until he has another big launch, though, Jackman can do no more spying among the islands, under pretext of pleasure-cruising, nor get word from men that he pays in South Uist and other places. And now there's no Seamus Donley to handle his explosives for him, though Royall and Jackman himself might make shift, if ever they find a good time and place to use them. And Jackman will be fearing that the fire was seen, and that inquiries will be made."

"How is it, Seamus Donley," Logan asked him, "that you've contrived to keep clear of Jackman on this little island for three whole days?"

Donley chuckled with a deep gratification. "There'll be a dozen caves in Carnglass; and faint cliff-paths that only a Kerry man could follow; and two ruined villages, and the two empty farmhouses, and the barns and outhouses and the rest. And the mist, the blessed mist. Would you believe, Mr. Logan, that I'm sixty-four years of age? No more would they. But old Seamus is three times the man that the best of them ever was. Oh, I can lay false scents: I broke a window at night in the New House, so they might think me hid inside, though I never entered; and I smashed the lock on the door of this black house — it was kept for a hunting-lodge on this shore — though I've not slept inside, to fool them again; and they cannot tell where I lay my head. After dark, they give up the hunt, huddling together in the Old House, for fright of Seamus. And in the day, they dare not seek me in packs of less than three, though I've but little Meg here against their rifles. Twice they've come near to finishing me, the last time only this evening; but the mist saved me again, and I climbed down the sea-face of the cliffs, and came round to this hut of yours when the tide was low. They'll be on the scent again so soon as there's daylight. For if Seamus got away from Carnglass with a whole skin, their game would be played out.

"What they hope, Mr. Detective Logan, is that old Seamus will be worn down by lack of victuals and broken sleep and being run like a hare all day; and then they'll bag him. And so they might have done, in a day or two more, had you not brought your dinghy to Dalcruach sands, Mr. Logan. But now I'll take French leave of them."

In his wild and ruinous way, this was a wonderful man, Logan thought. "I've another plan, Seamus Donley," he said. "It's this: I suggest that you and I go up to the Old House together, in the morning, and face them down."

Donley slapped his hand upon the table, approvingly; and then, remembering his situation, glanced uneasily toward the door. "By St. Patrick and St. Merin — whoever *she* was — you've a heart in your body, Mr. Logan! You'd do honor to the Republican Army. Get thee behind me, Satan Logan. 'Tis a temptation: and I might yield, if only we had a brace of rifles. Mr. Detective Logan to stand for the majesty of the law, and Mr. Seamus Donley for justice outraged! Ah, the pleasure of seeing Jackman's face, under the circumstances. Now tell me true: have you no gun hid anywhere?"

"I've nothing but a walking-stick and a long razor," Logan said.

Donley shook his bald head. "No, the thing won't do, sir. Look here: there's but three bullets left in old Meg." He swung open the revolver's cylinder. "The rest were spent, though I had a pocketful of cartridges, in keeping off Jackman's boys when they came within my range. Fine figures you and I would cut, Mr. Detective, with one little gun to the pair of us, tossing a sixpence for who might have the third shot at Jackman. No, they call me a reckless Irishman, but I'm not the fighting fool you seem to be. 'Tis away in your boat I must be tonight; and if you've mind as well as heart, Mr. Logan, you'll come away with me, and let me set you ashore in safety, to fight another day."

"I'm thinking of the women's safety," Logan said. Donley nodded. "But you can do one thing for me, Seamus Donley: let me write a note or two, and you can carry them with you, and post them the moment you reach a post-box; for I take it that I'll need help."

"That I will do," Seamus Donley said. "And more: the moment I reach a telephone-kiosk, Mr. Detective, I will telephone your damned police, and tell them there is trouble in Carnglass. But promise this much to me, that you'll not put my name into your letter. And you must hurry, for midnight's near, and I'll need the ebbing of the tide to take me clear of the skerries."

"Give me five minutes," Logan told him, "and your leave to light the lamp again, and you'll have my word. You can read the note, for that matter. And then I'll see you launched in the dinghy. But unless you're a better boatman than any I've met, I can't understand how you expect to keep clear of the rocks, and fight the currents, let alone cross open water, in an open boat."

"Seamus Donley," that modest man said, "is as skilled with boats as with explosives. Trust me, Mr. Logan: I'll bring your message to land."

In haste, Logan scribbled a few words to the chief constable, Glasgow, or any police-officer into whose hands the note might come, saying that a man probably had been murdered in Carnglass, and that more trouble might be expected, and that immediate action was required. He put the paper into a soggy envelope, and Donley thrust it into an inner pocket. "Now," Logan said, "I'm your man, Seamus Donley. But watch for that current just beyond the needle-rocks: with the wind we've had for these past four or five hours, the odds are that it may be too strong for you, and smash the boat against the western cliffs." Logan stripped off shoes, stockings, and trousers, for it would be drenching work to launch the dinghy. And then the two of them went cautiously out of the black house. So far as they could tell, they stood alone on the dark beach.

Though the wind had gone down an hour earlier, and the tide was flowing back toward that lonely sea, still two strong men would be needed to launch even a light boat in that surge on the beach. Neither moon nor stars showed through the blackness. Between them, with much panting and heaving, they dragged the dinghy to the water's edge, and then pulled her along the beach to a more sheltered spot behind an outcrop of gray, weed-shrouded stone, where there was a good chance of getting her really afloat. They staggered in water up to their waists; once Logan fell, taking in a mouthful of salt water. The dinghy having shipped some sea, Donley bailed her as best he could with her rusty bucket. Now the trial must be made, and they would thrust her against the surf.

Donley flung his overcoat into the boat. "If you've no strong objection, Mr. Detective Logan," he growled, "I'll take with me the remnant of your good whiskey: I slipped the bottle into my coat pocket as we left the hut. You've a brave heart, but no eye for sneak-thieves. Yet I'll give value for value." He handed to Logan something dark and weighty: it was the little gun called Meg, in a shoulder-holster with a strap.

Logan fitted the holster under his arm. "That's generous of you, Seamus Donley."

"She's a well-balanced weapon, Mr. Detective, and never was meant for a free gift to a policeman. But how bullets will prevail against Jackman's boys, I cannot advise you."

"Give me your hand," Logan said. The tremendous grip of the Irishman almost made him cry out.

"We should have been Dominicans together, Mr. Logan," Donley grinned. He let go Logan's hand. "Now put your shoulder to the dinghy."

They forced her bow against the comber, and Donley, rolling his great body over the gunwale, seized the oars. Logan flung his weight against the stern, running up to his nose in the receding wave. Now Donley was plying his oars: the shelter of the rocks helped him; yet only a man of his vast strength could have made head against that surly swell.

Then, suddenly, the crest of a wave was carrying the little boat outward: Donley got her round the rocks that had helped her launching. If he called out anything to Logan at the last, his voice was lost in the noise of waves smashing against stone and sand. The dinghy passed into the Hebridean night, and Logan wished that fierce man good fortune upon his nocturnal sea. A minute later, Logan caught one final glimpse of the boat passing over the inner reef, Donley rowing mightily. After that, the mist settled upon the face of the waters.

CHAPTER 6

S ome strange bird, perhaps a shearwater, swept high above Logan as he made his way back to the hovel: it shrieked like nothing canny. That cry was a fitting farewell to Seamus Donley.

How much might Logan credit of the gunman's story? While Donley had sat before him, sinister and humorous, talking in his Kerry way, even the more amazing parts of the tale had seemed fairly credible. But now Logan felt grave doubts. Donley was a terrorist, his hand against every man's. That someone named Jackman should have upon Lady MacAskival's money was not improbable; but Donley's assertion that Jackman meant sabotage, espionage, and murder would not quite go down: not in a quiet Scottish island owned by an old lady.

Yet there had been Logan's own encounter with violence in Mutto's Wynd, and that unnerving scene in the valley just back of the cliff, with the three men firing at Donley. And Donley's account of Lagg's end had the ring of truth. Logan barred the cottage door behind him. Whatever measures Jackman's people had taken with an escaped convict, surely they would not deal similarly with an American lawyer, known by several people to have been bound for Carnglass. Yet the feel of Donley's pistol Meg, snug under his arm, was a comfort. Well, he must spend five hours more in the black house, though he had risen from his long sleep only ten hours ago, and did not feel in the least tired, even after the launching of the dinghy. There could be no climbing the cliffs until dawn. He let the fire expire altogether, and did not re-light the lamp: Donley's warnings had that much effect upon him. Lying on the old bed with a blanket about him, Logan thought of what he must do as soon as the sun began to rise.

The odds were that Donley's pursuers would be out in force when light came; they had nearly caught or shot Donley the previous evening, and they would know he was tired, and probably almost out of ammunition. And if those men with rifles were even half so rough a crew as Donley had suggested, it would be more prudent for Logan to avoid a sudden encounter with them — particularly since they would take any moving figure to be Donley himself. The best course, it seemed, would be for Logan to keep to the cliff-tops, if possible, until close to the Old House; and then to descend and go straight up to the door. If they wouldn't let him see Lady MacAskival, at least they could not mistake him for Donley; and he could lay his cards before this Dr. Jackman — or as many of his cards as might seem prudent. In Jackman, at least, Logan took it, he would confront a rational being.

It was inconceivable that any such man could persist in plans of violence — supposing he contemplated any schemes of that character — once he knew that he was facing a responsible person who had come to Carnglass on legitimate business. And if Mr. Lagg should be alive still — Donley, after all, had admitted that he had not seen Lagg die — presumably Logan would find an ally in him. Yet it might be wise to reconnoitre the Old House before knocking at the gate.

It was possible to half-believe Donley's tale because of the deathly solitude that enveloped Carnglass. The island was like a great bony corpse. Even here within the thick walls of the black house, the whole drowned mountain seemed dehumanized — perhaps hostile to humanity. Small non-human night noises drifted through the hole in the thatch: the rustle of bracken, unpleasantly like sepulchral whispering; the cry, again, of that nocturnal bird of prey: the surge of the devouring sea against the cliffs. Listening to these, Logan fell into a restless doze, now and then rousing himself with a start. Fragments of nightmare beset him during the sporadic periods when consciousness drifted away. And one of those fragments was deeply disturbing.

❧

He found himself in some place utterly dark, and made all of stone, without door or window; and his hands, when he extended his arms, could touch the cold walls on either side. Whether he was lying or standing, it was hard to guess: time and space and gravity and equilibrium had no meaning here. Something was belted to his side — a sword. And he was not alone.

Something else, foul and malign, existed there in that oppressive dark space. Of this, he could perceive nothing but its eyes; and there were three of its eyes. It was a devouring thing. In that cramped dead place, he drew the sword, and he hacked at those eyes. Yet the sword rebounded, as if he were striking feebly with a blade of grass against some enormous hard-shelled insect. "Strike through the sham!" a voice cried within him. "Strike through the sham!" Frantically he thrust again the blackness below the eyes. He was in terror not so much for himself as for someone else; but the name and face of that other someone would not come to him. And then, trembling and suffering from cramp in one leg, Hugh Logan woke.

❧

Outside the black house, birds were singing at the first feeble gleam of light in the east. Still shaken by the vividness of that nightmare vision, Logan flung on his clothes and strapped his knapsack on his back and took up his stick. It would be well to vacate this cottage before the man-stalkers of Carnglass were up and about; for, considering the direction in which Donley had fled the previous evening, Dalcruach was the most likely target for them this morning. Donley's pistol, in its holster, Logan fixed round his shoulder under his tweed jacket; it seemed adequately concealed.

He climbed the landward cliff more easily than he had the previous afternoon, now knowing the neglected path; and when he reached the summit, and saw the valley empty before him, he turned to his left along the ragged crest of those titanic cliffs.

The cliff-top was no narrow ledge: rather, it constituted an irregular plateau, in some places only a few feet wide, but in most twenty or thirty yards, and here or there a good deal wider. Broken by great boulders and dotted with springs or pools — some of them almost little ponds — this summit was rough going; surely it would take Logan almost twice as long to reach the Old House by this route. Up here, no doubt, Donley had lurked much of the time. When the mists were dense, it would be next to impossible to track down a solitary man at the top of this little world.

This was one of those high places in which Satan offers the kingdoms of the earth, Logan thought. Because of the winds, and the lack of soil, nothing grew here except occasional clumps of heather and little ferns and rock-plants. For the most part, the summit-plateau sloped inward toward the valleys of the island; the sea-face seemed to be sheer drop, almost everywhere. Today the wind was fairly strong, sweeping the spring fog out to sea, and Logan had clear glimpses, half the time, of the interior of Carnglass. The island was much better wooded than are most of the Hebrides: thick plantations were dotted here and there below the screes, doubtless the work of old Sir Alastair MacAskival. Twice, as he made his precarious way over the wind-swept rocks, Logan saw red deer grazing near the cliff-foot. And everywhere was trickling water. Early spring in the Western Isles has its charms, but it made the rocks treacherous for Logan and soaked his boots through. He used his binoculars when he came to a bold promontory of cliff, looking northward, though he lay down to avoid making a mark of himself. Near the ruined farmhouse at Mucaird, a small flock of sheep was browsing, some straying upward upon the hill itself; yet there was no sign of any man.

But a quarter of an hour later, as he drew near to a jumbled mass of living rock and broken boulders covered with lichens, something moving against the heather of Mucaird caught his eye. Half sheltering himself behind a rock, he took out the binoculars again. Yes, it was three slim men with rifles, close to the derelict farmhouse and shielings, and walking in the direction of Dalcruach. Something in their movements suggested that they were very ill at ease. And at that moment Logan felt himself to be in peril.

For only fifty yards away, and scrambling toward him, came two armed men. Their attention was fixed upon the scene in the valley, as his had been, and apparently they did not see Logan. He slid quickly down behind his boulder. It scarcely was possible that this cliff-patrol should fail to detect him. Should he stand up and call out to them now, or wait until they should be right upon him? Either course had its perils. Then the decision was taken out of his hands.

Down in the valley, one of the men flung his rifle to his shoulder and fired into the bracken on his left. The other hunters in that party knelt and fired also. Having put his binoculars back into their case, Logan could not see whether there was any movement in that brush. Whatever could they be firing at? Mere nerves, probably, since they had no idea Donley had escaped from the island; or possibly a stray sheep or a deer, which they in their tension mistook for a man.

"Ferd!" one of the men on the cliff called out to the other. "Ferd!" They were so close to Logan now that they sounded almost on the other side of his rock. "They've flushed him!" Then the voices of his neighbors receded, and Logan risked a peek around the boulder. The two had turned about and were retracing their steps, apparently looking for some way down the cliff to the screes, and so to the valley floor. It had been a close call. As the two riflemen scrambled round a rock shelf and began a tentative descent, Logan crept toward the seaward side of the cliff and so on toward the west, sometimes on hands and knees, until he felt safe from their sight.

When next he ventured toward the inland side of the cliff and took out his binoculars, the party of three men in the valley was vanishing behind a knoll toward the northern cliffs, and the other two, who had so nearly stumbled upon him, were nowhere to be seen; presumably they still were groping for a way down. Now, Logan guessed, he would be secure from such patrols until he came close to the Old House. Likely enough, two or three men had been sent to search the northern line of cliffs, so as to drive the elusive Donley like a wild beast toward Dalcruach; and that would leave only a handful of men about the Old House, the New House, and the harbor — if, indeed, even these last, or most of them, were not out searching elsewhere. He ought to be able to get very close up to the Old House before being noticed.

Soon he was past the ridge or saddle that joined the cliffs to the hill of Mucaird; and now he could look down upon the further valley. Broader than the first, it also was less stricken by the plague of bracken; there were cattle grazing — yes, the shaggy Highland beasts, he could see. The ring of cliffs was lower here than at the other end of the island. At the southwestern extremity, those gray walls dipped down to the ocean, forming the neck of Askival harbor. On the northern side of the harbor, the cliffs rose again and merged into a steep hill, which must be the one called Cailleach, The Nun. At its foot he could make out the scanty ruins of an ancient village: here Duncan MacAskival's crofting ancestors had lived.

Askival harbor was a good deep anchorage. On either side of its mouth, an old pier of rubble ran out to narrow the entrance still further against the ravenous ocean. And at the quay nearest to him, the burnt yacht lay lurched against the rocks; it was low tide again now, and her deck, or what remained of it, was just awash. The New House, rather a modest and neat eighteenth-century mansion, stood close by the harbor, surrounded by plantations and over-grown gardens. Further up the valley, in the shelter of the southern cliffs on which he stood, there was another farmhouse, apparently empty, but in better condition than the one by Mucaird; and near it some cottages and shielings.

All this, Logan took in through a long, low sweep of the binoculars. Then he focused upon the object of this troubled journey of his, the Old House of Fear. A quarter of a mile back from the harbor, the stark gray walls of the Old House rose upon a massive outcrop of rock: a place of great strength once. No man was stirring about it.

Fine old trees grew at the very foot of the living rock on which the Old House was built; but the castle defied the wind in its naked power, showing no touch of greenery except a glimpse of leaves at the back, possibly in a small walled garden. The late-Victorian wing blended fairly harmoniously with the mass of the ancient tower, and seemed to close off the original entrance from the present exterior of the complex; the modern gate must front toward the harbor, and so lie hidden from Logan's view, from his present position upon the cliffs. Talk of castles in Spain! The Old House of Fear, here upon the desolate verge of civilization — at the limits, indeed, of human existence itself — had a brooding glamour denied to Roman and Saracen lands.

Here toward the harbor, the cliff-face was easier than the precipices toward the northeastern end of the island. If he were cautious, he might make the descent without alarming anyone at the Old House. Having climbed several summers both in the highlands of Perthshire and in the Rockies, Logan could avoid sending boulders thundering before him. Supposing no one chanced to make a target of him, he might reach the Old House about noon.

Now how might he descend toward the Old House unobserved? Coming down the cliff-face and the screes, if he should try it just now, he must make a fair mark; although when he should reach the cliff-foot, he might pass to the back of the New House through the plantations and then slink along a belt of aspens and firs which stretched from the New House to the wood round the base of the rock where stood the Old

House. First, however, he must make his way along the cliffs until he should come nearly abreast of the New House, and then seek for a way down. And the thing might be done, in this mistiest of islands, in this mistiest of seasons. For the breeze was subsiding again, and the sky had darkened; and once more the fog might settle over cliffs and hill-tops, though possibly it would not sink low into the valley.

It took Logan half an hour to discover — always taking advantage of cover — a tolerable fissure in the cliff down which he might make his way. Still no one was to be seen between him and the Old House. Twice he thought he heard gunshots in the distant northeastern valley; but, the wind being eccentric and generally against him, he might have been mistaken. And presently, as he had hoped, the mist began to settle like a shroud upon the cliffs. His tweeds blended with rock and heather. For twenty minutes more, he crouched at the summit, the fog slowly shutting off his view of harbor and New House and Old House. Then, carefully, he began the slippery descent. When he reached the talus-slope, he walked gingerly, lest he start a warning slide of rock debris.

Still he saw no one, nor heard anything. At length he was in the first of the outlying plantations of the New House, and moving swiftly toward the Old House. It was midday, on a Wednesday, a full week since he had left Michigan. And now he stood, sheltered by old trees, right below the Old House of Fear.

Immediately above him, nearly thirty feet up the steeply-sloping gray outcrop, was the little walled garden he had glimpsed from the cliffs; and a stout stone dyke about eight feet high enclosed it. The garden was set against the rear wall of the great ancient tower, the windows of which looked upon the wood, so that the moment Logan should emerge from the cover of the trees, he must be fully visible to anyone at those windows. Most of the apertures in the tower-wall — from this position below, it seemed like a skyscraper — were the original or at least medieval windows, perhaps a foot square, though now closed with glass panes; but the windows of the third story had been much enlarged, perhaps at the end of the seventeenth century, so that they were taller than a man, and fitted with double sashes of nine panes each. Crouching near the northeastern angle of the tower as he did, Logan could see the range of seventeenth-century buildings that extended to the smaller medieval tower, and beyond that the jutting bulk of the late-Victorian additions, which covered the whole surface of the seaward part of the rock. So long as he kept to the rear of the old tower, he could not be observed from the later portions of the mansion. And it stood to reason that some sort of postern-door must open from the old tower into the walled garden.

There drifted to him a sound of voices. Lying flat in the wood, Logan made out two men with guns, striding from behind the façade of the Victorian building in the direction of the hill called Cailleach; thus their backs were to him, or soon would be. The leader was a tall gaunt gawky creature, possibly Donley's "walking cadaver," Royall. So Logan knew that he had not yet been seen; and there were two less snipers to fret about for the moment. He let them go out of sight downhill. By hooking the handle of his stick over the lip of the garden dyke, he thought, he should be able to scramble up and into the little garden. It had best be now.

But at that moment, as he rose to step out of the wood and clamber upon the rock, he perceived someone at the nearest third-story window of the old tower. "Saints be praised," Donley would have said; for it was a woman's shape. If this should be Lady MacAskival herself, Logan's work might be made easier for him. He stepped into the open.

From high above, she saw him; and though perhaps she started a little, she gave no sign of real dread. This was the first calming thing that Logan had observed in Carnglass. Unhurried, the woman lifted the sash. Surely she could not be Lady MacAskival, for she was slim and graceful and apparently young; that much Logan could make out, though she stood so high above him. Could this be the "Young One" to whom Donley had referred vaguely? There had not been much time for asking incidental questions of Donley. Then she spoke, with a gentle lilt to her voice, and very low, so that her words just carried to Logan. "If you can come over the dyke," she said, "I will open the little door for you." Her shape vanished from the window.

Logan skipped up the great rock and hooked his stick upon the dyke, putting his feet against the wall; and up he went, and grasped the top — luckily there was no broken bottle-glass set into it — and pulled himself over, and sprang into the square of garden, which must have been wearisomely established by patient labor in this unlikely spot. There were a half-dozen flowering shrubs, and some small yews, and two neat beds of flowers. And beyond these lay a small heavy iron door set into the great wall. Logan waited a long minute before bolts grated back and the door swung inward.

76

"Quickly, now," that soft voice said, "and please take off your boots once you are inside." The foundation-wall into which the doorway had been cut must be at least ten feet thick. Logan slipped past the woman, who bolted the door behind him, and he had unlaced and removed his boots almost before she turned to him. They stood in an enormous empty vaulted chamber, in the earliest days of the stronghold a stable and storehouse, no doubt. At one angle, a stone stair wound upward into the blackness of the great wall itself. Though the only light came from slits three feet above their heads, he saw her fairly plain.

"Really, sir," she was saying, ever so quietly, but with an undertone of amusement, "you seem to have scrambled over the worst of Carnglass." Logan became conscious of his rock-bruises and his two-day beard. "Now what is your name, please, and who sent you?"

She was young, less than twenty, and a tiny beauty: her shapely head came scarcely above Logan's shoulder. The oval face with the high cheek-bones was a charming pink-and-white; the firm lips had an infinite grace and mobility, and the dreamy wide eyes were green. The nose, perhaps, was a trifle masculine in so small a face, straight and strong. And the flaming glory of her red hair, which descended to her supple waist! She wore a close-fitting simple suit, of the green tweed of the Islands. Blood tells, Logan thought: this girl is of the old line. She made him stammer.

"I'm Hugh Logan," he said, "representing Mr. Duncan MacAskival."

She clapped her slender hands noiselessly. "I knew you must come from him! It was I that sent for you, you know. Are there others just outside?"

Logan shook his head. This would be the Young One. But who was she?

"And I am Mary MacAskival," she told him. "Come away, and make no noise. I do not think we shall be long alone together. Carry your boots." She sprang to the twisting dark stair in the wall, with Logan at her heels. They were naked delicate heels, Logan saw, as they scampered up into the wall: she wore no shoes and stockings, as if the chill stones of the Hebrides were warm sand to her. The bare feet of Scottish girls, it came to him incongruously, had been one of the principal attractions of the land for French visitors in the eighteenth century.

In silence, they passed a shallow landing and a massive door; and hurried up another corkscrew flight, she pausing to whisper, "Do watch your feet here; it is the bad step — the place they made to trip enemies in the fighting with claymores, you know." Yes, the single step was two inches higher than the rest, to throw off balance a man leaping upward. They passed a second recessed landing and a second heavy door; and then Mary MacAskival swung open the door opening upon the third story, ushering Logan into a noble ancient vaulted chamber. "This is my very own parlor," she told him, with just a hint of vanity.

The square room had a ceiling painted in faded reds and browns, geometrical designs by men long dead; and there were a few good pieces of furniture, principally eighteenth century, and a crimson Victorian sofa. A door in the further wall gave entrance, probably, to the seventeenth-century domestic range of the Old House; and another led presumably, to a sleeping-closet. "Do sit down," the girl said, gesturing toward the sofa, "and you may put on your boots, if you like. I did not wish them to hear us on the stair." For herself, she settled nimbly into a window-nook opposite him, her tiny feet hid by her skirt. "Now tell me truly," she went on. "Are you a real American? I thought all Americans wore synthetic suits, and carried great cameras over their shoulders, and smoked cigars incessantly, and said 'You bet' and 'I guess,' and wore their hair sheared ever so close. Do you know, Mr. Logan, you could pass muster for a Scot? Now wherever are the others?"

"There's no one with me," Logan said. She still had him nearly tongue-tied, like an adolescent.

A little charming ripple of dismay passed over that lively face of hers. "No others? Then where are Mr. Duncan MacAskival and all his people?"

"I came alone from America, Miss MacAskival, and it was all I could do to make Carnglass by myself."

"No!" That sweet mouth rounded to give force to the negation. "No!" She threw back from her forehead a lock of red hair, bewildered. "Mr. Logan, I'm afraid I have made a serious error. You must understand that I am not very worldly; I'm sorry for it. I thought any American millionaire would come in his own grand yacht, and servants beside him, and perhaps policemen and soldiers and cabinet-ministers. I never guessed that you, or anyone else, might come all alone. I do fear that I may have fetched you into a dangerous plight." Her musical island English — and yet she must have been to a good school somewhere, too — was so pleasant to the ear that Logan almost neglected the warning in her words. "Now look here, Mr. Logan." A quality of decision came into her soft voice that had some connection with that high-bridged nose of hers. "Do you think you could pretend — successfully, I mean — to be an Edinburgh man? A young bank clerk? The British Linen Bank, shall we say?" Despite the girl's childish look, in some respects she was in advance of her years; just now she might have been a dowager duchess. "You can? Then you must do precisely that. I do hope you studied play-acting once upon a time. I did, you know, at the convent-school. You're very young, Mr. Logan — I had expected a very rich and very fat old man — but really, you must contrive to carry it off. Everything depends on it."

"Just a question or two, please," Logan said. "I met a man named Donley at the other end of the island."

"Of course." She smiled. "A great cheerful ruffian. And he said some things to you? They will not have caught him yet?"

"I don't believe they'll ever catch that man, Miss MacAskival. He told me that matters are dangerous here in the Old House."

"He told you truly. What else did he tell you?"

"He said that Dr. Jackman intends to — to have Lady MacAskival die."

Her eyebrows lifted. "O, no! Donley was mistaken. Lady MacAskival would not have been alive these past two months had not Dr. Jackman tended her with all his skill. He has been a good nurse. It's to his own interest that she should live."

Logan looked her compassionately in the eyes. "And Donley hinted that you, too, were to die."

The girl shook her bright head impatiently. "Donley did not understand. Dr. Jackman does not mean to have me die — not now, and perhaps never. Dr. Jackman means to marry me."

Logan had cultivated a calm courtroom presence, but now he blinked. "You're not joking?"

Mary MacAskival smiled ever so slightly. "Do you think Dr. Jackman shows bad taste? Hush, now!" She sat listening intently, her head inclined toward the door that opened upon the body of the Old House. Logan could hear nothing, but of course this girl's ears would be attuned to every footfall in that strange place.

"Stand up, please," she said; and then, silent on her nimble naked feet, she approached him. "I do hope you'll forgive me, Mr. Logan, but I am about to do something rude. I've done it seldom, and I may do it badly." There came a light tap at the door. "Hold me, if you please," she whispered, and pressed that lithe body against him, flinging her arms about his neck. Logan heard the door creak open, but he could not see, for the moment, who entered; and this was because Mary MacAskival's red lips were thrust upon his, and the glory of her red hair was all about his face. Then, as she let him go a trifle, over her shoulder he saw a man standing in the doorway.

It was a small man, sturdy enough, but with an indescribable air of deformity about him — perhaps a curious thrusting forward of the shoulders. With his forehead, too, there was something faintly wrong. But the eyes were splendid: black, and piercing, piercing. The man's face was one of those faces which never were young and never will be ancient. The face tightened, as if resisting shock, and Logan thought the man's right hand strayed toward the back of his coat; but it returned gently to his side.

The man's voice was controlled and well modulated. "I am surprised to find you have a visitor, Miss MacAskival."

Mary MacAskival let go her arms from Logan's neck and turned on her toes to face the man, with a wonderfully convincing air of surprise and embarrassment. "Oh, Dr. Jackman!" she murmured. "We must have looked dreadfully silly. Dr. Jackman, may I present Mr. Hugh Logan, of the British Linen Bank, Edinburgh? Mr. Logan and I are to be married."

CHAPTER 7

"Why, then," Dr. Jackman said, "Mr. Logan is a fortunate young man." The note of irony was faint. "I seem to recollect, Miss MacAskival, your mentioning that you met a young man at an Edinburgh party, last Christmas: I suppose this is he. And however did your betrothed contrive to come into this house, in this season?"

Whatever game the girl was playing, Logan thought, he too would have to play it now. And possibly he might carry it off. Jackman he took for an Englishman. Logan had some talent for languages and dialects; his courtroom years had taught him dissimulation; and since the war he had been in several amateur performances of the Players' Club. Now for his present role: he had best play the part of a rather callow, but ambitious, clerk from the Lothians. His speech ought to have a strong suggestion of Scots, but to seem an imitation of public-school English, and with a touch of what people called "la-de-da." A small moustache might have gone well with the part; it was a pity he hadn't been given time to cultivate one.

So Logan stepped forward rather stiffly, offering his hand to Jackman. "Now the fat *is* in the fire, isn't it? Rather. It's grand to make your acquaintance, Dr. Jackman, but really, I must apologize for coming informally this way. It's my fortnight's holiday, and I had promised Mary to come for a holiday as soon as ever I could. Somehow my letters hadn't reached her. The post is beastly nowadays, is it not? Some fishing-johnnies brought me over from North Uist, and set me ashore at

81

the other end of your wee island. Now I must see Lady MacAskival to-day and ask her approval. For Mary and I do not mean to wait another quarter, do we, Mary, darling?"

The girl had stepped forward with him; and now Logan, putting an arm about her waist, gave her an overdemonstrative squeeze in keeping with his new character. She did not seem disconcerted. "No, Hughie," she said, "we mustn't wait a day longer than necessary."

Dr. Jackman's thin lips contracted, but he took Logan's hand briefly. "You and I will have much to discuss soon, Mr. Logan," he said, "but just now, tell me this: if you came from the shore at Dalcruach, did you meet no one on your way?"

"Indeed I did see some men hunting," Logan replied, easily, "but they were away down in the glen, and their backs to me, so they did not see me when I waved." He was doing well enough with his assumed pronunciation, he thought; he threw just a suggestion of "awa' doon" into his words. "Then there were two sportsmen on the cliffs, and I called af-ter them, but the mist came up and hid them. I kept to the cliffs, the better for finding the castle. And Mary here" — he squeezed her again — "had told me her rooms were at the back of the house, so I went round, and Mary saw me and let me in." He felt sure that Jackman dis-liked him intensely. Who wouldn't, in his present role? He hoped he was convincing as a pushing, canny, and unmannerly junior clerk.

Jackman looked vexed, though not especially with him. "Mr. Logan," Jackman said, "did you ever dream that you were the commander of a gar-rison, for instance, with Red Indians all about your fort; but that the mo-ment you turned your back, your troops would vanish like shadows; and any shot that was fired at the enemy, would have to be fired by yourself?"

"No, sir," Logan replied, with what he trusted was a properly oafish perplexity, "I never did. The fact of the matter is, I never do dream."

"I should have thought of that," Jackman observed. "No, I'm sure you never dream. But to return to the heart of the matter: I dream a great deal. And the conduct of Lady MacAskival's servants is like a nightmare to me. What incompetence! Yet several of them saw service during the late war. If none of them spied you on the cliffs, they must be even duller than I thought. I suppose that Miss MacAskival has told you a very dangerous man is at large in the island?"

"She has, sir; and I am thankful I did not meet with him on my way. An Irishman, she says."

"Yes, Donley: an Irishman, and a homicidal maniac. Our people have been seeking to arrest him for more than three days, but he always escapes their net. Those were not sportsmen you saw, Mr. Logan, but our people tracking this Donley. Neither Miss MacAskival nor anyone else in this house will be able to set foot outside while that man is at large, unless accompanied by an armed guard. I regret to say, Miss MacAskival, that I must forbid you to visit your garden until the man is caught. And please have the goodness to remember to keep back from the windows. The man is armed, Mr. Logan, and a crack shot. Only Ferd Caggia, our cook, is his peer with a gun. To be defended by a Maltese cook in one's own castle! Ludicrous, isn't it, Mr. Logan? I suppose you wonder why we haven't summoned the police. But possibly Miss MacAskival has had time to tell you that the madman destroyed our boats, and we have been quite out of communication with the mainland. Presumably, however, our agents in Glasgow will send a launch to us in a day or two, by way of inquiry, and then we can call in the police. That launch, by the way, can give you passage back to the mainland, Mr. Logan."

"That's very thoughtful, I'm sure, sir," Logan said innocently, "but it's my plan to stay the best part of a fortnight, if Lady MacAskival will permit me."

"Lady MacAskival is in no condition to make decisions of any nature. As for your remaining here — why, we'd best go upstairs to my study and discuss certain matters, Mr. Logan. Will you excuse me, Miss MacAskival?"

That barefoot little girl stepped forward like a princess. "Dr. Jackman: surely you remember my Airedale, Tyke?"

"Yes," Jackman said with a frosty smile, "I do. A great pity, that rabbit-hunting accident."

"You took Tyke for a walk, Dr. Jackman," Mary MacAskival went on, dispassionately, "and never did you bring him back. I wish you to bring Hugh back to me. I intend to give him tea here in my parlor, one hour from now."

"Of course, my dear young lady." Jackman bowed slightly. "I shall bring him back safe in wind and limb: eh, Logan?" He clapped Logan lightly on the back. "And now, be so good as to follow me up these stairs. Mind the worn stone treads: they're treacherous. No one knows how many generations of MacAskivals have trodden that granite through.

There's a legend that the ghost of Old Askival snatches at one's ankles on those stairs. Eh, Miss MacAskival? I'm sure he'd snatch at yours, and small blame to him." Jackman nodded at the girl with a kind of paternal gallantry.

Mary MacAskival stood in the doorway as Logan and Jackman began to ascend. "I believe it was my ankles that you noticed first, wasn't it, Hughie?" Though the stair was dark, Logan thought that Jackman almost winced. "I suppose I really ought to tell you how it was that Hugh and I came to meet, Dr. Jackman. You've already guessed that it must have been during that wonderful fortnight Lady MacAskival and you let me spend in Edinburgh in December with Anne Lindsay, who had been at school with me. I happened to go into the Lawnmarket office of the British Linen Bank to change a five-pound note, and Hugh was so very helpful and we found that he knew the Lindsays of George Square; and . . ."

"Quite," said Dr. Jackman, "quite. Perhaps we had best leave the rest to my fertile imagination? Really, I am not in the least surprised; if you will pardon my saying so, Miss Mary MacAskival, the little episode is part and parcel with the traditional impulsiveness of ladies of your family. You understand what I mean. The inscription by the door of the old tower, for instance — we'll show you that incised slab later, Mr. Logan. Just now, I've only one thing to say to you, Miss MacAskival. I advise you to go in to Lady MacAskival and tell her that a young man has come to call upon you. As for any mention of marriage, the shock might put an end to your aunt; and you know as well as I do the certain consequence to your own prospects. Yet you had best mention Mr. Logan's coming, because old Agnes would tell her soon enough, in any event. I advise you to be extremely gentle and prudent in the telling. And while you are having your little chat with Lady MacAskival, I shall have my little chat with your Mr. Logan."

Mary MacAskival sent a glance from her disturbing green eyes at Hugh as he followed Jackman up the dark stair; and she gave him a demure wink. Whatever else the girl had or lacked, she had sufficient courage in adversity. Then she was gone, and Jackman led him round and round the twisting stair in the thickness of the wall, past several shut doors, to the topmost chamber of the tower. Upon three sides were windows, not so large as those of Miss MacAskival's room, but still big and handsome; and on the fourth wall was an immense fireplace, perhaps fifteenth-century work, with a ponderous chimney-piece carved crudely from basalt. On one side of the mantel, and standing two feet high, carved almost in the round, was the effigy of a naked man holding an axe; and on the other, a naked woman clutching a cross to her breast.

"A ponderous quaint affair, isn't it?" Jackman observed, nodding toward the fireplace. "There are similar figures set into the outer wall, by the door of this tower: Askival and Merin, they say. The Old House is so well preserved only because it stood empty, but not a ruin, nearly the whole of the nineteenth century: the proprietors lived in the New House. They used the ground floors of the Old House for byres and rubbish-rooms. Sir Alastair MacAskival, the present old lady's husband, restored the Old House — with his wife's money. It's far too large for such a household as she has now. The block that Sir Alastair added is all great drawing-rooms and dining-rooms and billiard-rooms and ballrooms, with the kitchens below; and the present servants sleep in the upper rooms of that wing. Lady MacAskival has a grand bedroom hung with Spanish leather, in the Renaissance range; and I have rooms in that building. But I spend much of my time in this study. For centuries it was the private chamber of the chiefs of MacAskival. There's a fine prospect; but I'll show you that later, Mr. Logan. And have you noticed the ceiling? But I presume you're no antiquarian."

Indeed, the ceiling was a wonder. Though the colors in which its panels were painted were much like those of the ceiling in Mary MacAskival's parlor, here geometrical designs alternated with scores of stiff representations of queer men and beasties: kings, perhaps, and knights, and ladies, and lions, and leopards, and griffins, and waterhorses, and unicorns, and things for which Logan knew no name — no two alike. "Late fifteenth century, perhaps," Jackman said, "and almost unique in the islands, this ceiling."

At the center of all these painted ceiling-panels was a panel with a dull red background; and on it, little faded, was depicted a very odd creature. It had the body of a man; but there were cloven hoofs instead of feet, though it showed human hands; and the head was the narrow malign head of a goat. The face itself seemed to be a dismaying blend of human and animal features, in which the cunning slit goat-eyes dominated. "I see you are looking at the Firgower — the central panel," Jackman went on. "A beast peculiar to Carnglass, it seems, the Firgower: half goat, half man. There's still a ruinous building upon the cliffs called the Firgower's house. I take it to have been the house of the last Pictish chief of Carnglass, before the Vikings came. There's some remote Pict strain, as well as Norse, in your own Miss MacAskival, Mr. Logan. She is of the old family, true enough — not that she has the faintest legitimate claim to the property, you understand. But I suppose you have little interest in fictions like the Firgower. These legends sometimes have meaning, all the same. Once an archeologist told me that the Firgower may be some island memory of the last Pict chieftain himself: an ugly brute, to judge from this portrait. The old islanders used to say that the Firgower never died, but lives on from age to age. And that's true enough, Mr. Logan, after a fashion — the goat strain, I mean. I don't scruple to say that a goatish strain has run through the line of MacAskival, from beginning to end. Gallant men and handsome women; but concupiscent, Mr. Logan, concupiscent. You understand me? There are vessels for honor, and vessels for dishonor."

"I can't say that I do understand, precisely, sir." The two of them were seated in leather chairs now, and Jackman was pouring sherry from an eighteenth-century decanter. What with Mary MacAskival absent, Logan could spend his time studying this unnerving Dr. Jackman. As Donley had told him, the fellow was clever, immensely clever; and more than that, wise, perhaps; and voluble. He made Logan uneasy to a degree Logan never had experienced with that gunman Donley. The little deformed man had a commanding presence. And still Logan was unsure of the nature of Jackman's deformity: it was something about the spine and shoulders, though not crippling or really noticeable. Yet Jackman's lean face had about it just a suggestion of that look of suffering and humiliation which one sometimes sees on the faces of congenital hunchbacks. And there was something dismaying about the man's forehead. Right at the middle of his brow existed a small and shallow depression, about the size and shape of a sixpence; and there seemed to be no bone behind the skin at that spot. Now and then the place seemed to stir a little, as if the skin lay upon the quick brain. In an unpleasant way, it was fascinating.

"Very good old sherry, this," Jackman was saying. "Sir Alastair kept an admirable cellar, and much of it still is below stairs. One has to watch the servants. There's a quantity — perhaps two bins — of Jamaica rum of 1800 or earlier, commencing to lose its savor now, alas. Another drop, Mr. Logan? You've been looking at the hole in my head: not that I mean to reproach you, for you'd have to be blind to ignore it. It's a souvenir of Spain. In the lines outside Teruel, a spent bullet went right through the bone. But there was a Russian surgeon in Teruel that day, luckily, and he got the bullet out, and now there's a bit of plastic set into my poor skull. I call the place my third eye. You've read the Hebridean legends of third eyes, Mr. Logan? No? I suppose you've little time for general reading, what with the getting and spending of your vocation. For that matter, I presume you know next to nothing of the Spanish trouble, more than twenty years ago: a youthful indiscretion of mine. But possibly that's just as well. Every man to his last. You will be twenty-seven years old, Mr. Logan, or perhaps twenty-eight? And earning seven pounds a week, like as not. And you aspire to marry the sole survivor of the old, old line of MacAskival. Not that I blame you, not in the least. In the coming world, Mr. Logan, there will be no rank and no class. And intellect will have its rewards. No, so far as social status is concerned, I offer no objection. 'A man's a man for a' that,' as you Scots say, Mr. Logan. Yet I would be no friend to you if I neglected to give you some description of the difficulties in your way."

His face and his facility of speech had served him well, Logan thought: Dr. Jackman had no doubt, it appeared, that Logan was indeed an Edinburgh clerk; and astute though Jackman obviously was, he had underestimated Logan's age by nearly a decade. The man could make mistakes. Logan intended that Jackman should continue to make mistakes, at least until he could discover more about Lady MacAskival and Mary MacAskival and Jackman himself. "Difficulties, Dr. Jackman?" Logan said, leaning forward and acting the pushing clerk, at once brash and smarmy. "Difficulties? Mary has told me more than once that there will be no financial problem, for she says she's money to burn. And look at this grand house. Aye, I'll take more sherry, and I thank you. Would Lady MacAskival raise difficulties, do you think, Dr. Jackman? Look here, sir: I ask you as a son to his dad. If Lady MacAskival's incapacitated, would it be asking too much for you to give away the bride, sir?"

That twist of the knife had been felt, Logan could tell: the skin twitched about the strange spot in Jackman's forehead; but the man's expression did not change, nor the tone of his voice alter. "Why," Jackman said, "before you and I speak of marrying and giving in marriage, there is some history I must tell you, Mr. Logan. And I fear I have been neglecting my duties as host in Lady MacAskival's absence." He put his

hand on an old-fashioned velvet bell-pull, and jerked it. "Among the difficulties of life in Carnglass, Mr. Logan, is the problem of staff. We take
men where we find them, and try to be thankful for small mercies. Life
in the remotest of the Hebrides isn't to the taste of modern servants.
Our butler, however, is rather a jewel; you'll see him in a moment. The
footman is a diamond, though rough. We may have to let the footman,
Anderson, go; for he has involved us in all this trouble, doubtless with
the best of intentions. It was on his urging that we engaged that Irish
brute of a gamekeeper, Seamus Donley, who was some connection of
Anderson's. I could see that Donley was three parts savage, but in a
lonely island like Carnglass, savagery may be a virtue in a keeper. What
I failed to detect was his insanity. For a man of his age, Donley is aston-
ishingly strong and quick — for a man of any age, so far as that goes.
And quite out of his head. He concealed his madness with a certain
Kerry wheedling wit. I must confess that I knew Donley had been in
gaol at one time; in Belfast or Derry; but I mistook him for a mere
simple-minded Irish rebel, relatively harmless. I've still some fellow-
feeling for rebels: in my younger days I was rather a radical — almost
an activist. I still have many acquaintances in the labor movement. You
are not a Socialist, by any chance, Mr. Logan?"

"Oh, no, sir," Logan demurred wholeheartedly, "that never would do
at the British Linen Bank. The manager never would allow it."

"Quite." Dr. Jackman nodded approval, with the merest suggestion
of a pucker about the corners of his mouth. "Quite right. Socialism is a
snare and a delusion, at least as socialism is understood in Britain. Hold
fast by your principles, Mr. Logan."

A tap at the door, then; and a small gray-haired man in a neat velvet
jacket entered. He almost stumbled upon Logan, and his mouth fell
open. "Blimey!" he cried; and then, to Jackman, "Begging your pardon,
that is, sir." This must be the Cockney butler Donley had mentioned,
Sam Tompkins; and he certainly did not look like a ruffian or a conspirator, though there was a shiftiness about the little eyes. South of Ma-
son's and Dixon's Line, Logan reflected, such a servant would be given
to "totin' victuals." Yet, the times and the place considered, a very decent-
looking butler.

"Tompkins," Dr. Jackman said, "this gentleman is Mr. Hugh Logan, a
friend of Miss MacAskival. He was landed from a boat this morning. We
shall put him in the brown room, opposite mine, and you are to see that

everything is in order. Take his sack and stick and cape with you. And you'd best tell the others as they come in, for fear of misunderstanding. Niven is standing guard at the door just now? Very well. Make sure he gets nothing to drink. And tell Miss MacAskival that Mr. Logan will be late for tea; he and I are having a very interesting talk."

As Tompkins went out, Jackman smiled at Logan. "Your arrival will be a nine-days' wonder below stairs. If you observe some surliness or fecklessness below, please accept my apologies in advance. I never tolerate deliberate rudeness; report anything of that sort to me. Whatever the deficiencies of these fellows, I suppose they make up a better staff than the mob of Anguses and Annies that must have slept on the stairs and in the kitchens of the Old House in the grand old days of the MacAskivals — before Donald MacAskival was sold up, I mean. Miss MacAskival has told you something of the history of the family? Quite so. And speaking of old Donald MacAskival, who died raving in the New House, I have a curiosity to show you." Jackman, going to a cupboard set in the wall, carefully drew out a heavy box and set it on the table before Logan.

The big box, or rather casket, seemed to be carved from a single block of stone, almost blue in color, but here and there shading into gray. The lid was of the same polished stone. "If the servants had the slightest notion of the value of these," Jackman remarked, "I should have to put the casket under lock and key." He lifted the lid and began to lift out strange stone figures, each some five inches high. "You play chess, Mr. Logan? I have a marble chessboard here — modern, I regret to say. But these chessmen are ancient, and Norse. They are called the Table-Men of Askival."

The little statuettes were marvellously carved by some master of the Viking age. Each was wrapped in cotton-wool, and Jackman put them deftly in place on the marble board. They were of the same blue stone as the casket in which they had lain; and, after a thousand years, they remained almost perfect, only three or four being badly chipped. "The chiefs of MacAskival would have slit a hundred throats rather than have parted with these toys," Jackman went on. "For more than a century, it was thought they were lost altogether, but Sir Alastair MacAskival discovered them when he was restoring the family tombs by St. Merin's Chapel. The casket was resting, of all places, in the stone coffin that is said to be Askival's own tomb. Perhaps Donald MacAskival hid them there when his creditors were hard at his heels, for even in the eighteenth century these things would have brought a pretty price. If so, they are all he left to his descendants. Sir Alastair died less than a month after the finding of these, and Lady MacAskival has told no one of them, so far as I am aware; so you are looking at works of art never photographed or catalogued by the museum-people. Do you ever go to the Queen Street Museum in Edinburgh? No? A pity. There they have walrus-ivory chessmen from Lewis, also Norse work, and perhaps as old as these. And there are others in the British Museum. You have not visited the British Museum? Once, like Marx, I went there daily. But I presume it is all *l.s.d.* with you, Mr. Logan. 'Put money in thy purse, and yet again, put money in thy purse.' So the world goes. Shall we make a game of it as we talk?"

Yes, fearfully and wonderfully made, these chessmen. The kings held drawn swords across their knees, and stared stonily out of bulging merciless eyes; the queens, with long wild faces, held daggers; the rooks were berserkers, biting on their shields; and all the other pieces, even the pawns were modelled from the life of the age of the Sea-Kings. One set of men had been saturated in some reddish dye or paint; the other retained its natural blue hue. To play with these priceless and timeless things was to sink into a remote past. "They're very nice, I'm sure," Logan the bank-clerk said, with what he trusted was a Philistine indifference. "Aye, I'll play you a game, sir, if you'll promise me I sha'n't miss my spot of tea with Miss Mary."

"Miss MacAskival will excuse you; and it occurs to my mind, Logan, that perhaps we can discuss certain delicate matters more easily in the progress of a match. But I warn you, Mr. Logan, that I rarely lose. Here: I submit to a handicap." Jackman removed his own queen from the board. "No protests: I think you'll find me an old hand at chess."

Logan advanced the pawn before his queen's bishop. "I've had many a grand match at the West End Young Men's Society for the Advancement of Chess, Dr. Jackman."

"Indeed." Jackman made a similar move with his king's bishop's pawn. "Now the question of marriage aside, Mr. Logan, I don't suppose you'd choose to live in a great rambling ill-lit place such as the Old House of Fear is, would you?"

"Oh, never in the world, sir." Logan moved again, and lost a pawn to Jackman. "No, sir, give me a nice semi-detached villa beyond Bruntsfield

Links, any day. Even the New Town of Edinburgh is too old and stuffy for my taste, Dr. Jackman. I like a bit of a rookery in the front garden, and an Aga cooker, and a fridge, and a parlor with a pair of Portobello china dogs by the hearth." He advanced his king's knight.

Jackman shot a sharp glance at him. Had he overplayed his role a trifle? Logan wondered. The Aga cooker and the Portobello dogs were spreading the butter rather thick. He smiled ingenuously at Dr. Jackman; and apparently the smile was fatuous enough to convince that alarming gentleman.

"That is precisely the sort of man I took you to be, Logan: my congratulations. And do you think Miss MacAskival would share these reasonable ambitions?" He took Logan's knight.

Logan captured one of Jackman's pawns. "I don't see why Mary shouldn't, sir; she's a canny lass, and the day of grand houses like this one is long past."

Having sent a bishop on a raid deep into Logan's territory, Jackman leaned back in his armchair. "Canny, Mr. Logan? Sensible? Miss MacAskival? Charming, certainly; beautiful, at least in many eyes; but canny is the last word I should apply to her. I consider her my ward *de facto,* you understand, and what I say now is for her good and your own, and is to be held in confidence."

Logan took one of Jackman's knights. "Perhaps you'll take the trouble to enlighten me, Dr. Jackman." He hunched forward, the picture of the respectful and hopeful young man on the rise.

Jackman frowned at the chessboard. "I take it that Miss MacAskival has given you to understand that she has large expectations, or possibly that she already has ample independent means? That she is Lady MacAskival's heiress?"

"Why, sir, we've not discussed the matter in detail, but I have assumed that Mary was to have her due."

"Her due, Mr. Logan? To be quite frank, Miss MacAskival is very little better than a waif. Her grandfather was first cousin to Sir Alastair MacAskival — though the closest male relative left to Sir Alastair, at the end of his life. But Sir Alastair and his cousin were on bad terms; and, in any event, Miss Mary MacAskival was born nearly a generation after old Sir Alastair died. This is a most tenuous family bond, you see, although it is true that the old line of MacAskival being almost extinct altogether, Mary MacAskival has a better claim than anyone else to be the head of her little dispersed and forgotten clan. Our Mary's father was a ship's second mate, and drowned off Naples in the late war. The girl, who cannot remember her father, was left with the widow at a village in North Uist. Had matters followed their usual course, probably she would have grown up knitting sweaters and milking cows, and have married some crofter. But then her mother died. The girl was left quite alone.

"Lady MacAskival is an old friend of mine, but I cannot say she has been known for openhandedness. A minister in North Uist wrote to her, however; and, oddly enough, Lady MacAskival agreed to take the child into her own household and provide for her schooling. Perhaps Lady MacAskival felt she owed some debt to her husband's name; she is oppressed by a sense of guilt where her husband is concerned, but I sha'n't enter into that. Whatever her reason, she took the girl Mary, and sent her to good schools — to the convent school at Bridge of Earn, most recently. I must make it clear here, Mr. Logan, that she did not adopt Miss MacAskival, nor make any provision for her future."

Jackman's narration did not take his mind altogether from the chess match. He played with assurance and even arrogance, while Logan lost three more pieces to him. Logan set his face in an expression meant to suggest alarm at both the account of Mary MacAskival and the match.

"What's in a name, Mr. Logan," Jackman continued, "or in the inheritance of family traits? The scientists have been at work on these things for a century and better, but nothing is settled. Possibly you followed the course of the Lysenko affair in the Soviet Union? No, I didn't suppose that was an especial interest of yours. As I said, these problems of hereditary traits are not settled, though for my part I feel confident that the Russians will give us the answers before 1965. Well, our Miss Mary MacAskival seems to offer some decided evidence that a certain type of character is conveyed from generation to generation within a family, whether the cause is genetic or environmental. Since time out of mind, the MacAskival men and women — the family of the chiefs, I mean — have been rash, spendthrift, fearless, and — why, promiscuous, shall we say. Sir Alastair was an exception, true, going to the contrary extreme. It has been a family exceedingly inbred. I think I am not venturing too far when I suggest that the stock is worn out. The qualities I mentioned just now were dominant in both Mary's father and mother. The beauty and the daring may survive long after the strength and the wits are gone."

"Dr. Jackman, what are you telling me?" Logan deliberately threw a strong burr into his words, to simulate dismay; and his disturbance was not altogether feigned. But he did not neglect to take Dr. Jackman's other knight.

Jackman compressed his mouth, as if pained at the necessity for speaking out. "Lady MacAskival, while she was still in full possession of her faculties, gave me a detailed account of the girl's conduct — sometimes she calls Mary her niece, out of kindness — from the age of seven upward. I have made some serious study in the realm of psychiatric disturbances, if I may say so, Mr. Logan. From the month Lady MacAskival took the child under her patronage, there was trouble with the girl. The reports from the schools — she changed schools a number of times — were disturbing. Mary was haughty, full of notions of her family's importance; shy, at the same time; and sometimes what I must call ferocious. Compensation, perhaps; no doubt she was very lonely. Lady MacAskival is not a cordial woman, and, besides, Mary saw her 'aunt' very seldom; and she did not make many friends at school. And now I am about to tell you something that may shock you, Logan, or may not. Did it ever occur to your mind that sexual overindulgence, like drunkenness, often is a retreat into a world of fantasy, caused by a deep unhappiness in this real world? Our Mary has fed on fantasies of one sort or another, it seems, ever since she was a baby. For her, the legends of Carnglass, for instance, are real: real in the most literal sense of that word. She might happen to identify you with her legendary ancestor, Sigurd Askival; and herself with his bride, Merin or Mann; and me with — why, the monster, the man-goat, the tyrant: the Firgower, that pleasant creature we see overhead."

"Check," said Logan. Jackman retrieved his situation promptly. "Aye, sir," Logan said, "I know Mary is dreamy; but that's small harm, if we've money enough for the whole of our lives."

"I scarcely think you understand how extremely and dangerously fanciful Miss MacAskival is, Mr. Logan; nor what consequences that sort of mental sickness may lead to. She may have let you think, for instance, that she's a great heiress, or rich already. In plain fact, she hasn't a shilling of her own, and I may have difficulty in persuading Lady MacAskival to leave her two or three thousand pounds. My old friend says she has given the girl — who is no kin of hers really — schooling and breeding enough to make her a governess or schoolmistress; and she owes her no more. What is worse, perhaps, Mary lives in her own ir-

93

rational private world of gods and devils. And that way lies . . . why, extreme eccentricity, at the least. And then there is the concupiscence, which may be an inherited tendency, or at least the next thing to a biological characteristic."

Logan took another pawn. "Oh, surely now, Dr. Jackman, you don't mean to say that my Mary's a wild girl?"

Jackman reached gently across the board and gave Logan a pat on the shoulder. "It's best to know these things early, Logan. I do mean just that. When our Mary was scarcely thirteen, there was — well, what I really must call an affair with a farm laborer here in Carnglass, in the summer. The man was dismissed as soon as the thing was discovered; he could have been sent to prison, I suppose. And yet he does not seem to have taken the initiative. Then there was a report from school that the girl was found with an hotel porter. I sha'n't say more concerning that. There have been two lesser incidents of the same nature — two that we know of. And finally, your case."

"Dr. Jackman!" Logan had half convinced himself that he really was a decent, ambitious bank-clerk, and threw corresponding indignation and bewilderment into his outcry. "Dr. Jackman! I'd never think of anything — anything not proper with Mary. I mean the girl to be my wife, Dr. Jackman."

Jackman raised his eyebrows. "Frankly, now: would you care to begin married life with a young woman of these tendencies? Possibly you don't quite believe what I've told you, though I could show you letters. Yet you'd discover the truth after marriage, if you refused to credit it before. So far as your own conduct is concerned, Mr. Logan, I'm satisfied that you have behaved decently. But look at the matter from another point of view. Here is a girl who throws herself at the head of a young man she encounters casually in a bank, because he is bold enough to say he likes her ankles. She invites him to her house without even informing her guardians. She conducts, I suppose, some clandestine correspondence with him. She rushes into his arms after not having seen him for three months. Really, Lady MacAskival ought not to have allowed Mary that Christmas holiday in Edinburgh."

"Dr. Jackman," Logan said, "I trust you, and I see you're an educated man. As for me, I never attended the varsity; it was not my line. But cannot this be all rumor and misunderstanding about Mary?"

"I don't mean to be harsh upon the girl; after all, she is as much of a daughter as I possess, Logan. Oh, check again, by the way. I am not condemning — only explaining. I doubt if the girl can help herself. I suspect the concupiscence is in the blood. And her loneliness contributes: as I suggested, sexual promiscuity sometimes is more a symptom of a disorder than a disorder itself. I will be entirely blunt, if you will allow me, Mr. Logan: in the legal meaning of the phrase, and in other meanings, Mary MacAskival is not sane. She is not sane where men are concerned, nor in certain other matters. She suffers from a variety of delusions — I give you, my word. She might suddenly tell you, for instance, that I, Edmund Jackman, desire to marry her — an absurdity, because it would be almost as if I were to marry my own granddaughter, of course. At times she has even come to me with — well, shall we say hints and invitations? That was when no younger man was available. It has been necessary to forbid her very strictly ever to be alone even with the servants; Mr. Royall and I take care, one or the other of us, to be in this house whenever she is. I'm sorry, Mr. Logan. But to tell you all this is the best service I can render you."

"I had no notion, sir," Logan told him. He took Jackman's king's rook. And Logan had no difficulty in looking perplexed. Jackman was a very different sort of being from the charlatan or bully he had thought he might be. Those fine black eyes of Jackman's looked candidly into Logan's.

"And I confess I am somewhat surprised, Logan," Jackman was saying, "that you got yourself engaged to the girl while she is a minor."

"Oh, surely, Dr. Jackman, Mary's old enough to choose for herself."

"I fear she already has chosen quite often, Logan; she began at a tender age, to put it somewhat coarsely. You do know just how old she is, I take it?"

"Not precisely, sir; she would not tell me her birthday. She said I ought not to spend the money for a present. Nineteen, nearing twenty, I suppose?"

"Then I have been unjust to you, Logan. If you had known . . . Miss Mary MacAskival is barely fifteen. She prevaricates on that topic, as on many others. Of course, as any man with eyes in his head can see, Mary is a well-developed girl. Again, it runs in her family, I am told. Physically mature, yes; but emotionally and morally immature; and always will be."

Why this disclosure affected Logan so deeply, he hardly could ex-

plain to himself. It was as if he actually had turned himself into the fictitious bank-clerk he was impersonating. In this matter, as in related matters, he might have been on the verge of making a great fool of himself.
He had begun to fancy himself in the role of Galahad — or of Sigurd
Askival — rescuing a beautiful maiden from a wicked enchanter. And it
seemed to be turning out that the maiden was no maid, nor right in the
head; and that the enchanter was by no means thoroughly wicked. He
had listened to a drunken Irish terrorist spreading scandals about an unknown Dr. Jackman. He had not the least proof, indeed, that Jackman
had any real connection with J. Dowie, Commission Agent, or with Captain Gare of the frightened eyes; they might be someone else's agents,
perhaps in the pay of those London connections of Lady MacAskival. It
remained possible, and even probable, that this Dr. Jackman had aspira-
tions after some of Lady MacAskival's money; but he doubted very
much whether Jackman was a conspirator, or a saboteur, or even a charlatan. Some sort of political radical, likely enough; and a dabbler in odd
learned subjects; but a keen and even likeable man. And for what had
Logan been paid to come to Carnglass? Not to criticize Dr. Jackman's
character, or to carry off young women — or children — of doubtful
morals, but merely to buy a piece of real estate for his principal. He
might have made a thoroughgoing fool of himself. Indeed, he had done
so already. He had put himself in a ridiculous light with Jackman by accepting the role of suitor which Mary MacAskival, in her madcap childish way, had thrust upon him. He had sent a silly note to the police in
Glasgow — though that would do no real harm, since surely Donley had
no intention of delivering it. He may have helped a murderer escape
from the island — almost surely he had done just that. He was almost
an accomplice, what with the Irishman's gun hidden in a sling under his
arm. Yes, he was a damned fool; and he might have to play the fool a
while longer, if only to extricate himself from this folly. He moved at
hazard on the chessboard; the glaring eyes of a berserker-rook con-
fronted him. One misgiving, however, did come into his head.

"Dr. Jackman," he said, "I understand there was a factor, a Mr. Lagg.
Where is he?"

Jackman seemed taken aback at this *non sequitur.* "Surely Mary has
told you . . ."

"No, we had only a moment together before you came into the parlor,
sir. She had simply mentioned a puzzle of sorts, with Mr. Lagg involved."

Jackman was solemn and troubled. "I am virtually certain, Mr. Logan, that Lagg has been murdered. We have searched every nook in the island for him, these three days; but not a trace. As I have pieced matters together, Donley drank too much and broke into Lagg's house in search of money. Lagg was very much of a Scot — if you'll pardon me, Mr. Logan — and the servants talked of how he hoarded five-pound notes in his kitchen. Perhaps Lagg returned from a visit to the farm while Donley was doing his mischief. From the wreckage inside the New House, we can only conjecture that there was a struggle. Donley, we know to our sorrow, was armed. He may have forced Lagg, at the point of his pistol, to the cliff's edge. But we cannot find the body. Then, after Lagg had disappeared and we had begun to question Donley, that Irishman broke away and ran into the bracken. In the evening he came down and burnt our boats, to keep us from reaching the police or in an attempt to get a boat for his escape; and we have been after him ever since. Presumably he is short of ammunition by this time. In the fight at the harbor, he threw burning petrol into the boats, and one of our boatmen was terribly burnt, poor fellow, and probably will lose the sight of at least one eye; I must dress his face again tonight. But Lagg? A gone gosling, I am very much afraid. And an efficient factor, for years."

This account of Lagg's end held together much better than did Donley's. And Logan had told Donley he might bear witness for him at any trial! No whisper of this Carnglass episode, he hoped, would filter back to America. At this moment, Jackman took Logan's queen. Yes, Hugh Logan had made a fool of himself through and through.

"But to return to a topic almost equally difficult for me, Logan: I think you will perceive that your marrying Miss MacAskival is wholly out of the question. To begin with, she simply isn't of age. Besides, the shock of an announcement of that sort might put an end to Lady MacAskival, who is very old and very sick. And for your own sake, Logan — and I rather like your face and your ways — don't be rash. If you still care for the girl after what I've told you, give her time to reach moral womanhood, if ever she can. I don't say you need to break off the affair altogether. Be gentle with her; go back to Edinburgh; exchange letters now and then, if you like. But marriage, for the next two or three years, would be a catastrophe, I assure you."

"Perhaps you're right, Dr. Jackman," Logan replied, still in his bank-clerk role.

"I usually am right," Jackman told him, smiling. "And there's this: it is worth something to Lady MacAskival to have a decent young man treat her ward decently. My recommendations happen to carry considerable weight with Lady MacAskival. Mary does not need a husband or a lover, but she does need a friend. And I can see that you mean to move ahead in the world; and you deserve to, Logan. So if you can contrive to act as I suggest, where our Mary is concerned, I think I can guarantee that Lady MacAskival will give you a cheque for fifteen hundred pounds. I have no intention of bribing you: I know you're above that. But you deserve some compensation for the disappointment you've had, and for my part, I'd not be sorry to give you a leg up in the world. Don't feel insulted, Logan. I put it to you plainly: will you do us the honor of accepting that cheque?"

What Logan might have done had he truly been the fictitious bank-clerk, he did not know. But as an experienced lawyer, he was disturbed by this offer. It was too much money for no real service. If once he had been inclined to mistake Dr. Jackman for a thorough scoundrel, it would not do now to make a model philanthropist of him. Of course he could not really take the money, being Hugh Logan; yet he could accept the cheque as the fictitious Logan and destroy it later. What he said was, "If you'll allow me, sir, I'll sleep on your offer and give you my answer to-morrow."

"A sound policy." Jackman lightly tapped his shoulder again. "And I believe I know already what your decision will be, Logan. Ah: check-mate." Jackman had won the match with the thousand-year-old chess-men, despite his handicap.

Dr. Jackman rose. "We dine at seven, here in my study, Mr. Logan. In the Old House we have neither electricity nor running hot water — Lady MacAskival does not care for modern comfort — but old Agnes will bring hot water and a lamp to your room. I'll show you there in a moment. But before the sun goes down, shall we enjoy the view from the battlements? I think the mist has lifted a trifle, though you come to us in a clouded month. By the way, Miss MacAskival will be at dinner with us. I ask you to say as little as possible to her about my observations, should you talk with her alone before dinner, or later — for her own interest, you understand, Logan. A personality as unbalanced as hers might be permanently affected by imprudent reproaches. I trust to your Scottish discretion. Just up the stair, now."

They emerged upon the lead of the roof from under the conical-capped turret. A narrow walk led round the gabled cap of the great tower, between the stone slabs of the gable itself and the machicolations of the battlements. Before them was Askival harbor, the sunken yacht black against the pier; and beyond, across the foggy ocean, the sun was descending in a diffused glory. Despite its climate, Carnglass was a beautiful island. A corncrake flew low above the tower. Far below, in the policies, a jungle of rhododendrons was in bloom. And five armed men were walking up to the gate in the Victorian block of the Old House of Fear.

"Mr. Royall!" Jackman called. The five looked up, and the leader, that "walking cadaver," formed his thin hands into a trumpet. Even at this distance, his pallid face and protruding teeth were ugly in the extreme: a queer sort of secretary, this skeleton-like man with a rifle slung over his shoulder. "Mr. Royall!" Jackman cried out. "What luck?" The five men below stared in astonishment at Logan, beside Jackman at the battlements. The four hangdog faces behind Royall aroused a vague discomfort at the back of Logan's mind.

"Rab and Carruthers have strayed, Dr. Jackman," Royall called back. "Can you see them from the tower?" Though Jackman and Logan looked to north and east, there was not a sign of the other two men.

"Is there no trace of Donley?" Jackman shouted. Gesturing dispiritedly, Royall shouted back, "I'll explain when I come up."

"I doubt whether we can give you a decent dinner, Mr. Logan," Jackman said as they turned back to the turret-stair. "Our cook, you understand, has been out with the searching-party, and we have had to press the butler into service in the kitchen. Have you ever lived in a state of siege? A mad island, this Carnglass."

"Fish and chips would do nicely, thank you," Logan told him. "I've not had a bite these twenty hours." He still was the bank-clerk; it might be difficult to abandon this play-acting.

"Really, I scarcely think Miss MacAskival would care for fish and chips week in and week out, Logan." Dr. Jackman said it drily. The man, after all, was doing no more than his duty in sheltering his friend's ward from an unpromising suitor. Suppose, Logan thought, I were to tell him what I really am: how would he act then? Yet an impulse cautioned Logan to play this little deception according to its rules until he had talked with Miss Mary MacAskival, the girl of fifteen with the green eyes, the red hair, and the spotted past.

CHAPTER 8

On those cold and dark stairs, Miss Mary MacAskival met them, her quick and rounded little body, her rosy cheeks and lively eyes defying the barbarous spell of the old tower. She sent Logan a darting, inquiring glance, but it was to Jackman she spoke. "I heard the men outside," she said. "Really, you ought to let me lead the search. I know every bush and cranny of Carnglass, but they're stupid townfolk."

Jackman frowned. "I may have to lead them myself, Miss Mac-Askival: Rab and Carruthers seem to have lost their way. I'll have a word with Royall. Will you be good enough to take Mr. Logan to see Lady MacAskival for a moment? And then bring him to the study for dinner. Don't be long." He sent out a hand as if to touch her lightly on the shoulder, but the girl drew back cleverly, almost as if unintentionally, against the curving stair-wall, and Jackman passed by her, ignoring the repulse. "Don't forget the advice I gave you, Mr. Logan," he said softly, disappearing down the spiral of the stair.

At that instant, a most unpleasant recollection came into Logan's head. An hour earlier, in the painted study, he had given his rucksack to Tompkins to be carried to his room. And in that pack were his passport and other papers. That man Tompkins, by the look of him, would pry into everything, even had he been only butler in a normal country house; and this was no normal place. The moment Jackman talked with Tompkins, Logan's real identity would be known; and then there would be trouble — though just what sort of trouble, Logan was not quite sure. His dismay showed in his face.

Mary MacAskival was looking at him in concern. "What is it, Hugh?" (So it was "Hugh" even in private now, Logan thought, and on very short acquaintance, which seemed to confirm Dr. Jackman's account of this odd little girl's very forward ways with men.) Whatever else she was, she had a quick mind, though; for she added, after a moment's pause, "Are you thinking of your rucksack? You needn't. I met Tompkins on the stair and took it from him before he had any chance of a look into it. And I took your papers and put them into a hidie-hole — the Old House is mostly hidie-holes — where only I could possibly find them again. Then I put the rest of your things into your room. Do you mind? I can get the papers for you whenever you like, but we mustn't let Dr. Jackman know you're from America. You'd not be safe then. You're not particularly safe even now. I'm sorry." Those mobile red lips framed the "sorry" with a pathetic beauty. Indeed, it was a pity that Mary MacAskival was what she was.

"Thank you, Miss MacAskival," Logan said. "Probably I'll need the papers after dinner. Shall we go down to Lady MacAskival now?" His voice sounded cold even to himself. He needed a little time to think. The girl's charm — her glamour, literally — was too near to him on this clammy sepulchral stair. How did those rosy little feet of hers endure the damp, attractively bare as they were? But he must get his mind off the girl: she was only fifteen, and bad medicine.

"Hugh!" Mary MacAskival spoke his name reproachfully, and now a little haughtily. "Hugh! It's not only your papers you're thinking of. What is it? This is a house of secrets, but you and I mustn't have secrets from each other. You weren't sent to me to keep secrets from me. What is it?" Logan hesitated, and the girl's mind leaped swiftly to the usual conclusion any woman reaches when two men have been talking seriously in her absence. "What is it? Were you and Dr. Jackman talking of me?" In this instance, the woman's instinct spoke truly.

Logan looked her full in the face. "Yes, we were."

Over the girl's delicious heart-shaped face, with its high cheek-bones and rather deep-set green eyes, spread a crimson flush, suffusing all the delicate white skin. It would have been a beautiful thing to watch, Logan thought, if it had not been a mark of guilt. The finely-moulded nose and chin went up. "Then you heard nothing good," said Mary MacAskival, deliberately. She turned, as if to avert her tell-tale young face, and led the way down the stairs. "Dr. Jackman is the father of lies. But now I will take you to my aunt."

A doorway in the immense thickness of the medieval tower-wall led into the Renaissance range of the Old House. Here the plaster ceiling of a great book-lined corridor was moulded into baroque shells and swags and Lord knows what fantastic designs. An odor of damp and musty leather came from the shelves; this library could have been used little since Sir Alastair's time. The little barefoot beauty walked beside him, still a trifle flushed and defiant, but apparently not hopeless of winning him over; Logan thought for a moment she actually meant to take his hand, but if she did have that impulse, she thought better of it. "After dinner," she murmured, "if we can be alone, there are things that must be told you. Not here: there's not enough time, and we could be overheard." She noticed his glance at her exquisitely narrow bare feet, which here trod upon Oriental carpet, in utter silence; she smiled a trifle coquettishly, and said, "I was reared barefoot, and don't like shoes and stockings in the house. Besides, when I'm this way, I can scamper all over the house, and *they* don't know where I am — nor when I'm listening to them. Do you mind? I know it's not the way to receive foreign guests; but you are our first foreign guest, and I don't think you stand on ceremony. Here's my aunt's bedroom; she never leaves it now. Only Agnes will be with her." The girl pushed open a heavy carven door, and they entered an immense gloomy room.

There the walls were hung from cornice to floor with square panels of leather, stamped in gold leaf with some intricate pattern of dancing figures; Logan thought be made out the figure of a capering goat in this design, but could not be sure in the twilight of the room. These hangings must have been long neglected, for splotches of white water-stain showed here and there, and some of the panels had pulled almost loose from the stitching that held them one to another, so that the stone of the walls showed through the gaps. Nearly in the middle of the room stood a vast ancient canopied bed, the curtains drawn back. Beside it, huddled on a stool, an old serving-woman looked with lacklustre eyes at Logan, cringing aside to let him approach the bed: this would be Agnes, the shawlie. Certainly she was timid — could she be trembling, or was it a slight palsy? Then he made out the shape under the rich covers upon the bed.

Lady MacAskival lay with closed eyes, and she was very nearly a corpse: almost bloodless, and her face and hands grotesquely wrinkled. Could this pallid immobile thing once have been a beautiful woman of fashion, no better than she should have been — like little Mary MacAskival, perhaps? At their best, Logan suspected, the features must have been slightly vulgar. Mary MacAskival slid between him and the bed-rail. "Aunt!" she whispered, very low. "Aunt, Mr. Logan has come."

The wrinkled eyelids slid back, snakelike. The fingers of the desiccated left hand stirred slightly. The withered lips writhed, almost as if the ancient creature would have burst into a scream, but no sound came forth.

"Aunt," said Mary MacAskival, "he may be trusted." Those purblind eyes of the failing woman flickered, for a moment or two with intelligence. But Logan could not have meant much to her; possibly he was but a dream within a dream, drifting through limbo, less unpleasant than the terrors that often clustered round the bedstead. For either this old woman was drugged, Logan thought, or else she existed, tortoise-like and impotent, in a realm of perpetual terror. In those weary eyes was frozen fright, fright grown so familiar that it was almost identical with consciousness. What kept her alive? Surely she would have been happy to escape from this terror — unless she fancied that worse horrors lay in wait for her beyond the grave.

Now her lips moved, and very faint sounds came forth. "Not Alastair," Lady MacAskival whispered. "Not Alastair. Good. Go — go with him, Mary. When I am done. He is not the goat, no. Is he Askival? Is he flesh? In Carnglass it is all mist." The lids slid back again; the left hand ceased to claw at the covers; one would have thought the woman dead, had not nostrils and chest stirred ever so slightly with her labored breathing. Mary MacAskival drew Logan through the still room to the door.

They were back in the book-lined corridor. "Is she under drugs?" Logan asked.

"No," said the girl, calmly enough, "only hypnotism — and terror. If you had seen the chairs rise up of themselves in this house, and eyes glowing in the dark where no living thing could be, and heard the footsteps in this hall, and if you were very old — why, I think even you would lie there like my aunt, Hugh."

"Who did these things?"

"Dr. Jackman and Mr. Royall — who else? They have come near to putting me out of my wits. And now and then they put Dr. Jackman himself out of his wits. He believes, in part at least, though Mr. Royall does not, I think. Dr. Jackman has said he will call old Sir Alastair from under the stone by St. Merin's Chapel. He has said he has made Sir Alastair walk down this very passage where you and I stand."

Logan looked involuntarily over his shoulder: but of course there was nothing but mouldy books and hangings and family portraits. In this strange place, minds might scamper after any vagary. "Does your aunt wish to see her dead husband?"

"Not she. She feared him while he lived, and she feared him more once he died; and things lie heavy on her conscience. She will give Dr. Jackman anything he wants, so long as he keeps Sir Alastair this side of her bedroom door." The girl was almost conversational about it all: surely she was either quite mad, or had a grip upon her nerves stronger than that of any woman Logan had known. What lay at her heart, Logan could not even guess; what could be seen was delectable enough, but Logan put no trust in her. Yet, trollop though she might be, Logan resolved to play his masquerade a little while yet, so far as Jackman was concerned, for her sake and his own.

"Now tell me this, Miss MacAskival," said Logan, "just how old . . ." Then he heard something in the passage, toward the tower; and so did the girl; and they turned simultaneously. Logan felt tempted to reach for the little gun under his tweed jacket, but refrained. And, after all, it was only that shifty butler. "Dinner is served, Miss MacAskival," Tompkins murmured, quite deferentially, and withdrew back toward the tower.

"Later," Mary MacAskival said, very low, as they followed Tompkins. "Later I'll tell you everything that can be told. Now you must meet Mr. Royall." They went up the ancient stairs again, and passed into the study. It was dark now, but the study was cheerful enough. Many candles, in eighteenth-century silver candlesticks, had been lit; a square table was laid with a cloth and good china; there was soup being kept warm by a paraffin lamp on a sideboard. Tompkins had gone down somewhere to the kitchen, assisted by a footman whose grumbling voice Logan could hear below — Anderson, perhaps; and Jackman and Royall were not yet in the room: doubtless the two of them were discussing Hugh Logan thoroughly. Mary MacAskival, leaning gracefully against the piano which occupied a corner, pointed a little finger toward the painted ceiling.

"Do you know what *that* is?" She meant the painted monster called the Firgower, only dimly visible by the candlelight, away up there in the shadows. "Oh, Dr. Jackman told you? He should: for he is the Firgower, you know. Why do you look at me so queerly? Of course Dr. Jackman is the Firgower; he'd tell you so himself, if he were candid. He has told me so. You saw the hole in his forehead: that's his third eye. He sees Sir Alastair MacAskival with his third eye, and tells my aunt." She took a candlestick from the table, and, standing on tiptoe, lifted it as high toward the ceiling as her little body could reach. "Now come here, Hugh Logan, and look close."

The painted horrid goat-face of the Firgower stared down at Logan; it seemed to smirk and leer and scowl all at once. "Its forehead — look," the girl went on.

Now Logan could make out that in the middle of that painted forehead, with horns sprouting above it, was a third eye, faintly visible. It was much less distinct than the two normal goat-slit eyes, but it was very like them. "I don't know whether it was painted so," Mary MacAskival murmured in Logan's ear, leaning a pretty hand on his shoulder, "or whether that nasty third eye wore on the nerves of Sir Alastair or someone else, so that perhaps someone put a trifle of white paint over it. It's no less an eye than Dr. Jackman's. Do you understand? That's Dr. Jackman's portrait, so to speak. I'm ever so glad you do not have a third eye."

Logan turned his head to look at this queer little lovely creature. Was she lunatic, coquette, or infinitely subtle? They two stood so close together that his nose touched hers. His right arm almost went round her, as she stood there on tiptoe; but just then boots sounded on the stair, and Miss MacAskival drew away. "My poor bare feet!" she said. "I'm forgetting my manners. Whatever would they say at the convent? They never let young ladies dine there barefoot, you know. I leave you to Dr. Jackman and his secretary, but I'll be back before the soup has gone quite cold." With a little swirl of her skirt, she sprang, rather than stepped, through the heavy doorway, and was gone.

She must have passed Jackman and Royall on the stair, for they came in immediately. "Mr. Logan," Jackman said, "Mr. Royall, my secretary." The death's-head secretary nodded curtly. Once the man began to speak, Logan perceived with relief that he was an Englishman, like Jackman, though probably from Yorkshire; had he been a Scot, he might have seen through Logan's masquerade. Logan would talk as little as possible to the Scots among the servants, lest he give himself away.

Royall made some perfunctory observations about the hunt for Donley, the weather, and all that. A cold fish, but a keen one, Logan hazarded. He was well educated, surely; Logan suspected that he might once have been a fairly high-ranking civil servant; somehow there was the mark of Winchester school upon him. Yet now he was secretary to this pseudo-doctor, in an island at the back of beyond. Why? Had Royall been dismissed from some civil post — for unreliability of sorts? The man was sick; the signs of a gnawing illness were plain upon his pallid face; and yet Logan guessed — though perhaps he was becoming fanciful, in this house of shadows — that the real cause of his trouble was some sickness not of the body, but of the spirit. Could one trust Royall? If one were of the same faith, undoubtedly; on the man's grim features was set fanaticism, not simple criminality.

"Do you have a taste for letters, Mr. Logan?" Royall inquired abruptly, in his hoarse voice. Jackman had said very little, but stood back in the shadows, watching, as if he had agreed to let his secretary do the prying this night. Tompkins came round with a tray of sherry-glasses, and Logan sipped before he replied.

"Why, now, Mr. Royall," Logan said, "I must admit I am fond of Rabbie Burns. Burns, sir, is the poet of the Scottish nation. No nonsense for Rabbie Burns. I don't mind saying, Mr. Royall, that at the British Linen Bank, Lawnmarket Branch, we know an honest man's the noblest work of God. How does Burns express it, sir? 'The rank is but the guinea's stamp . . .'"

Here Mary MacAskival returned, with neat shoes on her feet, and cotton stockings. Jackman and Royall bowed to her slightly, and the four of them sat down to dinner, Tompkins putting the soup before them. Without bothering to taste his soup, Royall pursued the topic.

"I suppose you know, Mr. Logan, that Burns is perhaps the most popular English writer in the Soviet Union today." Royall's sunken eyes seemed to expect some significant response to this.

"Indeed, sir?" Logan said, ingenuously. "Why, now, I would have thought there would be difficulties in doing Rabbie Burns into the Russian tongue."

"The Soviet Russians, Mr. Logan, are masters of translation. Yes, they appreciate Burns. At a conference in the Crimea, not so very long ago, I had the honor to be asked to read Burns aloud, in English, to a group of intellectuals. I found they especially enjoyed the final stanza of 'For a' That and a' That.' How does it go —

> 'For a' that, and a' that,
>   It's comin' yet, for a' that,
> That man to man, the warld o'er,
>   Shall brothers be for a' that.'

Do I have it quite right, Mr. Logan?" Royall gave him another long stare.

"Aye, as I mind it, it goes so, Mr. Royall. Very sound sentiments — brothers the world o'er." Logan smiled at him.

Royall hesitated; then, "Would you care to give me a gloss on those lines, Mr. Logan?"

Logan looked puzzled, as indeed he was. "A gloss, sir? Now how do you mean? A commentary?"

"Mr. Royall thought some remarks might occur to your mind, Mr. Logan," Jackman put in. "Concerning international brotherhood, perhaps."

"Why, no, Dr. Jackman, I do not believe I could add anything." Logan turned, simpering, to Mary MacAskival. "Do you think of a proper commentary, Mary, darling?" The girl shook her head slowly; her eyes, their lids half lowered, moved uneasily from Jackman to Royall. "Nevertheless, gentlemen," Logan went on, still very much the Edinburgh clerk, "we've had many a serious discussion of Rabble Burns in the West End Young Men's Discussion Club. There's profound meaning in Rabbie Burns. Profound."

Royall's eyes never had ceased to stare at Logan. Now Royall said, "An acquaintance of mine who sometimes visits Edinburgh is an admirer of Burns. Possibly you have met him: a Captain Gare."

Logan's training as a lawyer served him well at that moment, for his fatuous smile did not fade, nor did he start. "No, sir," he told Royall, "I don't believe I've had the honor of making the gentleman's acquaintance."

"And then," said Royall, "I think of a commission agent in Glasgow, a man of the people, who often has Burns on the tip of his tongue. Perhaps you have encountered him. His name is Dowie, Jim Dowie."

"Dowie? I know a solicitor's clerk of that name in Dalkeith; but he reads only American thrillers, sir."

"So, Royall," Dr. Jackman interjected, "it seems that our Mr. Logan here is not a member, after all, of the little circle you had in mind. You were quite mistaken, I fear; I told you he wouldn't be. Mr. Logan is a very honest and industrious rising young bank-clerk, I'm sure. But speaking of your national poet Burns, I call to mind a verse you might take to heart —

'My love she's but a lassie yet,
My love she's but a lassie yet,
We'll let her stand a year or twa,
She'll no be half sae saucy yet.'

Apropos, Mr. Logan?"

The butler brought the main course, boiled mutton and potatoes, before Logan had to reply. Logan noticed, as Tompkins served, that Mary MacAskival's face had gone crimson at Jackman's quotation, and then white again.

"Tompkins," Jackman said as the butler served him, "I take it that Carruthers and Rab have returned by this time?"

"No, Dr. Jackman." Logan saw that Tompkins' hands trembled slightly. "Neither of them, sir. Not hide nor hair."

Jackman bit his lip. "Royall, where do you suppose they've got to? It has been quite dark for more than an hour."

"Ah, well, sir," Royall answered, "so long as the pair of them hang together, no harm can come to them. They're both armed with good rifles, and they weren't reared in ladies' boudoirs. Rab knows rough country well enough, and something of this island. I suppose they may have been hot on Donley's scent when the sun set, and bedded down in one of the farmhouses or keepers' cottages. I last saw them toward St. Merin's Chapel. No doubt they'll report in the morning." But Royall seemed to have no appetite for his mutton.

Jackman shrugged. "No doubt, no doubt." That unpleasant patch on his forehead twitched, almost as if he were trying to lift the lid of the third eye. He turned toward Logan. "As you were about to say . . . ?"

"Why, Dr. Jackman" — but Logan smiled toward Mary MacAskival

— "I had thought of another verse from Rabble Burns, that I like better than yours; and it is this, sir —

'Gaist nor bogle shalt thou fear;
Thou'rt to Love and Heaven sae dear,
Nocht of ill may come thee near,
    My bonnie dearie.'"

"I think that's very pretty, Hugh," Mary MacAskival told him. She looked toward Dr. Jackman: "'Gaist nor bogle . . .' A good phrase for the Old House, is it not, Dr. Jackman? But whatever can have become of Rab and Carruthers?"

Jackman looked blacker still. "Leave that to us, if you please, my dear." He seemed about to add something when Mary MacAskival rose and walked to the piano.

"How very slow Tompkins is in bringing the sweet tonight! May I play until he comes? Hugh, will you sing with me?"

"You know I've no voice, Mary, darling," Logan said, also rising, "but I'll play to your singing." He did, indeed, play the piano reasonably well. Miss MacAskival behaved as if she had always known it: wondrously clever, that girl, for fifteen years.

"I'll set you the tune, Hugh," she told him, seating herself at the piano, "and then you can take my place here, and I'll sing you a song from Burns, if you like. Dr. Jackman, can you endure it? Mr. Royall?"

"Of course," Jackman told her, somewhat absently. He ran his lean hand slowly over his forehead. Royall said nothing: he had stalked to a window, opened it, and was staring uneasily into the night below.

Miss MacAskival played pleasantly — an air Logan knew well, "Charlie He's My Darling." Logan took her place at the piano then, and she stood and began to sing. Her young voice was full and tolerably trained, and very sweet.

"An' Charlie he's my darling,
My darling, my darling,
Charlie he's my darling,
    The young Chevalier."

The night air of Carnglass crept into the ancient room through

Royall's open window. There came the cry of some night bird, winging past the Old House, and the heavy beat of the sea upon the pier of Askival harbor. Mary's voice swelled up:

> "Sae light's he jimped up the stair,
>   And tirled at the pin;
> And wha sae ready as hersel,
>   To let the laddie in."

Then, above the noise of the ocean, there came an unnatural sound, echoing perhaps from the other side of the Old House. It was a burst of horrid laughter, or so it seemed, ending in a desperate sob; then silence; then the high dreadful cackle again. "The devil!" cried Jackman, and leaped to join Royall at the window. Mary MacAskival shivered, but sang the last verse:

> "It's up yon hethery mountain,
>   And down yon scroggy glen,
> We daur na gang a milking,
>   For Charlie and his men."

To Logan, the girl's relative composure was as strange as the dreadful yelling outside, but he played loyally on until "Charlie and his men" died away. Then Mary swept from the piano to the window, and Logan was right behind her. The laughter, if laughter it was, had ceased; and nothing at all was to be seen through the mist. But in a moment, a shot was fired; and then three more shots, in quick succession, seemingly not far outside the Old House. Jackman and Royall ran for the stairs, and Mary and Logan after them.

Through that great chill hodgepodge old house, past Lady MacAskival's room, through an interior courtyard that had been roofed over, into the enormous Victorian block, they ran, stumbling through passages and down flights of stairs, until at last the four of them burst into a big Victorian entrance-hall. About the closed door were clustered Tompkins and Ferd and Anderson and a fourth man whom Logan took to be Niven. They all had rifles at the ready, but no one had ventured to open the door. Jackman dashed among them and flung back the bolts: "See what it is, you fools." None of the four seemed eager to investigate, but they followed Jackman and Royall a little way into the dark, and Mary MacAskival and Logan tagged after. A massive knob of the great rock on which the Old House stood jutted up close by the door, and Logan urged the girl toward it.

"If anyone fires from out there," he whispered to her, "we'll be so many sitting ducks."

"No one will fire at us," the girl said; but, obediently, she crouched behind the rock, peering round in the direction the men were looking.

There came one more screech of hysterical laughter, and then a figure came into view, reeling, stumbling, slipping, but still holding a rifle. Only a few yards from the Old House, the man swung round to face the darkness from which he had emerged, brought his gun to his shoulder, and fired three more shots, wildly, toward nothing visible. There was as much chance of his hitting the moon, with the aim he took, as of winging any living thing in Carnglass. Then the man dropped his rifle altogether and came lurching on toward the entrance of the Old House, falling at last in a heap right at Jackman's feet, giggling, moaning, choking.

"Rab!" cried Jackman. "What the devil, Rab?" It was a very young man, thick-set and heavy-featured, with a great shock of hair. He was covered with little cuts, and his clothes were in rags. To judge by his gasping and gulping, he had run for miles. And he was quite out of his head. He squirmed at Jackman's feet, and mumbled obscenities, and then burst once more into his screaming and terrified laugh.

"Something has run him like a hare," Royall said. "The wits are gone out of the man." The four servants, hard cases though they looked, bunched together like so many rabbits. Stooping, Jackman took Rab by the shoulders and shook him mercilessly.

"Rab!" Jackman hissed. "Rab! Speak, man, or I'll give you worse than you've had already." But Rab only sobbed for breath. "Pick up his rifle, Mr. Royall," Jackman said, prodding Rab with his foot. Logan suspected that he gave the order to Royall for fear that none of the servants would obey it. Stooping, Royall slipped into the heather, groped for the gun, found it, and hurried back, glancing over his lean shoulder.

"Anderson and Ferd, lift this lump," Jackman called out, "and drag him inside." The whole party retreated through the wide doorway into the Victorian courtyard, and then back into the formal entrance-hall, barring the gates behind them; Anderson was left as sentry inside the great door. "Now you, Niven and Ferd, hold up this thing before me."

They supported the muttering Rab between them. Jackman slapped Rab's bleeding face with his open palm, terribly hard. The young man ceased to moan; his eyes rolled. "Rab," said Jackman, slowly and distinctly, "where the devil is Carruthers?"

"O, it took him, it took him!" cried Rab, and lapsed into incoherence.

"I'll have the heart out of you, Rab, if you don't speak up. What took Carruthers?" Jackman slapped him again.

Rab's dull eyes widened. "It took Carruthers! Lagg took him, auld, wet Lagg! Lagg it was!" With that, Rab sank into a kind of fit, and Ferd and Niven pushed him down upon the floor.

Dr. Jackman stood rigid. "No," he said, perhaps to Royall, perhaps to himself. "No. Not Lagg." Then he looked round, his face stiff and white, upon the little ring of men, and upon Logan and Mary MacAskival beyond them. "Get this creature to bed," he said to Niven and Ferd. "Tie him in, if you must. Ignore his ravings. The fellow's lost his nerve; Donley must have been after him. Royall, post someone atop the tower, and tell him to fire at anything that moves. Miss MacAskival, this is no scene for you. See if your aunt has been disturbed, and then get to your room. Logan, Tompkins will show you up. Stay in your rooms until I have you called for breakfast." Then Jackman went out into the courtyard again, calling to Anderson.

Tompkins, carrying a petrol lantern, led the girl and Logan through the passages toward the Renaissance block. Outside Lady MacAskival's room, Mary paused. "I'd best look in here, Hugh," she said, "so I tell you good-night now." Tompkins moved discreetly a few feet further down the passage, but Logan only pressed the girl's hand. She contrived to smile at him. "Do you recollect that last stanza I sang?" she asked:

> "'It's up yon hethery mountain,
>   And down yon scroggy glen,
> We daur na gang a milking,
>   For Charlie and his men.'

Take care this night, Hugh." Then she was gone into the bedroom hung with Spanish leather.

Tompkins led him to a decent smallish chamber on the floor above Lady MacAskival's room, wished Logan a civil goodnight, and slid away. There was no key in the lock upon the door, and no bolt. To shove furniture against the door, Logan felt, might seem unduly suspicious to Dr. Jackman; but he did it, all the same, jamming a chair-back under the doorknob, and reinforcing it by a small chest. He looked out his two windows; they were high and small, and almost impossible for anyone to reach even with very long ladders, for the rock fell sheer away below this portion of the Old House. The bed, if rather damp, was tolerable. He slid his pistol Meg under the pillow, and was dozing off in short order, with only the wind at the panes to break the stillness, and the distant growl of the combers. Logan was too tired to think of Rab, or Lagg, or Jackman, or Royall, or even of the green-eyed girl — to whom, in a fit of sympathy at the dinner-table, he had promised that she need fear neither ghost nor bogle while he was near. It was an unsecured pledge of questionable validity to an insecure girl of questionable antecedents.

CHAPTER 9

Much later — it must have been past three in the morning — Logan was waked from his troubled sleep by a curious sound. His nerves on edge, he sat up in bed, scarcely knowing where he was, and befuddled by finding himself tangled in an old-fangled nightshirt, until he remembered that Tompkins had laid out for him this antique garment. The only source of light in the room was the extinguished candle, of course; and Logan reached for the candlestick, thought better of it, and listened.

The noise was the sound of slow sliding. Blinking, he looked toward the door. So far as he could see anything at all, it seemed to him that the door was very slightly ajar. And then he knew the source of the sliding-sound: someone must have dislodged slightly the chair he had used as barrier, must have got a hand round the edge of the door, and must be quietly shoving chair and reinforcing chest inward, so that whoever was outside might squeeze within.

Logan snatched his pistol from under the pillow. It wouldn't do to use the gun except in the last extremity, though. He slid silently out of bed to the floor, and rolled under the bedstead. If someone meant to cut his throat, there in the blackness, whoever it was would stab an empty bed.

That sliding-noise had ceased now; what had wanted to enter presumably had glided in. To Logan, taut on the floor under the bed, came the thought of Old Askival, who was supposed to walk the narrow passages of the Old House, and had driven the wastrel Donald to the New House. Whatever had entered surely made no noise at all: a thrill ran through Logan's body. Holding his breath and straining his sight, after what seemed like a quarter of an hour — really some five seconds, probably — he made out the dimmest of dim shapes bending over the bed, its legs right before Logan's nose. Gripping the pistol in his left hand, Logan seized an ankle of the intruder and gave a mighty tug.

A stifled cry, and the thing was on the floor beside him, and Logan flung himself upon it in a tangle of arms and legs, thrusting the pistol against the thing's head. The shape made very little resistance. Shape? The body under Logan was not a man's shape. And most certainly it was not Lady MacAskival or old Agnes. "You've hurt my head," the shape murmured, resentful and panting. In the faintest of whispers — "Really! Are men always so violent when they're waked in the middle of the night?"

It had been a near thing; that little pistol, thrust against the girl's temple, might have gone off. "Oh!" said Logan, shocked and embarrassed. "Did I cut you?" He ran his hand through the mass of her hair, searching for a wound.

"I think not," the girl said, brushing aside his hand. "You were good enough merely to stun me. Now do you mind sitting somewhere else than on me? I'm rather out of breath. Sit on the bed. How queer you look in that nightgown! It must have been one of Sir Alastair's, who was twice your size; I wonder it hangs together still. And keep your voice low, for Dr. Jackman walks the passages at all hours, like a wraith, and he *would* put an end to Hugh Logan if he found me with you. I'm ever so sorry to put you in danger — or more danger — and to wake you from a sound sleep, and to invade your bedroom; but you and I must talk tonight. There, that's much better! You do look silly, perched in that old nightgown on that old bed, but it can't be helped. Oh, you have a little gun? That's clever of you. I wish I had one of my own. I have keys — although Dr. Jackman doesn't know it — to nearly every room in the house except the gunroom, and the cellars where they keep those explosives: Dr. Jackman put new locks on those. Do you mind if I sit on the other end of the bed? The floor's rather hard. Thank you: now we can make matters clear."

The minx — Logan's eyes, adjusted to the dark, could make her out vaguely — was fully dressed, except that she was barefoot, as usual. Either she was an idiot, which he doubted, or else she was the bravest woman he ever had come upon. "Miss MacAskival," he said, "what is outside this house? What drove Rab out of his mind? It may be, I suppose, that Donley was forced back to land, after he took my boat; but he was a tired man when I saw him last, and I can't imagine him knocking Carruthers on the head and chasing Rab right up to the door."

"Now that you have knocked *me* on the head," said Mary MacAskival, "and have sat on me, you may as well commence calling me Mary, Hugh Logan. We've not time, just now, to talk of what may be outside; for I must tell you of what's within. You have no faith in me, have you? You've been talking with Dr. Jackman. What did he tell you of me?"

He had no faith in anyone in the Old House, Logan thought; indeed, he had begun to doubt his own sanity. But he would be blunt with this girl, and see if she could make a case for herself. "He told me, Mary MacAskival," Logan said, "that you were eccentric."

There in the dark, the girl laughed softly; she was a cool one. "Why, that's true enough, Hugh Logan: all the MacAskivals have their oddities. I fancy that old Mr. Duncan MacAskival, who sent you to me, has his peculiarities."

"That he has. But he's no girl of fifteen."

"Fifteen?" She sounded startled. "Whatever do you mean?"

"You are fifteen, aren't you?"

"Fifteen!" She stifled her merriment. "I'm past twenty, Hugh Logan, though it's little I am. Whatever possessed Dr. Jackman to tell you such a thing?" Her voice rang true.

"And he said you were too fond of men."

"Fond of men? I'm not fond of Dr. Jackman, I can tell you. I never see any men to be fond of, here in Carnglass. Dr. Jackman's crew are half afraid of me — particularly Niven the tinker, who knows I am a witch — and I'm thoroughly afraid of them, although I never let them guess it. With whom am I supposed to be infatuated?" A tone of suppressed anger had come into her voice.

"When you were thirteen, Jackman said, you — why, you loved a gardener here in Carnglass."

At first Logan thought she had begun to sob; but then he realized she was choking in an endeavor to keep from breaking into imprudent shrieks of laughter. "Malcolm Mor MacAskival," she managed, at last. "Malcolm Mor! Of course I loved him. I do still. He carried messages for me and contrived to get them posted in Loch Boisdale, and so they discharged him. And he worships the ground I tread, because I am The MacAskival. He has a great white beard, and is upward of seventy. Are you jealous of him?"

It was impossible not to believe her: Jackman was plausible, but Mary MacAskival was all candor. "What a consummate liar Jackman is!" Logan played with Donley's little gun.

"To be sure he is; didn't I tell you so, Hugh? He lives by lies. But into nearly every lie he works a tiny grain of truth, for the sake of appearances. Well, then: what other mischief have I been working, according to your friend Dr. Jackman?"

"He implied, Mary MacAskival, that you suffer from delusions of grandeur. He said you must have told me — by 'me' he means our fictitious bank-clerk, of course — that you were to inherit Carnglass and all the rest from your aunt, while in truth you are a pauper."

"Would it matter to you if I were a pauper?" She was serious now; he thought her firm chin went up.

"Not in the least."

"Well, then, as a matter of fact, Hugh Logan, I have more money than has Lady MacAskival. She never has loved me, but she has no one else who signifies; and so, more than five years ago, she gifted Carnglass to me, and more than half her securities. She told me that would baffle the Exchequer; for in this country, you know, one can escape death-duties by giving away one's property, so long as one does it five years before one's death. Five years ago my aunt still had her wits about her — enough to make a lawful will, at any rate; and she put Carnglass and the rest into trust for me; and six months from now, when I am twenty-one, I can do what I like with my own."

This revelation reminded Logan of his proper business in Carnglass, which the troubles of the past few days had almost driven out of his head. "Then Lady MacAskival couldn't sell Carnglass to my principal even if she chose? It's yours? And will you sell?"

"Hugh Logan! Here we sit whispering, with a gang of murderers and conspirators in the house, and The MacAskival honoring you with a call at four in the morning in your bedchamber, and you talk of title-deeds! You *are* a man of law. But no, I wouldn't sell: Carnglass is my world. Yet Duncan MacAskival being an old man, and a kinsman, and having his heart set on the matter, I might arrange for him a life-tenure of the Old

House. And I, and any husband I might choose to have, could live at the New House. When I wrote Duncan MacAskival that last letter — the note that brought you here, Hugh — I made up my mind that I would not bring him here upon a wild-goose chase altogether. If a lease of the Old House will satisfy him, he shall have it. But Dr. Jackman will be a nasty tenant for us to evict, Hugh Logan."

And then, in part volunteering the story and in part prompted by Logan's questions, the girl gave him her account of Dr. Edmund Jackman. Three years before, when Mary still had been at school, old Lady MacAskival had gone to London for a month, in winter. For half a century, Lady MacAskival had been very odd; and now whatever rationality remained to her was giving way. On her infrequent London visits, she had tended more and more to surround herself with peculiar company: Indian pseudomystics, and fortune-tellers with pretensions to decent manners, and mediums of various sorts. Lady MacAskival detested anything resembling orthodox religion, but rejoiced in any oddity which flirted with faces that glowered up from the abyss; and she believed, or half believed. She was ignorant, superstitious, vain, and rich — and she had a bad conscience. Moreover, she was extremely lonely. To her, in time, was presented a Dr. Edmund Jackman, "a scholar, my dear, and a progressive politician, and a diplomat, and a man who knows *all* about the occult. He has just come back from a trip to Roumania." Dr. Edmund Jackman spent a great deal of time in Lady MacAskival's London drawing-room, that winter three years gone. In the spring, he was invited to Carnglass, and came for a visit of two months. And then there was another visit, lengthier; and another.

By the end of the year of lengthy visits, Edmund Jackman was wholly master of Lady MacAskival's mind, or what remained of it; and master, too, of her money, and of Carnglass. Dr. Jackman was useful in many ways. He kept her avaricious London kinsfolk from troubling her. He took her affairs out of the hands of her ineffectual solicitors, and gave them his personal attention. Gradually he dismissed her feckless Island servants, even the farmhands, and reduced household costs, and brought in some hard-featured, but doubtless dependable, men from London and Glasgow, until only old Agnes remained of the former staff. He spent much of her income, too, on "schemes for political education."

This Mary MacAskival had learnt from the mumbling lips of her old aunt, in that darkened room hung with Spanish leather, listening to the ramblings of that stricken brain, convinced sometimes that she was near to madness herself. This she whispered to Hugh Logan, curled at the other end of the bed. And she had learnt other things from Dr. Jackman himself, and from Royall, and from scraps of servants' conversation overheard in the passages.

Her solitary years with Lady MacAskival had given the girl an insight into the old woman's mind and soul, Logan perceived, so complete that she could speak almost for, rather than of, her dying aunt. She understood, and nearly shared, the terrors of that room hung with Spanish leather. And she knew what talents gave Jackman his power over the old woman.

More than all his other services, what made Dr. Jackman indispensable to Lady MacAskival was this: he kept Sir Alastair away from the door of her room. Lady MacAskival always had suspected that Alastair was lurking outside that door, even though she had buried him under the great stone in St. Merin's Chapel so many years ago. Every day she sent the footman with a message for Alastair to be placed in the tomb at St. Merin's Chapel, imploring Alastair to forgive her, and to stay up there at the top of Carnglass where he belonged. Yet twice she had glimpsed Alastair, unrelenting, in the narrow passages. He *would* come back, and gobble at her bedroom door on windy nights, and she lay in dread that one night he might cross the threshold.

Dr. Jackman had saved her from that: he had bound Sir Alastair by a mystical chain, he told Lady MacAskival, and so long as she possessed the loyalty of Dr. Jackman, no tall stern old man, who ought to be in his tomb, would cross the threshold. Of course it was essential to retain the wholehearted loyalty of Dr. Jackman, and that could be secured by agreeing with him in all things. Once or twice, when she had demurred from some plan of his, Dr. Jackman had come to her bedside, with Mr. Royall beside him, and had described in awful detail what would be the consequences if Sir Alastair made his way in. She had fallen into a fit, and old Agnes had been too terrified to speak. At all costs, Dr. Edmund Jackman must be kept in a good humor; and sometimes the costs ran very high. It was a great pity that willful girl Mary did not take to Dr. Jackman.

For months now, Dr. Jackman and Mr. Royall had lived at the Old House all the time, except for brief cruises about the islands. Dr. Jackman demonstrated to Lady MacAskival his control over the risen dead by certain seances in her room. Tables rose, and chairs fell over, and horrid white shapes loomed up — but never, Dr. Jackman promised, the shape of Alastair. And presently Dr. Jackman revealed to her that he always had been in Carnglass; and had been there infinitely long before she, as Miss Ann Robertson, had been married to Colonel Sir Alastair MacAskival. For Dr. Jackman was not simply human. He was a part of Carnglass, and its master from time out of mind. He had been there before the Viking rovers came. He was the Firgower, the Goat-Man. And he saw all things, past, present, and future, through his Third Eye, which quivered in the middle of his forehead. By watching Lady MacAskival with his Third Eye, he could relieve her of all pain, and put her to sleep at will.

Yet it did not seem quite right that Dr. Jackman should marry her niece. He had told Lady MacAskival many times that he must do so; that the thing was ordered by the Presences under the rocks of Carnglass; that thus Carnglass would be his in the eyes of the puny law of men, as well as by the decree of nature. Still, it did not seem right. Mary belonged to the living, not to be a being beyond good and evil. Lady MacAskival dared not deny Dr. Jackman, however; she said only, in great fear and pain, "Then you must ask Mary herself."

Dr. Jackman did not neglect Miss Mary MacAskival. Upon her he bestowed much valuable time endeavoring to instruct her in progressive social views and in a proper understanding of occult lore. He had compelled her to come to him in his study at least an hour a day, to listen to his peculiar talk. Almost always he had been quite civil but once or twice he had threatened her, and then he had been ghastly. He talked politics and necromancy to her, a queer mixture. The one, she thought, was as mad as the other, or perhaps the politics was a little the madder.

"If I had known the least little bit about politics and economics and all that," she said to Hugh, "Dr. Jackman would have converted me. But I was utterly ignorant, so he could make no impression. I was altogether too stupid." The politics, so far as Logan could determine from Mary's imperfect exposition, were Marxist, or a variant thereof. "He has been so eager to have me serve the Party," she said. "But the Party, so far as I could make out, meant to destroy a great many people to bring about peace everywhere, and meant to make everybody precisely alike so everyone could be perfectly happy, forever and ever. That's nonsense. You're a solicitor — or is it a barrister, Hugh? — and you know. I don't at all want to be like Dr. Jackman, or like Niven the tinker; and I don't want them to be like me. So after a time I simply stared at Dr. Jackman, and said 'Indeed?' now and then, and he grew discouraged. My tactics worked like a bomb."

"Like a bomb?" asked Hugh Logan, startled.

"Oh, you know — that's one of the things we said at school, 'like a bomb.' Everything good or successful is like a bomb. You know, don't you?" Sometimes this astounding girl seemed old as the hills, and at other times younger than the fifteen years Jackman had assigned to her. She was a hoyden of sorts, but quite innocent. "Don't you ever say 'like a bomb,' Hugh? But then, I suppose you never attended a girls' school."

So Jackman had abandoned his endeavor to enlist Miss MacAskival in The Cause. Yet he had persisted in his instruction in the occult. "He really believes in it all, Hugh. Mr. Royall doesn't believe, or believes only a little; but Dr. Jackman is stranger than my old aunt. He was shot in the head in Spain — oh, did he tell you that — and I think that he has been more clever and more dangerous in various ways since he came from the hospital; but also he sees things that no one else sees, and hears sounds that no one else hears. And he has become a part of Carnglass. I mean that. He has read everything that may be read concerning Carnglass; and all the old tales have got into his brain the way romances got into Don Quixote's head: but so evilly, Hugh. He did not say he was the Firgower simply to frighten my aunt; he believes it. He frightens even Mr. Royall. And then, of a sudden, he will drop that weird talk and begin discussing politics. Or he may become quite sensible, and make plans to scout round the islands, and to keep in touch with people on the mainland, and to send messages to the Continent, and to set off gelignite when he's ready."

"Explosives?"

"Oh, yes, he has a crypt full of it; but I'll tell you of that presently. He didn't mean me to hear about the explosives, but there are places in my Old House where I can eavesdrop, if I must." She seemed to take a schoolgirl satisfaction in that art.

Royall, to judge by Mary MacAskival's description, was what someone once called "the humanitarian with the guillotine." Wholly devoted to Jackman, he was forever talking of the sufferings of the working classes. But he spoke of the men who served him and Jackman, and sometimes of people in general, as "that scum." Systematic and humorless, once upon a time he had been a successful civil servant. Then, however, political fanaticism had swallowed him, and there remained of the man only an emaciated body and a hatred of life, which he disguised from himself as hatred of the "expropriating classes." Mary MacAskival thought that Royall would have snuffed out her life, if it had served his interest — or the Party's interest — with no more scruple than as if she had been a mouse.

Edmund Jackman was more subtle and interesting. Possibly, Logan thought as he listened to the girl, Jackman once had known the good and had deliberately chosen the evil — and ever after had been haunted by that memory. "Evil, be thou my good." Fearless and very clever, somewhere early in life he must have taken the sinister track. And never had he contrived to turn back.

"When the horror is upon Dr. Jackman," Mary was whispering, "I think I would faint, only that he reminds me of Rumpelstiltskin in the fairy tale, and that makes me laugh inside, even though the rest of me is shaking." The horror came upon him once or twice nearly every day, and then he looked like a damned soul. "I think he is remembering the things he has done. Once, when he meant to break my will, he hinted at what he had to do in Spain. I think he killed patients in hospitals with doses of poison, so that they would not tell tales. Perhaps, in the beginning, the people who gave him his orders saw the streak of good in him, and so they hardened him by ordering him to do all the worst things that could be done." The girl shivered.

After the civil war in Spain, it seemed, Jackman had vanished into eastern Europe; and had reappeared in England for a time during the Second World War; and next had turned up in Roumania. There, somehow, he had fallen into disfavor with the people who gave him his orders. Possibly he had gone too far in his measures, having come to love terror for its own sake. Or perhaps he had been chosen as a scape-goat, during a period when there were official pretenses of moderation. In any event, he had fled out of Roumania, four years ago, returning to London; and then he had come to Carnglass. Royall, it seemed, had been with Jackman in Roumania, and the two of them had done things there of which they preferred not to speak even to each other. "Royall is like a ghost: I mean that he has no conscience left. But Jackman, I think, has memories of the difference between wrong and right, and so the horror comes upon him."

Suddenly the girl leaned closer to Logan, who had been about to speak, and put her little hand upon his mouth. "Hush!" — this scarcely more than a hiss. Her ears, attuned to the creaks and echoes of the place, had detected something his had not. Yes: now there were stealthy, footfalls in the passage. Someone moved outside the door of the room; seemed to hesitate there; passed on. The girl's fingers were gripping Logan's shoulder, and his hand shook as he held his pistol ready. But whatever had been outside was gone elsewhere in the labyrinth of the Old House.

How ever had Mary MacAskival endured, in her solitude, the dread strain of this perilous ordeal, month on month? "I say," she asked him, abruptly, as if she had read his mind, "do you think I'm mad myself?" He squeezed her little hand for answer. "Sometimes I wonder if I am," she went on, "for it seems like one unending nightmare: until you came, that is."

Once Jackman had said to her, "Miss MacAskival, felicitate you on your strength of mind." Considering what the man was, he had been almost gentle with her; probably his admiration was genuine. He tolerated no rudeness toward her from any of his rough men.

"I don't think he is interested in women as most men are," Mary MacAskival went on. Did she blush in the darkness? "He is in love with power and terror. He wants me only because with me he could have Carnglass a while longer, and because I have money. And, I suppose, because he enjoys crushing other people's minds. He has tried to crush mine. Had he not been so busy with other things, I believe he would have defeated me long ago."

So long as her aunt continued to live, Jackman had no urgent motive to compel the girl to marry him: his ascendancy over Lady MacAskival gave him Carnglass and enough money. But as Lady MacAskival sank, now rarely rising from her bed, the day grew near when Jackman must marry the girl, or else run the danger of exposure and ruin.

"Once I was rash," Mary said. "I told him and Royall that I had tolerated them only because they held my aunt's life as security. I said that when she was gone, I'd tell everything I knew to the police.

"Dr. Jackman smiled a horrid smile. 'Who would believe a mad girl?' was what he said. And then he told me that if he should fail to persuade me to remain loyal to him, he and Royall might do things to me — 'painful measures, Miss MacAskival, painful for all of us' — that would make me into a different person, so that I could never be the same again. There were 'special mental disciplines,' he told me, and 'certain shock treatments.' It would be ever so much pleasanter if I simply did as he told me to. And he could be sure that I would do as he wished if I were to marry him. That was once when the horror came upon him."

Here, at last, the girl burst into suppressed sobs. Logan's arm went round her shoulders. "Sometimes I have thought," she mumbled, "that I ought to give way. So much easier! But I suppose I was too proud."

The fierce old blood of the chieftains of MacAskival, Logan thought, was strong in her; she was a sport in more ways than one. It would be a pleasure for him, if ever he got the chance — which, at the moment, seemed slim — to settle accounts on her behalf with Edmund Jackman.

Why, until she wrote to Duncan MacAskival, had she made no attempt to expose Jackman, or to escape? Because it was only gradually she had come to understand what Jackman and Royall were after; and she had known, too, that her aunt's life was in their hands, and that they would not hesitate to snuff it out if they were pushed. From the moment Jackman established himself in the Old House, it had become increasingly difficult to send any message out of the island; a fortnight ago, it had become virtually impossible; and since Donley's flight, she had not been permitted even to leave the house.

And there was another reason: that room in the cellars full of explosives. She thought that Jackman was eager to use them, if there were any chance for it, to destroy certain mysterious things that the government was building in the Outer Isles; but Royall was trying to restrain him. "Dr. Jackman," she had overheard him say once, "you know what exceeding instructions has brought us already. Until word comes from Bruhl . . ." Royall was willing, she suspected, to rest content with gathering what information they could about those mysterious projects, and transmitting it to someone in London. But in Jackman there was some terrible compulsion to blow everything apart. "If he could, I do believe, he would explode all the world into little bits."

So there was this: if Jackman were brought to bay, and had the opportunity, very probably he would set off the gelignite in the crypt. The Old House would go, and everyone in it; and for Mary MacAskival, the Old House and Carnglass were the center of the universe. "I know nothing about politics," she told Logan, rather apologetically. "I suppose Jackman and Royall are traitors, and might do terrible harm to the country. But Carnglass is my country. I think of the Old House first." Jackman would destroy himself and everyone in the Old House, almost certainly, if he despaired. "What was it the old Greek said: 'When I am dead, let earth be mixed with fire'? I learnt that at school. Well, that is how Dr. Jackman thinks."

She had lived with the terror, hoping vaguely that Jackman's plans might alter and he and his men go away; that the authorities in London or Glasgow might discover the scheme and descend before Jackman could act. It was only as her aunt had sunk toward her end that the girl had been roused to some plan of action, what with her own imminent danger. And so she had got off the note to Duncan MacAskival, a schoolgirl's design; yet it had succeeded so far as to bring Logan to her. "Until you came, I had no one at all to talk with." Her sobbing broke out again.

Jackman and Royall, she was convinced, had no notion of what she had done or of Logan's real identity. Once Logan had told her of his encounters with Dowie and Gare, she said that Duncan MacAskival's cablegrams could not have reached Carnglass. The storms, and the fortunate burning of the boats, had prevented that. There was a wireless in Old House and Jackman sometimes used it, cautiously, in sending messages in code to people on the mainland; but some ten days before Lagg and Donley disappeared, part of the wireless set had slipped out of sight. "They thought Lagg, who was acting strangely, must have stolen it," she said. "He didn't. I did." This girl was a paragon. "I do believe that if they knew who you are," she went on, "they would make away with you, just as they did with Mr. Lagg" — for Logan had told her, hurriedly, what Donley had said of Lagg's end.

In a very little while, Logan realized of a sudden, it would be dawn; and Mary MacAskival must be gone from his room before then. "Mary," he said, "what is this about Lagg? Could he be alive? Could that fellow Rab really have seen him? Who is outside this house? Is it Donley, or is it only these fellows' imagination?"

She hesitated. "I do not know," she said. Was she concealing something? "Perhaps I ought to — but there isn't time now. Listen: someone's stirring already, somewhere below. There's so much more to tell you, but it must wait. Jackman will keep us apart if he can, but perhaps he'll be out with the men today, hunting for Donley. Now I must run." There were, indeed, the first faint flushes of the Hebridean spring dawn visible through the windows. She leaned toward Logan. "You may kiss my cheek, if you like, for being a brave man."

Logan did that, but he said, "You seemed to be friendlier yesterday." She sprang up, averting her face, and went to the door, and pressed an ear against it; then she opened it a crack, and peered out; then waved a little hand, and slipped through, and was gone. With this sudden vanishing, Logan almost doubted that the strange little creature ever had crouched sobbing beside him.

Logan lay awake on his bed after that, as the sun came up, full of dreads — more, perhaps, for the girl than for himself, but sufficiently concerned for Number One. About seven, there was a rap at his door, and Tompkins, that pillar of varnished iniquity, brought him morning tea. Logan would not have been surprised to be knifed as he took the tray, but Tompkins said only, "Foggy again today, sir," and closed the door behind him. Leaving the tea untasted, Logan shaved with the hot water Tompkins had brought, hurriedly dressed, and found his way downstairs to the book-lined corridor, where for a few minutes he idled about, with a feeling of complete helplessness. Then Royall appeared from somewhere, glancing at him suspiciously; but Royall was civil enough, in his deathly way, and told him that he could breakfast in the study in the tower.

He breakfasted alone. Of Mary, there was no sign; and Tompkins told him that "Dr. Jackman and Mr. Royall and some of the men have gone out, sir, hunting that Donley person." The breakfast was meagre, porridge and a scrambled egg of sorts — powdered egg, Logan thought. In a besieged house, supplies soon ran low. Outside the small windows, the mist clung to the gray stone. He would have liked to pry into the drawers of desk and table, but Tompkins or someone else might enter at any moment. His pistol was invisible under his heavy tweed jacket; that was something. How would it all end? He was a pawn in this deep game, and presently someone would sweep him off the board, unless Donley had got to the mainland and delivered his note to the police. And even if a police launch should put in at Askival harbor, could that devil Jackman be prevented from sending everyone in the house up in smoke? To ponder these things, in a deceptive calm, really was the strangest part of the nightmare into which he had got himself.

About half-past eight, Mary MacAskival ran into the study — shod, for a change, and her face glowing with excitement. The nerves that girl must have! Logan put down his pipe, not knowing whether he was expected to shake hands or to kiss her; but she gave him time for neither. "Hugh," she said, "Hugh Logan, I saw them from my window! Jackman and Royall and the others: they're bringing something up from the shore, dragging it. Come down with me, and we'll go out to meet them."

Through that immense house they ran, out into the enclosed courtyard of the Victorian block. By the big door, or rather gate, three of the men were standing: Tompkins, and Anderson the footman (who looked unpleasantly like his Gallowgate brother), and a dark grinning man, supple; and compact, who must be Ferd Caggia, the cook. A rifle lay at an angle against the wall by the door, back of Anderson. Caggia had just passed an odd green bottle — was it the old rum? — to Anderson, who took a swig from it. The three men stared at Logan and the girl, Anderson leering as he wiped his mouth with the back of his hand.

Mary MacAskival marched straight up to the door, Logan by her side, she quite ignoring the men until she stood right before Anderson, who barred the way. Yes, it was rum Anderson smelt of. "Open the door," she said, calmly.

"Mr. Logan and I are going out to meet Dr. Jackman."

"What'll ye gie me if I do?" Anderson's words came thickly; the man was drunk. Anderson winked at Tompkins and Ferd for approval.

"Be good enough to open it." Mary MacAskival's green eyes glittered.

"Not for a young hizzie, not me." Anderson laughed harshly, leaning against the door. Mary MacAskival reached past him and pulled at the bolt; it slid back.

Then Anderson took her round the waist, staring defiantly at Logan. "Ye'll gie me something, whether I let ye oot or no, ma fine leddie." With one raw fist, he pulled at the girl's jacket. Logan took a step forward and gave Anderson the back of his hand.

Caught off balance, Anderson crashed against the door. His big head jerked back, his arm flew away from the girl, and he fell.

The next second, Anderson was up from the flagstones, and everything happened at once. "Davie, you know what Dr. . . ." Tompkins began, in mild remonstrance. Ferd Caggia glided to one side, still grinning, as if he were a spectator at a match for his especial amusement. And tall

Davie Anderson, rising, had grasped the rifle; already its muzzle was swinging upward, toward Logan, and there was killing in Anderson's tipsy eyes.

Logan's reaction was instinctive and the product of his army years, not prudential. Very swiftly, he sent his hand into his armpit and flashed out the little pistol. "Anderson," he said, distinctly, "don't move. Don't move at all." The girl stood fixed by the unbolted door, her eyes wide, very pale. Anderson's mouth opened; the rifle in his grip sank toward the ground. Out of the corner of his eye, Logan saw Caggia glide smoothly toward his back, and saw Caggia's hands slip down toward something protruding just above his belt; but still Caggia smiled. "Caggia," said Logan, "bide where you are, man." Tompkins quivered.

Then, behind Anderson, the big door opened, and Dr. Jackman stepped softly in, his eyes sweeping across the little tableau. Without hesitation, Jackman snatched the rifle from Anderson's hands and dealt the footman a terrible blow in the jaw with the butt of it. The man fell, stunned, and a tooth flew out of his mouth as he struck the flagstones. Behind Jackman, Royall entered; and after him, two more men, dragging something, and staring at the tableau as they came.

Jackman kicked Anderson in the face. "I told you, you ape, to mind your manners. Caggia, get this fellow to his quarters. Powert, relieve Anderson on duty at the door" — this to one of the men behind him. "Mr. Logan, I was not aware that junior bank-clerks carried revolvers on their social calls." Jackman's words were smooth, but his face was twisted cruelly. Rumpelstiltskin, Logan thought. "Mr. Logan," Jackman went on, even more suavely, "now that I have disposed of Anderson, you have no more need that pistol. Be good enough to give it to me." Jackman held out his hand.

Royall was beside Jackman now, carrying a rifle; and Caggia was out of Logan's line of vision, probably right at his unprotected back; and the girl, surrounded by men, was exposed to any shooting; and the odds were too great. Logan extended his palm, with the little pistol lying up it, toward Jackman.

Then Royall drew in his breath. "Dr. Jackman," he said, hoarsely, "see what gun that is!"

Plucking the pistol deftly out of Logan's hand, Jackman examined it. "Quite right, Royall," he observed. "It's Donley's gun Meg, isn't it? Mr. Logan, my apologies: I was quite deceived by you — an excellent performance on your part. You are a young man of talents. After you took the gun from Donley, did you shoot him or drown him?"

Only then did Logan see what the men had dragged into the courtyard. It was the battered dead body of Donley, still streaming with water. "Don't look, my dear," said Jackman to Mary, considerately. "A bit of flotsam, washed up near the pier."

CHAPTER 10

Two more men had come into the courtyard, and stood staring. "Simmons," said Dr. Jackman to one of them, "help Niven to get this body into the cellars, for the time being. Miss MacAskival, be so good as to go to your rooms and remain there until I send word. Well, Rab! Up and about? I take it that Donley here wasn't on your heels last night? No, of course not. We haven't yet found your friend Carruthers, but I trust that we will. Caggia, *do* get Anderson to his bed, for he's sprinkling blood all over the flags, and there's a lady present."

The sight of blood seemed to put Edmund Jackman into excellent form. Shock-headed Rab gazed at him vacantly, as if still dazed by his last evening's encounter with shadowy pursuers. "Well," Jackman went on cheerfully, "poor Till — he's lost the sight of one eye forever, I'm sure — is quits with Seamus Donley now. Go up and tell him the news, Tompkins."

Mary, in the midst of this hard crew, was looking at Logan with dismay in her eyes. "Hugh," she said, "Hugh . . ." and stretched out a hand toward him. Jackman shot a malign glance at her.

"You'd best go, Mary," Logan told her, with what assurance he could summon up. She turned and fled into the Old House.

Logan could conjecture the fate of Donley. Tired and wounded, the old terrorist must have been flung on the skerries by that cruel sea; the boat would have broken up; and his body, beaten against the rocks, had washed round to the harbor at the other end of Carnglass. In this grim moment, Logan had little time to pity Donley. It could not have been Donley, then, returned, who hunted Rab and Carruthers through the night. Rab might have fired only at imaginary stalkers, in this eerie island. But then what had become of Carruthers? Lagg had taken him, Rab had screamed in his hysteria last night. Was it possible that, after all, Lagg had not been killed? But if he had not, how could he have existed alone and invisible these several days; and how could a sly fat Galloway factor have made away with one seasoned ruffian and driven another out of his wits?

Except for Powert, standing sentry at the gate, Logan now was left alone in the courtyard with Jackman and Royall. "Well, Mr. Logan," Jackman was saying to him, "there are few things in this vale of tears more interesting than an accomplished adversary. I prize you." He was playing with that little pistol Meg. "Royall, we'll take Mr. Logan up to my study, and there he'll supply us with valuable information, I'm sure. He should be able to tell us, for instance, who disposed of Carruthers. He has done us one service already, in evening our score with the late lamented Seamus Donley; now we'll discover just who sent Mr. Logan to us, and why."

It might be folly to go on pretending he was an Edinburgh bank-clerk, Logan thought: Meg had given him away. Under the circumstances, and considering the habits of Jackman's gang, naturally Dr. Jackman assumed that Logan had disposed of Donley. But what new role could Logan play? To have lapsed into his American speech would have suggested to the quick mind of Jackman that this young fellow had been sent to manage the purchase of Carnglass. And, having learnt too much about Jackman and Company, Logan then would be a candidate for extinction.

He dared not pretend to be an Englishman, for his mastery of English accents was not up to it, and Jackman would have detected him at once. Their French, too, might be better than his own. There seemed to be nothing for it but to keep speaking in a genteel Scots, though he might expand his vocabulary beyond the usual range of a fictitious junior clerk. "Well, Dr. Jackman," Logan said — he made the word almost "weel" — "I confess I do find myself in predicament."

"Really," said Jackman, "really now, my dear fellow, you needn't continue to talk as a Lothians counter-jumper would. You didn't ring quite true in that role, but yours was a valiant try. You're a cut or two above that sort of thing, eh? I doubt whether you're a Scot at all. An English-man, possibly? Or even a German? A university man, probably. Just walk on the other side of our Mr. Logan, if you will be so good, Royall. We shall have Mr. Logan resident in Carnglass for some time now: per-manently, perhaps, depending on his degree of co-operation with us. Among the many things about you which puzzle me, Logan, is how you contrived to become acquainted with Miss Mary MacAskival. We shall have to interrogate the young lady on that point, eh, Royall — unless Mr. Logan is so gallant as to save us the trouble? I hadn't guessed that Miss MacAskival numbered among her friends any person formidable enough to do in Seamus Donley, late I.R.A. Well, up to my study, if you don't mind. On the stair, Mr. Royall, pray walk directly behind Mr. Lo-gan, with your gun at the ready. We mustn't underestimate his talents a second time."

For all the gravity of this situation, Hugh Logan felt more confi-dence in himself than he had known since he landed in Carnglass. He had begun to understand matters, and to struggle against the tide of events; his ineffectuality of an hour ago had given way to action of a sort. And time was running out for Jackman. A few more days of silence from Carnglass, at most, and someone — the police, or a passing ship or plane — would suspect that things were amiss in the island, and there would be investigations highly embarrassing to Jackman. They would not be so embarrassing, however — sobering thought — if Hugh Logan somehow should have vanished from Carnglass before any official in-quiries might be made. It was some comfort to reflect that Duncan MacAskival, if no one else, soon would begin to wonder where he was; and there was the faint possibility that the Glasgow police, desiring him for a witness in the affair of Mutto's Wynd, might commence to look for him. Everything, conceivably, would depend upon how the next few minutes with Dr. Jackman happened to go.

In the study, Jackman indicated that, as on the first occasion, Logan was to sit at the chess-table. "I don't think you'll be needed, Royall," Jackman said to that cadaverous secretary, "but you might look in within the hour. We have a very clever guest here: devilish clever. It's as well I have Donley's pistol in my pocket now." Royall hesitated, as if to offer some objection; but, at a dark glance from Jackman, went out.

Once again Jackman poured sherry for Logan, and set out the Table Men of Askival. "Really, Logan, I think you were pulling my leg at our last game of chess, as you were in so many other matters. I'll not accept any handicap in this match. It's rather pleasant to play during a casual discussion like ours, don't you think? We never may have an opportunity for another match. That depends upon you, of course, Logan." Jackman showed every sign of being in good spirits, as if he enjoyed this contest with an able adversary; but well below his urbane surface, Logan suspected, a gnawing disquietude was at work in Jackman. He knew the man much better after Mary's account of him.

As for Logan, he made his first move in the match with seeming indifference, smiling at Jackman. The only thing that could suffice to save him, Logan felt, was to dismay Jackman by a show of complacency and mysterious assurance. He had this sole advantage, that Jackman had not the faintest glimmer as to who Logan really was. "Oh, no, sir," he said to Jackman, still with his assumed Scotish burr, "I fancy that the question of our future encounters, Dr. Jackman, already is settled by people from beyond Carnglass."

Jackman scowled. "I told you you needn't play at little games with me, Logan, or whatever your name is. It's pointless now for you to talk like a smarmy bank-clerk that never existed. Why not out with it all? Who are you?" He advanced a rook.

"That, Dr. Jackman, you'll learn in the fullness of time. Lest you grow rash, let me remind you of one thing: you may be sure that I'd not have come to Carnglass, knowing you and your men were here, without having taken precautions. There are a dozen people who know precisely where I am, and why, and who will come looking for me if I don't return when I ought." He let that observation sink in as he meditated his next move. He wished there were any truth in it; but Jackman could not know its hollowness.

"As for that, Logan" — here Jackman castled — "it would be entirely possible for you to be lost, accidentally, in the wild waters. No witnesses would swear to your having met with any harm in quiet old Carnglass. Not one. You might, for instance, have gone mackerel-fishing in a small boat with Lagg and Donley; and the three of you might have been caught in a squall — there are mishaps enough in these waters — and drowned; and two of the bodies might have been recovered, Donley's and yours. A death by drowning is quite natural. A quarter of a mile off the western shore of Carnglass is a ragged reef that would offer a wholly convincing explanation."

133

Logan extricated a bishop from a tight corner. "But suppose, Dr. Jackman, that my friends ashore are not the sort to be satisfied by the formalities of a coroner's jury, or, indeed, by Scottish courts of law? Suppose they might hold you privately accountable, and presume you guilty until proved innocent?"

Jackman stared at him. "Logan, I put it to you bluntly now, Royall was sounding you out last night, of course, with his bits from Burns, and our other signals. You evaded him. Now tell me out and out, for I've no time to waste: are you one of us? If you are, why cannot you say so and have done with it, and transmit your instructions to me, if you've any to give? Perhaps you're from London; perhaps from Paris; perhaps from further East. I've been expecting some such inquiry, of course. Why this cat-and-mouse rubbish, if you are one of us?"

Jackman's nerves were wearing thin. To assume the new role of a member of Jackman's conspiratorial circle would be much the safest dodge for him just now, of course — if only Logan knew how to play it. But, lacking knowledge of the ring, all he could undertake was to cast out dark hints from time to time. "Why, I'll tell you merely this, Dr. Jackman: I am not authorized to make any regular communication to you until certain events have taken place, and until a certain time has elapsed. Until then, consider me simply as your casual guest." He took a rook of Jackman's.

"You *are* a cool chap, Logan. I needn't tell you I have ways of extracting a statement from you. I know all the ways, Logan."

"Of course you know them. But suppose I am the sort of person I may be: if you did me any hurt, it might be awkward for you afterward, eh? I have a long memory, Jackman."

Jackman bit his lip, and lost another pawn. "There are other ways of getting round you, Logan. Have you ever heard a lady scream? A full-throated scream, from exquisite agony, I mean. It's rather distressing for a gentleman who happens to like the lady in question. And it is the ladies, the gently-bred, soft-skinned ladies, who scream loudest, Logan, and talk soonest and most. Imagine a young lady accustomed all her life to deference, who hadn't had a hand laid upon her in anger since she was a naughty small child; and then think of her, to her surprise and chagrin, abruptly treated to the worst that the human body can stand. How she would scream, Logan, and babble all she knew, and beg to be let off; and you would have the interesting experience of watching the process, though unable to intervene. Suppose Miss Mary MacAskival were the young lady? I'm sure she could tell us a great deal about you." Jackman's marvellous eyes glinted. "Torment is the great leveller, Logan: in torment, the colonel's lady and Judy O'Grady are sisters under the skin. There are no class distinctions in agony; our Miss MacAskival would behave like the lowest trull from Piccadilly, except that she would scream louder and talk sooner."

It required a considerable effort, but Logan kept a smiling countenance. If he protested, or showed any sign of weakness, Jackman would take precisely this course; he was being sounded. Indifference on his part, just now, was the chief hope for Mary.

"Ah, well, Dr. Jackman, you and I are playing for higher stakes than a slip of a girl, aren't we? If you must, you must; but I may as well tell you that you'd be wasting the time of both of us. Miss MacAskival knows only just what I found necessary to tell her, which is precious little. As for my being racked vicariously by her discomforts — why, you and I got past that a good time ago, didn't we, Jackman? 'O had ye been where I ha' been, and seen wha' I ha' seen . . .' When fellows like us have supped long on horrors, another squeal or two doesn't much matter. Besides, I doubt whether you have much taste for twisting ladies' arms, Jackman, I know you did your share of the disagreeable business, that very sort of business, in Barcelona and Bucharest — oh, I know all about you, Jackman" — here Jackman grimaced, taken aback — "but really, though you make such operations sound jolly, they aren't very good fun, are they, now? One never quite grows accustomed to them; they stick in the craw; and what's worse, they stick at the back of the brain, don't they? Even our friend Royall, I suspect doesn't relish that business as he should."

"Even so, Logan, I wouldn't have to turn my own hands to the work, you know. Those strapping fellows downstairs would jump at the chance. They've been somewhat inhibited from their accustomed earthy pleasures here in Carnglass, poor chaps, and some haven't had their way with a woman for months. Your recent little *contretemps* with Anderson, for instance — I'm certain Anderson would perform the task with enthusiasm. They're a trifle coarse-fibred, my men, and to apply the *peine fort et dure* to a young lady would be quite their cup of tea."

"No doubt, no doubt, old chap." Here Logan took a knight from Jackman. "I have limitless confidence in their aptitude for such work, if for no other. But the powers that be still would tend to hold you person-ally responsible, wouldn't they, now? And suppose the interrogation should all be in vain — why, however could you explain? Nothing does a diligent man's reputation more serious damage than an unauthorized and unnecessary atrocity. *You* ought to know that by this time, Jackman."

"The things I did, others told me to do, Logan." Jackman's lips worked. He lost another pawn.

"Quite. But you went rather beyond specific instructions, didn't you? I don't advise you to exceed instructions here in Carnglass."

Jackman ran a hand lightly across his forehead, distractedly touch-ing the little round soft patch in the middle with a forefinger. He ven-tured out a rook too far, and lost it to Logan. Then he looked, silent, into Logan's eyes. The gaze of those great glowing pupils of Jackman's was hard to bear. Into Logan's mind came the sentence, "And if thy light be darkness, how great shall be that darkness." It was just possible that he might prove a match of Edmund Jackman now, though the odds were against him. The man's brain must be damaged, and under Jackman's outward imperiousness, Logan suspected, vacillation was gnawing away. Logan thought also that had he encountered Jackman at the height of the man's powers, Mary would have had a sorry knight-errant. But now the merciless energy and talent which had been Jackman's were flickering in the socket, like enough, and Logan had to deal only with the remnant of a bad man. In Jackman's ears sounded the wings of the Furies, and his mind sank further into doubt and dread. Or so Logan surmised, looking into those splendid, troubling eyes. It was just barely conceivable that Logan might defeat this failing master of deceit.

Logan started, and shook his head to rouse his consciousness. Had Jackman been attempting to mesmerize him? If so, the attempted paral-ysis of will had not succeeded, what with Logan's own mind being full of plots and stratagems. Yet Jackman might have come near successful hypnosis; Logan had a feeling that the man had been asking him ques-tions, in a low, almost friendly voice, to which Logan had given no an-swers as yet.

Just now Jackman was saying, ever so softly, "Who *are* your friends outside the Old House, out there in the wet and the dark?"

"Friends?" Logan spoke shrilly, alarmed at his own near-slip into rev-erie or trance. "Friends? Whose friends? If anyone's outside, they're no people of mine." Logan regretted this admission as soon as he had made it; it would have done no harm to keep Jackman wondering whether he had an accomplice or two hidden in the bracken. Indeed, perhaps Jackman had begun to extract the truth from him by hypnosis, and Logan had escaped from the domination of those black eyes only in the nick of time.

But Jackman shook his head slowly, in disbelief; and his eyes went to the window of that room high in the tower, almost as if he feared to see some face pressed against the pane, far above the living rock of the Old House's foundation. It was borne in upon Logan that Jackman's unease was greater than his own fears.

Jackman licked his thin lips. "Why, Logan, who do you expect me to believe they are?" If the mystery back there behind the bracken had shaken Jackman this much, the panic must be worse among the men below stairs, with Rab's hysteria to work upon them. "If they were police or intelligence people," Jackman said, almost as if he expected to be overheard by some presence in that dusky painted chamber, "they would have swooped upon us long ago; they wouldn't skulk about, picking off first one man and another."

"Rab told you that it was Tam Lagg: old Lagg, Dr. Jackman, that you sent over the cliffs a thousand feet down to the rocks and the sea, while he screamed of his wife and his bairns."

Jackman looked at Logan astonished. "You, Logan — were you watching then? But no, you'll have had that from Donley, before you finished with him. Lagg? What are you talking of? I saw him strike a crag halfway down, and bounce off like a ball, and then fall to the sea. Such a thing doesn't walk again."

"Not alive," Logan replied. "No, not alive." Jackman's eyes dilated. Yes, he could sound this note, Logan decided: the black beast was upon Jackman's shoulders, and the conjuror was bewitched. If ever a man was haunted, it was Jackman, stalked by Spanish victims and Roumanian spectres, and now with the wraith of Lagg at his heels. "See here, Jackman: you raise sham bogles to frighten old women, and you laugh up your sleeve. But when you play with things from the abyss, you run risks. In this dead island of Carnglass, all round us things are ready to stir, if they're called. I felt them in Dalcruach clachan. In Carnglass the dead are more than the living. And why shouldn't Tam Lagg rise? You gave him the death that he feared most to die. If ever you set a spirit to walk the night, it was when you tossed that screaming man from the headland at the back of St. Merin's Chapel."

As Logan spoke, a nasty change came over Jackman. His face went a sick white, and his eyes closed, and he slumped in his chair. The horror must be on him. His breath came hard. Logan began to think of closing with him as he sat motionless across the table. But after a moment, Jackman gasped, blinked, and fumbled for the pistol in his pocket; he drew the gun and laid it before him, beside the chessboard.

"Then you feel it, too," Jackman muttered, very low. "All about us, eh? Oh, this is a damned house, a place of dreams, horrid dreams. Listen: last night I walked the passages, for I didn't dare to sleep, until I was worn out. In the end, I lay on my bed, not closing my eyes. And then it was not a bed, but a long, close tunnel or cave, and I was stumbling along it. Away at the end, I could see something standing. And it came to me that I myself was standing there, even though I walked toward the thing. The Edmund Jackman at the end of the cave was the Edmund Jackman that I might have been, if — if I had taken another turn at the beginning. And as I came up to myself, wanting to see the face, and the beauty of what I might have been, the thing turned, and looked at me. Its face was the face of a goat. Ah, the slit eyes! And I became one with it, and woke, and the horror still was on me."

Infected by the man's loathing of himself, and his fright, Logan also lowered his voice to a whisper. "Would you rather have died in the cave than have become one with the goat?"

"Yes," said Jackman, "yes. It would be better to lie dead, dead like Lagg. I thought then of the gelignite, and I think of it every day and every night." At this, Jackman shuddered, seemed to collect his wits, scowled at Logan, and glanced dully at the Table Men of Askival on the board before him.

"Your move," Logan reminded him. Edmund Jackman moved almost at random. "So!" Logan shifted his queen. "Checkmate, Dr. Jackman."

"Hell!" cried Jackman, reaching out his hand as if to sweep the pieces to the floor.

"Easy!" Logan said, intercepting Jackman's hand with his own. "There's but this one set in the world, you know."

Once more their eyes met in a long, strange stare; then Jackman, to Logan's surprise, glanced down at the table. "Logan, or whatever you are," he said, almost pleadingly, "I don't know whether you can understand me. You're a Party intellectual, I think, and the Party believes it knows all things. Yet in some matters the Party is blind. Just now I said 'Hell.' In Carnglass, I have learned that Hell is real. That's heresy in the Party; but I have looked on Hell. There is no Heaven, but there is Hell."

Jackman's eyes were vacant now; he seemed to have forgotten to whom he spoke. "Hell endures," he went on. "I have been in Hell always. This Carnglass is Hell. Don't you know you were here in Carnglass before, infinitely long ago? We fought here then — and I lost. In Carnglass there is no time. Eternity is real here, and change is the delusion. I know this in the nights, when I walk the corridors. It is only in the day I can pretend that I am alive, or that what things I do can possibly save me from the torment. In the nights it is Hell that is real, and the Party is a sham. Do you understand that? And I know that you came here to send me to the torment, as you did before."

Many times, Logan had heard the phrase "possessed of a devil." But not until this moment, as he sat opposite Jackman with the chessmen between them, had he perceived the full and dreadful meaning of the words. The dark powers had claimed Edmund Jackman long since, and what sat opposite him was only the husk of a human being. Even the husk was crumbling now. Yet out of that desiccated scrap of mortality, dry and empty as the armor of last summer's locust, there echoed now and again cries of anguish, the vain contrition of the damned. Whatever traditionary spectres might throng round the Old House of Fear, here right before Logan sat the ghost of what once might have been a vessel for honor.

Again Jackman's eyes had closed, and the man or devil did not stir in the chair. What visions came and went behind those fallen eyelids, Logan preferred not to think. Jackman had drifted somewhere beyond this world of sense, for the moment. In the middle of that pallid forehead, the nasty round spot, the Third Eye, seemed to pulsate faintly, as if keeping night watch upon Logan.

Hugh Logan fought clear of the contagion of madness. Minutes, precious minutes, were slipping away. By a heap of chessmen lay the little pistol. Should he make a try for it? Or was this some sort of trap that Jackman had set? No, the damned man's trance was genuine. If he chose, Logan could leap up, snatch the pistol, and make for the stairs. But that gang of murderers was below. And where might Mary and he run to? Well, let him get his hands on a rifle, and he might hold the old tower against them for a time. It might be possible to keep Jackman a hostage. The scheme was fantastic, but the only probable alternative was torture and death for Mary MacAskival and himself. Rising silent from his chair, Logan stretched out a hand toward the gun.

"As you were!" It was Royall's harsh voice, at Logan's back. A revolver-muzzle pressed into his spine. Royall's long, almost skeletal arm reached past him and snatched up the little pistol by the chessmen. "Over to the wall," Royall said, "and stand there till I tell you to turn round. I've been behind the screen these ten minutes past, Logan."

CHAPTER 11

It would have been a lunatic try anyhow, Logan thought as he faced the wall. Behind him, Royall was ministering to Dr. Jackman, but Logan felt sure that if he swung round, Royall would not miss.

"Here, a little brandy," Royall was saying, rather in the tone of a nurse. "Come round now, Dr. Jackman. It's no time for fancies." There was a sound as if Royall were gently slapping Jackman's cheeks. "That's it, sir: are you quite awake now, Dr. Jackman?"

Jackman's voice came choked and faint, but grew in power after the first few words. "Askival," Jackman was saying. "Askival — where is he? And Lagg?"

"Take hold of yourself, Dr. Jackman. We've this fellow Logan to deal with. Very well, Logan: come over here and sit down."

For the present, Royall had assumed command. With his revolver he gestured toward the chair in which Logan had sat during the chess-match, and Logan took it without protest. Royall continued to stand. On the other side of the table, Jackman seemed in possession of his faculties again.

"We'd best search this man," Royall said. He slipped a hand inside Logan's jacket, still standing at Logan's back, and found his wallet. Logan did not move: Jackman was watching him keenly, his hand on the pistol. They would find no identification in the wallet, for Logan had put his passport and anything else with his name on it into the knapsack.

"No, sir, there's nothing with a name, worse luck," Royall murmured.

"Stand up and take off your jacket, Logan." Logan did as he was told. In a moment Royall thrust the jacket back to him. "And no labels, Dr. Jackman. The man must be an old hand at his game."

"Tompkins searched his room this morning?" Jackman asked.

"Yes; and he found nothing but a razor and the like. No papers — and not even the canvas sack this man brought with him. I suppose he burnt it in the fireplace, or else flung it out of the window and down the cliff to the sea."

"Have a man look along the rocks at low tide," Jackman said. "Yes, our friend Logan undoubtedly has had experience as an agent of some sort."

"You needn't bother to have a man risk his bones on those weedy ledges," Logan told them. "I burnt the sack on the coals, last night." He trusted that Mary had tucked away the pack in some really secure hidie-hole.

"For your circumstances, Logan," Royall muttered, "you seem unreasonably cheerful. I shouldn't care to find myself in your present situation." Royall ran his hands carefully along Logan's trousers and into his pockets. "No, Dr. Jackman — no knife, and no papers stitched into the linings."

"Why," said Logan, "I suppose a man might as well laugh as cry. And then, don't you know, it's not I who need to fash — as we true-born Scots say. It's you gentlemen who will have to make your peace, if you can, with the men that will be here all too soon for your comfort."

"Sit down again, Logan," Royall ordered. "You needn't sing that tune for us. If you had any people at your back, we'd have seen them before this."

"Oh?" Logan answered, amicably. "And who do you suppose took Carruthers? Donley was dead hours before you missed Carruthers, remember."

Jackman and Royall stared at each other, silent. In that moment, Logan almost felt a touch of pity for them. Both must have been reared and educated well enough — very well, indeed. What flaws of character or intellectual false turnings had brought them into this ruthless business, he could not tell. They might have commenced, like others, full of humanitarian sentimentality. And then, perhaps, demon ideology, with its imperatives and its inexorable dogmas, its sobersided caricature of religion, had swept them on to horrors. Ideological fanaticism had made of

Jackman the goat-man, mastered by lust: but not the lust for women's bodies. Jackman's was the *libido dominandi,* the tormented seeking after power that ceases not until death. And in the flame of that lust for power, Jackman and Royall would be burnt up, today or next week or next month: they were at the end of their devil's bargain, and the fiend would claim his own.

Now, in this oppressive silent moment, the conviction came to Logan that these two artists of disintegration were more frightened than he. He felt surprised to find himself thinking clearly enough, almost ruminating, in this tension that made electric the ancient room with the painted ceiling. Because frightened, Jackman and Royall were the more dangerous; but also their brains were stagnant with dread.

Fear, it crossed Logan's mind, is the normal condition of man, after all. Quiet ages and safe lands are the rare exceptions in history. Nowadays the tides of disorder were gnawing at whatever security and justice still stood in the world, quite as the swell round Carnglass sought to bring down that heap of gray stones to the mindless anonymity of the ocean. With growing speed, the brooding spectre of terror, almost palpable in Carnglass, was enveloping the world. This island was the microcosm of modern existence.

And here in the haunted stronghold of the Old House of Fear, Jackman and Royall and their gang found themselves caught in their own snare. Even the dull criminals below stairs, huddled tipsily by the kitchen fire, were unmanned by a dim sense of catastrophe, caught up in a horror of the empty island, where mist and silence seemed to have made away with time, so that Glasgow and Liverpool and London were fancies out of an illusory past.

Jackman himself, with his distraught imagination, his ruined talents once near to genius, fancied himself snared here by destiny, condemned to give reality to a myth. And was he wrong? In the Old House, Logan doubted where the realm of spirit ended and the realm of flesh began.

In this dead island, all Jackman's cleverness lay frustrated, and the strange chance or power that had brought Logan to Carnglass on this day seemed to fill the close air in that forgotten tower-room. For Edmund Jackman, Logan might be something not quite canny, at once a man and an occult agent. Even for Royall, Hugh Logan must seem a retributive figure, from Party or police, mercilessly calm with the knowledge that others were not far behind him.

For all their effort to behave as if they still were masters of the island, a tautness almost hysterical had crept into Jackman and Royall, and their voices were strained. What for years they had dealt out to others, now waited for them; and they had forgotten the meaning of mercy. There was no justice to which they could appeal. By fear they had lived; and now the fear which they and their sort had carried throughout the world was claiming them also. Having murdered order, these two at last were cast into the outer darkness.

Jackman was speaking. Had something like a quaver crept into that urbane and sardonic voice? "Well, Royall," he was saying, "what will we do with this Logan?"

Royall shifted uncertainly behind Logan's chair. This man, it occurred to Logan, saw the growing madness in his leader, and yet was loyal — his last link with old-fangled human affections.

"Dr. Jackman," Royall said, "I have a theory concerning our friend Logan. I believe he's one of Vlanarov's people."

Jackman now spoke with his old decisiveness, as if another spirit had entered into that sinister body, and as if what had happened during the preceding half hour had quite washed away from his memory. "Possibly," Jackman commented. "Quite possibly. The thought had crossed my mind, too. If he should be, perhaps we can arrive at satisfactory terms. Well, Logan?"

Logan devoutly wished, at this juncture, that he had studied more attentively the recent history of Eastern Europe. If he had fought in Europe, rather than in the Pacific, that might have been of some help; or had he been in intelligence, rather than the infantry. As it was, the name Vlanarov told him a little, but not enough. If memory served him aright, Vlanarov was such a one as Jackman, but a much bigger fish. Logan rather thought that Vlanarov had been at Bela Kun's side in Hungary, a generation ago, and in Madrid during the Civil War, and after 1945 a terror in Poland. Through all the vicissitudes of Party feuds and all the eddies of ideology in the buffer states, the shadowy but formidable figure of Vlanarov had glided scatheless. No one ever saw a photograph of the man. It had been his peculiar talent to anticipate the triumph of particular factions within the Soviet states, and to shift masterfully in precisely the proper moment from one interpretation of Marxist doctrine to the corrected version. Whenever a vanquished clique fell to its ruin, Vlanarov sorted through the wreck for such survivors as might still do mischief to the new Party orthodoxy, and clipped their claws and their wings for them — or something worse. Certain Trotskyites called Vlanarov "The Vulture."

This much, Logan recalled. And he could see that conceivably the pose of being one of Vlanarov's people, at watch upon Jackman's schemes, might save his neck. But the great difficulty was that he knew far too little of Party intrigues to play this role to the full. For that matter, he was not precisely sure that Vlanarov still was alive: Royall might be setting a trap for him.

"Yes," Royall was saying, "I fancy that he's a Vlanarovite, sent over by Bruhl from Brussels, to report on our work. Only one of that sort could have made away with Donley so efficiently."

Jackman, now tense and erect in his chair, nodded. "Logan," he said, "if you come from Bruhl or Vlanarov, with instructions for us or perhaps for a survey — why, tell me now. After all, you can't expect to remain anonymous much longer, because tomorrow or next day I should receive word from Glasgow, and perhaps from Paris."

"No, Jackman, I don't think you will." Logan had resolved to sound as much like a Vlanarovite as possible, without being expected to furnish proof positive. "You've contrived to get your boats burnt for you by a stupid old Irishman. You've had part of your wireless stolen" — Jackman started at this — "and you've no way of sending word to shore. And you saddled yourself with the clumsiest of agents that ever I set eyes upon. Gare, that drunken incompetent; Dowie, who's fit only for filching sixpences from slum boys; Jock Anderson, all swagger and no nerve. We gobbled the lot of them." Logan opened his right hand wide and closed it hard, as if crushing something within. "They're awa' doon the water, Jackman. An old hand like you! One would think you had turned to drink. But you've turned to old wives' tales, instead."

Jackman bit his lip. "Do you mean — do you mean they been taken?"

"Liquidated is our word, Dr. Jackman. They were, after all, depreciated assets. And were I you, Jackman, I'd look sharp. What have you accomplished here in Carnglass? The rags and tags of information you've collected in foraging round the islands are next to worthless. We have better ways of mapping those missile sites. And playing with gelignite, like a boy with firecrackers! You'd never get the stuff past the guards at the installations, if you seriously tried: these hangdog fellows you've collected here in Carnglass haven't the heart or the mind for it. You drove out your only experienced man, Donley, so that he had to be liquidated for fear he'd talk. Unauthorized enthusiasm! It will be your ruin, Jackman."

"But after all," Royall put in eagerly, "Bruhl himself gave his consent to this project."

"Tentative consent is one thing," Logan said; "approval of blunders in operation is another."

Jackman ran his fingers across his forehead in his old gesture of incertitude. "Logan," he said, "I believe you really are from Vlanarov's people. You're a Party intellectual: you've the look and tone of it. In short, you're a man we can talk with. You must know as well as we do what has gone wrong with this scheme. The people in the Continent want action from me, but they'll take no risks nor spend any money. For that matter, they'll give me no men. I am expected to extort the funds from old women, conscript a set of criminals and hold them together by blackmail and intimidation, and pay the penalty by myself, with my own neck, if everything falls in pieces.

"For years those people have used Royall and me in this way. Edmund Jackman, who ought to be forming policy at the upper levels, set to leading a gang of banditti at the back of beyond! It's enough to craze a man. As one intellectual to another, do you see any justice in that? Bureaucracy on the one hand, fanatic ideological rigidity on the other; and the best minds in the Party, like yours and mine, fallen between the stools. In my situation, what would you have done differently?" He was almost wheedling.

"I'm not authorized to offer any opinion on that subject, as yet," Logan said, with what he hoped was an enigmatic smile.

"Perhaps I had better make it clear, Logan," Royall put in, "that Dr. Jackman's association with Beria arose solely from necessity, and from his obedience to Party discipline. We regret as much as anyone does what happened to Vlanarov's father."

"Do you have a cigarette?" said Logan. "I suppose lunch will be ready soon."

"Logan," Jackman demanded, intensely, "are you here to supplant me? If you are, why this shilly-shallying? Can't you have the decency to present your instructions?"

"Why, I'm in no position as yet to give definite orders, Jackman. The decisions must be yours; I decline any responsibility. But this I will suggest: disarm your men, lock up the guns, and give me the keys to the gunroom and the cellars where you keep the gelignite. Send all the men down to the New House except Tompkins and Royall. Light a beacon, or send up flares, and put Carnglass in communication with the mainland through ordinary channels. Leave me in charge of the Old House. Then wait the turn of events. If you do this, I'll put in my good word for you with my superiors."

This was spreading it perilously thick, Logan thought, but one might as well be taken for a tiger as for an alley-cat.

Jackman sucked in his breath. "You ask too much, Logan, whoever or whatever you are. Is this some plan to make Royall and me the scapegoats? To hand us over to the police or intelligence, possibly, by way of covering someone else's blunders? I've been treated that way before, Logan, and I'll not endure it again. Sooner than that — sooner than the gaol or the gallows — I'd walk into the cellars and detonate the gelignite. I'd rather blow Carnglass into pebbles than be the dupe once more."

"You asked for suggestions, Jackman. I told you I'd assume no responsibilities." Logan had not dared to hope that Jackman actually would fall into his impromptu snare; but at least it served to bewilder Jackman and Royall.

"And if we did disarm the men," Royall thrust at him, "who would keep off your friends outside? The ones that made away with Carruthers, and sent Rab mad? What's your scheme, Logan — to liquidate all of us in Carnglass? To send us to join Gare and Dowie and Jock Anderson and Donley? To make sure that no one here ever has an opportunity to furnish evidence to the government?"

Inadvertently, he might have carried the game too far, Logan saw: he might get himself drowned for a commissar instead of a police-agent.

"Damn it," Jackman almost shouted, the patch in the middle of his forehead twitching, "are you really from Vlanarov? Do you have another name?"

"I'll tell you when there's need for it," was all Logan answered him. For Jackman was losing control of himself, and it was conceivable that he might shoot Logan where he stood.

"Now, now, Dr. Jackman," Royall murmured, "if he *is* from Vlanarov, we'd best not . . ."

"No!" Jackman cried, his air of power returning to him. "No, you'll tell me soon enough. If you're sent by that mutual-admiration circle in the Continent, I'll have that news out of you, and make you pay for it. And if you're something worse, I'll twist that truth from you. I know your medicine, Logan. You're going into the Whiskey Bottle; there's no man who can endure that place long. You'll talk with me, and thank me for the chance."

"Dr. Jackman, I really do think . . ." Royall began, uneasily. But Jackman cut him off.

"Mr. Royall, get Anderson and Caggia. We'll put our friend Logan away below stairs. The responsibility is mine. And while I'm at the Whiskey Bottle, you make the rounds of the house, Royall, and make sure all the men have ammunition enough."

It never would do to let Jackman see any sign of weakness in him, for the man subsisted on others' dread, and was most merciless, Logan guessed, when they were most piteous. Deliberately Logan gathered up the Table Men and set them in their casket. "I thought you had a taste for sherry, Jackman," he said, "but you seem to have whiskey in mind for me." Jackman answered nothing. Then Anderson and Ferd entered. Anderson's jaw was bound up in a bloody handkerchief, and the man looked murder at Logan.

In silence, Jackman and Anderson and Ferd Caggia took Logan down the worn stair in the thickness of the wall. They took him to the ground floor of the old tower, where first he had met Mary MacAskival only yesterday about this hour, though it seemed an age ago. And they shoved him toward one corner of that great vaulted empty room. In that corner, flush with the flagstones, a small stair twisted downward, below the level of the rock on which the Old House stood. Anderson thrust him forward with a curse, so that Logan staggered down the short flight, the three men behind him.

The place below was wholly dark. Caggia carried a petrol lantern, and he lit it and swung it round. This crypt, hollowed from the rock, apparently contained nothing but what looked like a broken windlass in a far corner, and what seemed to be a coil or heap of rope in a near corner. And in the middle of the floor was a circular lid or cover of stone, with an iron ring set into it. Caggia and Anderson commenced to drag back this lid.

This being, perhaps, his last appearance above ground, Logan thought he ought to improve the shining hour. "I do hope, Anderson," he said, "that your jaw doesn't pain you." Anderson responded with an obscenity. "I am acquainted with your brother Jock in the Gallowgate," Logan went on. "A lively man, Jock. He kicked me in the jaw not long ago."

"Gude for Jock," growled Anderson. "I'll soon gie ye anither."

"But we caught him, Davie Anderson," Logan continued, "and put him where he'll kick no more. We caught Jim Dowie and his wife Jeanie, too, and the others. And now all the world knows of the criminals of Carnglass."

"Enough of that, Logan," Jackman put in. Anderson and Ferd were standing by the open mouth of a pit or cistern, staring attentively at Logan. Jackman pressed the muzzle of the little pistol into Logan's back and urged him toward the gulf. This must be the pit, for dead herring or dead men, described in Balmullo's account of the Old House.

"Dr. Jackman," Logan said in some haste, "I do trust that when, tomorrow or the next day, you decide in despair to blow up the Old House, yourself, and everyone round about, you will allow these two fine fellows to join me in this well of yours. It will probably be the safest place for some miles round. I doubt whether Anderson and Caggia are so ready to die as you are."

Ferd Caggia's perpetual grin diminished. He glanced appraisingly at Dr. Jackman. "Ferd," said Logan, "presumably you will be brought to trial for treason, at the least, if you escape Dr. Jackman's gelignite. They tell me that you are an excellent shot. If I were you, I should endeavor to persuade Dr. Jackman to remain a comfortable distance from the crypt where he keeps the explosives."

"Logan," Jackman muttered in his ear, "do you want a bullet in your spine?"

"By no means, Dr. Jackman. And try not to forget that there will be people asking after me, very soon." Would they try to throw him into the pit that stood open right by his feet?

"Kneel down," Jackman told him, "and you may have a glimpse of the Whiskey Bottle. Do you know the Mamertine prison in Rome? This is very like, Logan, but deeper."

Caggia had tied a long cord to the lantern, which now he lowered into the hole and swung in a circle, slowly, so as to show the interior of the place. Kneeling reluctantly, Logan made out an immense dry depth. The pit was shaped roughly like a bottle, narrow at the mouth and gradually widening, and going down, down. It was irregular, however, with bulges and depressions here and there in its sides, as if more the work of nature than of man. From the mouth, one could not get a clear view of the whole interior. The lantern sank lower and lower into the abyss, and still Logan could not perceive the bottom; then Caggia hauled it up. In this place, according to Balmullo's history of Carnglass, had been found the deformed skeleton that the crofters had called the Firgower. If ever the pit had been filled with salt herring, it must have enabled the Old House to withstand a siege of months, supposing there was fresh water enough to drink.

Logan stood firm upon the lip of the Whiskey Bottle. Nothing but audacity, he felt, would discourage Jackman from indulging in a new atrocity at this moment. "Look sharp that our friend Dr. Jackman doesn't put you, too, down this well, Caggia," he remarked. "It must tell on one's nerves to have a lunatic bent upon self-destruction for an employer."

"There you'll stay, Logan, until you feel inclined to talk with us," Jackman said, rolling the words thickly. "If I don't forget you. You'll not eat or drink until we let you out — if we do. I won't say when we'll come back to inquire after you: it may be hours, or it may be days. A man does not stay sane very long in the Whiskey Bottle. If you come out in time, there's not harm done. Scream when you wish to come out, and perhaps we will hear you. Better men than you have gone down and not come up alive. Down with you, now."

Anderson had dragged from the corner a long rope ladder. He made it fast to two iron rings sunk in the floor of the crypt, and let the rope fall into the pit. "There you go," said Jackman. "Goodnight to you, Mr. Logan."

"I think I'll not go," Logan told them. They scarcely could carry him down the swaying rope ladder.

"In that event," Jackman remarked — and Anderson sniggered — "we would have to pitch you in, and it's nearly fifty feet to the bottom, so you would be broken. Or we would have to lower you in at a rope's end, head first, with risk to your skull. I advise you to choose the ladder."

There was nothing else for it. Logan set his feet and hands on the swaying ladder, and began to descend. As he went down, the feet of the three men disappeared from view, and presently he was in blackness. After what seemed eternity, swinging and twisting about on the ropes, he felt no rung-slat under his foot, and halted, twirling back and forth like a top in space. Did they mean him to fall and break his legs or back? "It doesn't reach," he called up. The echo was melancholy.

"Jump for it," Jackman's voice sounded ever so faintly above.

"I'll be damned if I do," Logan roared back.

"You'll be damned if you don't," called Jackman, "for we'll loose the ladder at this end, and you'll fall anyhow, and there'll be no way back."

Waiting was no comfort. Logan relinquished his hold on the ladder, expecting his end. But he fell only six or seven feet, bruising his back on the jagged stone floor, which was quite dry. He could hear the rustle of the ladder being hauled up. The light of the lantern glimmered at the top of the Bottle, and a head was thrust over the mouth of the shaft, silhouetted against the petrol glare.

"Should auld acquaintance be forgot," Jackman said, "shriek when you care for our company." He laughed. Then he said something else, more faintly; but Logan thought it was, "Once you put me here, Askival." There came a scraping sound from above, and the lid was dragged back over the Bottle's mouth, cutting off Logan from the world. He was shut into the tomb now, as in his dream on the second night in Carnglass. As if the stone cover had not been coffin-lid enough, an iron door had stood ajar, Logan remembered, at the entrance to the crypt, a big key in lock. No doubt they would turn the key. Goodbye, Mary MacAskival.

CHAPTER 12

In the Whiskey Bottle, it would not do to brood more than a man might help, for that way lay despair: especially when one thought of what might be done to Mary MacAskival, high above. So Logan busied himself, at first, in creeping round the circumference of the Bottle's floor, feeling everywhere. There was nothing to feel but lumpy naked rock, everywhere gouged by ancient chisels.

The batter of the circular sides made it impossible for him even to think of climbing, fly-like, toward the mouth. These pleasures soon were exhausted. His watch had not worked well since he splashed ashore in Carnglass, and perhaps that was to the good. Already he was hungry and thirsty; but this last must be chiefly a psychological oppression, as the damp air of Carnglass made it unnecessary for a man to drink much water a day.

Although he had been in the place but a quarter of an hour, probably, the problem of fresh air began to worry Logan. It was silly to think about it so soon, of course: the immense cubic capacity of the Bottle would give him oxygen enough for a long time, and conceivably enough to support life leaked beneath the rude stone at the mouth, anyway. But one thought about such things in the Bottle, for lack of aught else to do.

In all that dead island, the Whiskey Bottle was the deadest place. Not even an insect could live here; and the place was so dry that, perhaps, not even a lichen could cling to the sloping walls. One could think only of dead things: of the deformed skeleton found on this floor, and the presences that drifted through Jackman's guilty brain. It wouldn't do for a man to think such thoughts: not for a man who meant to keep his wits about him. If ever they let him out of the Bottle, he would need all the wits and all the strength he could muster. The best thing to do, then, was to sleep. Luckily, Logan was very tired from the strain of the past several days, and from having had so little sleep last night, what with his colloquy with Mary MacAskival. And sleep never had come hard to him, in the worst of times and places. He groped about the rough floor until he found a tolerable area upon which to stretch himself, and there he lay down, his head on his arm, and soon drifted off. Dreams came, hideous dreams; but afterward they were all a blur to him. Now and then he tossed and woke imperfectly; then, like a sick man, he sank back into the sanctuary of the unconscious.

How many hours later it was that a noise woke him, he could not say. What could make a noise in the Bottle? Nothing living. It was a faint dragging noise. Then high overhead, he could perceive the faintest half-moon of light. Someone was dragging back the stone lid of the Bottle, slowly.

Would Jackman and Royall pull him out and put him to more direct torture? If they had tormented the truth about him out of Mary MacAskival, the odds were that they would put him into the sea, as a man who knew too much of them, and whose death might be explained with tolerable ease. It might be easier for him to refuse to come up, and hope that aid might come from the mainland in time. They could descend, of course, and tie him, and haul him to the top; but that would mean a fight. If they shot him, that would be evidence of foul play, supposing his body were washed up.

Now something scraped and rustled, and barely brushed the top of his head: it must be the rope ladder. Reaching up, he grasped the thin strip of wood that was the bottom rung. Still Jackman, if he were above, said nothing. But light probed downward toward Logan; someone up there held an electric torch. He had might as well take this dubious chance. Although it had been long since Logan had gone in for gymnastics, he had strong arms, and so contrived to pull his chin up to the level of the bottom rung, get a fresh grip, and bring up his legs. And then he commenced the swaying climb toward the Bottle's mouth.

As he neared the top, the torch dazzled him. Then a hand caught his, helping him over the edge to the floor of the crypt. No sooner had Logan got to his feet than a pair of arms was flung around his neck, and a small body hung for a moment upon his, in fright and delight. "They've broken no bone of you, Hugh?" said Mary MacAskival. Before he could reply, she kissed him, and then flashed the electric torch the length of his body, as if to be sure he were all there. "Don't speak above a wee whisper," she murmured in his ear, "and come over here, for we must be off." Taking his hand, she led him through the dark toward a corner of the crypt.

"One glimpse of you, anyway," said Hugh. Taking the torch, he sent the beam over and behind her. She was barefoot but with a pair of little walking-shoes slung round her neck. On her back she had Logan's own rucksack, looking as if it were crammed with things. Her back was to what seemed to be the low circular coping of a well, with a derelict windlass above it.

"We daren't talk now," the girl said, "for we'll have but a quarter of an hour, at best, before Niven gives the alarm. He's sentry at the garden door on the floor above. I told him I was taking you food and water, which you're not supposed to have, and he let me pass, for he knows I am a red-haired witch. Jackman will thrash the poor fellow within an inch of his life when he finds we're gone. Niven never thought I could get out with you, of course. If he'd known that, even I couldn't have seduced him."

"Seduced him?"

She chuckled. "Oh, don't be silly. Has Dr. Jackman been telling you more lies about me? I mean, subverted his loyalty to Jackman. I gave Niven five pounds and nearly a full bottle of rum. All right now, Hugh: take off your trousers."

He was bemused. "Whatever for?"

"Why, silly, we're going down the cistern, and there's water in it, and you might catch your death of cold outside, with wet trousers. I think you may keep your shirt on; we sha'n't go so deep, I hope. Here, take the pack, and carry it, and stuff your trousers in it. I can kilt up my skirt once we're at the level of the water, but you could hardly slip off your trousers in the middle of the shaft. You'd best take off your shoes and stockings, and sling them round your neck, the way I have, too. You needn't be shy: I'll go down first, and I'll point the torch the other way."

Logan stared into the cistern. In the beam of the torch, he could see rusted iron rungs set into the masonry, leading downward; but they ended in still water. "If we're to drown, Mary," he said, "it had might as well be in the sea."

"What with the gutters of the tower being half clogged," she went on, "the water level down there is very low nowadays — twelve or fifteen feet, at best — and I feared they might find the arch, but they haven't. It's perfectly feasible: Malcolm Mor and I did it four years ago, like a bomb. Why, it's a lark, Hugh; come along. The last one down is an old maid." Hiking her skirt halfway up her white thighs, Mary MacAskival stepped over the well-coping, swung round, and began to descend the slimy iron rungs. "I locked the crypt door on the inside, for I have keys, you know," she whispered up, "but Niven may be pounding on it any second, so be quick with you."

There was nothing for it but to obey this madcap. Down Logan went into the cistern; he hoped the old rungs would hold. Once his foot caught the girl's fingers, and she suppressed a cry. He heard a faint splash of water below, and turned the torch downward, looking between his bare legs. Mary MacAskival, her skirt held up almost to her shoulders, was more than waist-high in the black water. "There is nothing in the world," she volunteered, "quite like a cold tub. Now do as I do, and mind your head, for from floor to ceiling is scarcely more than four feet." She vanished.

Dismayed, Hugh Logan descended to his waist in the cold water. Then, on his left, he saw the arch of which Mary had spoken: a round-headed masonry arch, very old. The cistern water came to within two feet of the crown of it. Gingerly, Logan stretched out a leg, found the floor of a passage under the arch, gripped Mary's outstretched hand thrust back from the passage, and swung himself from the iron rungs to a low tunnel nearly filled with water; he had to stoop so that his face cleared the surface by only a few inches, and his little pack, strapped to his back, scraped against the roof.

Squeezing his hand, Mary MacAskival pulled him along the black passage, the torch-beam gleaming on the water. She had her skirt twisted round her neck. "One thing's certain," she panted, "they'll not hear us here. In the old days this place was flooded altogether, except when The MacAskival let water out of the cistern so that men could enter the passage. Malcolm Mor — he was the old gardener, remember? — told me that his father's father's father's uncle knew of this place, though no living man had seen it for a hundred years and more. Malcolm and I found it out together. We had grand larks."

After six yards or so, the floor began to slope upward, fairly sharply; and after a dozen yards, they were free of the water. "No trousers for you yet, modest Hugh," Mary said, though she had let her skirt fall into place. "There is water still to come." A moment later, they entered a small square rock chamber, beyond which loomed another narrow passage. "The Picts made this, as they made the Whiskey Bottle, Hugh. Look there." She pointed the torch toward one wall, and by it Hugh made out a faint band of carving on the wall: little hooded and caped figures, faceless, some riding on queer little ponies. "This was a chapel, think, or a tomb; but we haven't a moment to spare just now." She led the way into the further passage, the floor of which sloped downward again. "We're far beyond the Old House now, Hugh."

The passage shot abruptly downward, and then ended in a solid barrier of living rock. Did the girl mean them to crouch here indefinitely, on the chance that help might come from the mainland before they starved? "I think the Picts dug all this for a temple," she was saying, "or a king's tomb; but the MacAskivals used it as a sortie-port in time of siege, or a way of escape if worst came to worst. Oh, I'm not strong enough. Tug at it, Hugh!" She was kneeling on the rough floor. Handing the torch back to her, Hugh Logan felt under his hands a thick stone slab, roughly rectangular. He tugged. It could be slid to one side, far enough to allow them to squeeze through to whatever lay beneath. And beneath was more water. But this water splashed and sucked, and the strong stench of seaweed came up from it; and from beyond came the roar of the wild Carnglass tide.

"We're to go into that, Mary?" But Mary MacAskival already had swung her handsome bare legs through the gap. The water just below snarled and surged in the cave, as if full of murderous desire.

"It's past midnight, Hugh, and the tide has ebbed." She jumped down.

After all, Logan found when he followed her, the water came only to their knees. At high tide, the passage would be impossible. He scratched a foot on some sharp submerged stone. Roof and floor of the cave now angled downward, and the water deepened; but by the time they reached the entrance, it was no higher than their waists. "In the old days," Mary said, "little coracles came into this at low tide. There is another cave like this on the northern shore, but larger, and far harder to reach from the land." She plucked a bit of seaweed from a rock. "This is the carrageen. In a better time, I will make you a pudding of it." Then she ducked through the low mouth of the cave, Hugh Logan behind her, and they were in the night, by the ocean, a cliff at their backs, a splendid moon overhead.

For the first time in many days, the mist and drizzle had lifted from Carnglass altogether; and for these islands, the sea was calm. But the clear beauty of the night was small comfort to these two fugitives: Jackman and his gang might hunt them down by that round moon. Mary splashed through a rock pool toward the relatively low cliff of gray stone that met the ocean at this point. "I think, Hugh, that by this time they will have searched the Old House for us, and Jackman will know we have got out. But they will not know the way that we have gone, and perhaps Jackman cannot make the men follow him out of the house this night, for they are afraid of every shadow now. Here we're too close to the Old House for safety. We'll pass between Cailleach and the sea-cliffs, and so up to St. Merin's Chapel; that's best." When the two of them had got to the foot of a faint path that seemed to wind up the cliff, Mary put on shoes and stockings. "Now, Mr. Barrister Logan, you pillar of respectability, you may wear trousers again."

They climbed; they scrambled; they trotted; when they could, they ran. From the cliffs they descended into the glen that twisted round the hill of Cailleach, and hurried through heaps of stones along a forgotten trail; here, once, had been a village, and Duncan MacAskival's people had lived under the thatch of one of these ruins. The girl was agile as a deer; it was all Logan could do to keep up with her, for his rucksack was curiously heavy. The moonlight helped them to make speed, but also it would leave them naked unto their enemies, should Jackman and the rest come this way. For more than an hour they hurried, until they had crossed a valley and saw before them the steep way up to the highest point of Carnglass, the headland on which stood St. Merin's Chapel, with the graveyard round it. Then Mary flung herself exhausted on the heather, and Logan sank down panting beside her. Two or three strange white shapes scurried away from them; Logan started. "Are those things deer or goats?"

The tired girl laughed at him. "Carnglass sheep, like no other sheep on earth. Long legs and long necks, and great leapers, and altogether wild." Everything in this forgotten island, it seemed, defied the tooth of time.

But it was no hour for philosophical observations. So soon as they had got a little strength back, they must be away to the top of the island. And what they could hope for there, aside from a brief respite, was more than Logan could see. Unarmed, they would be much easier game than Donley had been. Jackman and the rest would have their blood up. This girl, it might be, had destroyed herself by trying to save him. "Here, Hugh," Mary said, "you'll want this." She took from the rucksack a paper in which were wrapped some scraps of meat, two boiled potatoes, and a piece of bread, all this salvaged furtively from Lady MacAskival's dinner-tray. Logan, indeed, was ravenous, and he ate the lot, Mary insisting that she had got down a late supper. As he ate, she told him what had passed since he went down the Whiskey Bottle.

When Jackman and Royall had taken Logan to the study at gunpoint, Mary MacAskival had run to her room and locked herself in. It was only much later in the day, when Jackman and most of the men were searching for Carruthers, that she had bullied out of Niven the fact that Logan was shut in the Whiskey Bottle. In her room, she had taken out of a chest the only weapon she had, the ancient dirk that was said to have been Askival's, and had sat with it in her lap, expecting all the time to have Jackman and Royall turn upon her next. But Jackman had only tried her door; and, not being able to enter, had called out that he would deal with her later. And then he had gone out to comb the island for Carruthers, whom they did not find; nor did they find anyone else. The men returned after sunset, Jackman and Royall going back to the study, where they sat talking for hours. The girl had crept to the study door and had caught fragments of their argument.

No, they had not found Carruthers; but they had turned up something. When Donley's body was searched in the cellar, one of the men discovered in a pocket a water-soaked note. It was nearly illegible; but they could make out Logan's signature, and that it was addressed to the police. On this evidence, Jackman and Royall abandoned their notion that Logan was an agent of Vlanarov; they now took him for a detective. The question remained as to what they ought to do with the man in the Whiskey Bottle. Royall thought it best to hold him there until they could get some boat, and then to run for it, abandoning their whole project. But Jackman was for death: Logan knew too much, and must go over the cliff. The two exhausted fanatics still were debating when the girl slipped away, but she believed they would dispose of Logan in the morning, if not sooner.

So she took Logan's pack, with what food she could get her hands upon, and a pint bottle of paraffin, and Askival's dirk; and she bullied and wheedled Niven, on guard in the old tower; and to her immense satisfaction, she had got Logan clean away. Jackman and his people had no notion of the existence of that passage out of the cistern; Lady MacAskival herself had not known of it. When she ran, Mary knew that she left her aunt in danger, but Jackman's fanatic voice behind the study door convinced her she dared not delay; Jackman would act before his time ran out altogether. And here she was, lying beside Hugh Logan on the heather.

Behind them bulked the northern heights where St. Merin's Chapel stood. They could hear a little waterfall tumbling in that still night, from the cliff tops. The burn ran through the heather and bracken close by them, lower down joining a stream that entered the sea by Askival harbor. Now they must climb to their last forlorn refuge. First they drank from the peaty burn; then Logan shouldered the rucksack, and up they started. They hardly spoke in the course of that hard nocturnal climb.

From the summit, nearly an hour later, most of Carnglass was dimly visible to them in the moonlight. They could make out specks of light away to the southwest: lamps burning in the Old House. "Hugh," Mary said, laying a hand on his arm, "Carnglass is the oldest place in the world, and the loveliest. Do you hate it? You've seen only fright and death here. But it was Dr. Jackman that brought the terror. If — if we live, Hugh, I'll show you Carnglass as you ought to see it. Can you forgive me for having drawn you into this terror?"

"One crowded hour of glorious life," Logan told her, "really is worth an age without a name. And if I'd not come, I'd never have met Miss Mary MacAskival, would I?"

"No," she said, with a little sob, "no. But we can't loiter here." She took Askival's dirk from the rucksack. "Hugh, take this, and cut some branches off the trees around the chapel, as quickly as you can; and I'll scrape together some dead sticks and bits of dry heather; I made a little pile of them here weeks ago, on the chance that I might need to light them one day. We can burn the rucksack, too, and my jacket. They'll make no grand beacon, but we can do no more. The paraffin I brought will start them blazing."

Logan stared at her. "Who'd see the fire, except Jackman's boys?"

"There's a chance, Hugh. The night is clear. Besides, what other scheme is there? And my people will come. They may not come soon enough, but they will come."

"Your people?" The girl must be sunk in a Carnglass fantasy.

"Hurry, Hugh," was all she said. "It won't be long before dawn."

They built their poor futile beacon, with what fuel they had on that hilltop, and they poured the paraffin upon it, and they set it alight with one of Logan's matches, and they added to it the rucksack and Mary's tweed jacket and Hugh's coat. It flared somewhat better than Hugh had expected. But what possibility existed of this being seen by any vessel passing in the night, or of being acted upon? And it was almost certain that it would guide Jackman.

"We're only targets here," Logan said. "At the chapel, we'd have some shelter." They climbed still higher on that cliff-plateau, until they came to a low drystone dyke. Beyond it were tombstones, white in the moonlight. This was Carnglass graveyard; and in the middle of the graveyard stood a long, low medieval building, St. Merin's Chapel, battered by five centuries. Away to their right, a tall ruin, infinitely older than the chapel, round, nearly forty feet high, windowless and roofless, loomed at the brink of the cliff.

On its rough stones flickered the light of their little impromptu beacon. "They call that the Pict's House," said Mary, "or sometimes the Firgower's House." The tower's circular wall slanted slightly inward, all round, for some twenty feet of its height; then it shot perpendicularly to its summit. It was what was called a broch, a strong place, Pictish work beyond question. "I do not think that really the Pictish chief lived here," Mary went on, "for that room and the passages under the Old House, have the look of his palace. The Picts lived underground, you know. This was a watchtower, and a place of refuge."

She turned toward the chapel. The firelight was reflected, between them and the medieval building, upon a great Celtic cross, perhaps fifteen feet high, carved with grotesques and convoluted interlacing bands; and it leant heavily to one side. This was the Cross of Carnglass, set up by the missionaries of St. Columba in the dim Irish age, St. Merin's Cross. Mary led Logan toward it; and, as they came close up, she pulled from one of the stunted rowan trees which brooded over that windswept graveyard a little twig, on which the first leaves of spring had opened. She thrust it into the topmost buttonhole of Logan's shirt. "The rowan keeps off wraiths and evil spirits, Hugh," she said, "and St.

Merin's kirkyard is famous for them. Niven thinks I am the chief of them. Look at me: am I a witch?"

Mary MacAskival stood before the Cross of Carnglass, her red hair brushing the white stone, her haughty nose and firm chin marking her as the last of an old, old, fierce line: perhaps, truly, the descendant of the Merin whose bones lay beneath one of these grass-grown grave mounds. "If anyone could call spirits from the vasty deep, you could, Mary," Hugh told her.

She smiled queerly. "It may be I will do just that, Hugh Logan. But here, I'll show you the chapel." She took him through a Gothic doorway — the wooden door, ajar, sagged on its hinges — and flashed the torch-beam over the tombs within. A grotesque stone face, rudely carved, stared at them from a niche. Directly before them stood up an ornate modern tomb of marble. "Sir Alastair is beneath that. And here's his postbox." She pointed to a slot in the marble surrounded by a carved funerary wreath; and she slid her hand into the opening. "Oh, there's nothing within now!" she said, as if really disappointed. "For years, you know, my aunt used to send letters by the butler or footman to Sir Alastair in his tomb. And I used to post my letters here, too, when I wasn't watched."

Post her letters there! Mary must have read the amazement on his face, for she added, as if to reassure him of her sanity, "Oh, yes. The letter I sent Duncan MacAskival, that brought you here, was posted here in Sir Alastair's postbox." Was this some macabre witticism of the uncanny little beauty, or a delusion grown out of dreams and isolation? "But we daren't linger here, Hugh. If Dr. Jackman sees our fire, he'll come up the cliff straight away." She pointed to the old dirk, which Hugh Logan had thrust into his belt. "That was Askival's. You must be my Askival, Hugh. I am Merin, you know: Merin of Carnglass, who's haunted this place since time began." She was half playful, half in earnest. The dirk, Logan thought, might be small use against the guns of Jackman's men, but it was some comfort. Then he followed Mary MacAskival out of the silent chapel, and toward the towering broch by the precipice. Their fire still leaped against the night sky of lonely Carnglass, but in a few minutes only embers would remain.

"The Pict's House," Mary was saying, "is the best place we can hide. By the sea, away below these cliffs, is a great cave; but even I could not lead you down the path to it in darkness; and besides, the tide is coming in now, and the cave will be full almost to the top. It must be the Pict's House for us. One still can climb the stair to the top of it." She was quite calm, as if, having done all that she could do, she abandoned herself to fate and fortune. "And from the Pict's House, we can see nearly all of Carnglass, once the sun is up."

They entered the tower through a square doorway ten feet above the ground; a worn timber, sea-drift, propped against the wall just below the door, made this scramble possible. The doorway was capped, by way of lintel, by a great stone slab; the Picts had not known the arch. Empty and roofless, the round interior cavern of the broch was before them, but Mary turned into the wall itself: a circling stair led upward, its steps vast rude slabs. By it they came to the crumbling summit of the broch, and Logan observed, while they climbed, that no mortar lay between the cunningly-placed stones of the tower; this was the work of men in the dawn of history, and beside it the Old House across the island was a thing of yesterday.

Round the top of the broch ran a stone platform. "Stoop down behind the parapet, Hugh," the girl told him, "so Jackman won't see us, if he comes this way." The earliest hint of a spring dawn glimmered in the east; a corncrake fluttered up from the parapet. Right below them, the tremendous cliffs, the cliffs over which Lagg had gone, fell sheer away to the ocean. From this point, the last Pict chieftain may have watched the long ships of the Vikings as they swept inexorably out of the sea-mist to the north. On that sea, nothing was visible this morning but whitecaps breaking on a submerged reef.

"No, there's nothing, no sail," Mary MacAskival said anxiously, almost as if she had expected one. "Do you know the tale of the fairy boat, Hugh, that sails through the mists? If a girl glimpses it, she vanishes before nightfall. I wish one could carry me off — and you. Now you see my Carnglass, Hugh Logan."

He looked landward. Far to the west-southwest, beyond Cailleach, the Old House stood grim on its rock; lower down, the New House, among its plantations. Between them and the Old House stretched glen and hill, heather and bracken, boulder and peat-bog, waterfall and burn. On this lovely morning, the mists were quite gone, and there was revealed to him the unearthly beauty of the forgotten island. The girl took his arm. "Hugh, were it yours, would you live here always — or almost always?"

"That I would, Mary MacAskival." Carnglass, for good or evil, set its mark on men.

She faced him squarely, putting her hands on his shoulders. "We may be under that sea tonight, Hugh Logan. But if we are not, why shouldn't Carnglass be yours? I've known you but thirty-six hours, Hugh. You're all the man I need to know. Do you fear me? Some men do, though I'm so little." She kissed him then, and said, "Hugh Logan, I have kissed you more times than I have kissed all other men in all my life. Do you mean to ask me to marry you?"

Torn between love and doubt, in that high place, Logan looked long into her green eyes. "They would say, Mary, that I took advantage of a lonely girl who had barely met me, for the sake of her money."

She tossed her bright hair at that. "Don't be so canny, Hugh! Do you know the MacAskival motto, over the door of the old tower? 'They have said and they will say; let them be saying.' The MacAskivals, man or woman, have no concern for what they say in Glasgow or Edinburgh or London or all the wide world." Then a look of fright came into her flashing eyes. "Is it that you are married already, Hugh?"

"No," he said, "but I will be, if we get alive out of this." And as the sun rose, he took her in his arms. Rash, proud, and strange that girl was, perhaps a little mad; but in that moment he loved her more than all the kingdoms of the earth.

She clung to him, sobbing and laughing softly in her moment of triumph and surrender. But abruptly he thrust her back, and pulled her below the level of the parapet. "Mary, Mary! They've come!" For three armed men were climbing the slope toward the chapel, and Jackman was the first of them. Logan thought that they two had not been seen. No shots were fired, at least.

His arm around the girl's waist, he ventured a second glance between two heavy stones that teetered precariously on the parapet's brink. Yes, Jackman and Anderson and Powert. The men got over a low wall that ran round the graveyard, close by the remnants of the burned-out futile beacon. Then they entered the chapel.

"Mary, girl," he whispered, "they'll be on us in three or four minutes, I think." She did not cry, but kissed him once more, and then composed her young face, as if The MacAskival ought to meet enemies without flinching.

"Hugh," she said, "every second we can delay may help us." He did not see why, but she gave him no time to dissent. "Back down the stair, Hugh, and if they try to come in, we'll cast down the timber by the door." Yes, they could do that, though without guns they could do no more than delay Jackman briefly. Back down the stair they went, and crouched by the empty archaic doorway. It wouldn't do to push away the timber-gangplank that led up from the ground unless they must, for the noise of its fall would bring Jackman and his men.

Now they heard Jackman's voice; he was coming right round the broch from the chapel. Anderson's sullen Gallowgate mutter replied to Jackman. And in a moment the hunters stood just below the broch's door, though Logan dared not look out. "All right, Powert," Jackman said, "up with you." At that, Logan and Mary MacAskival shoved against the timber with all their strength. It slid sideways and fell to the ground. They showed themselves for an instant as they pushed, and someone fired, but the bullet passed over their heads into the broch.

"Ah, well," came Jackman's voice from below, "you *did* lead us a chase, didn't you? Anderson, Powert, take hold there." The timber was heaved back into place; Logan could not risk rising again to push it off, for Jackman would have a gun trained on the doorway. "Powert, Mr. Logan is not armed," said Jackman. "Quick, now!" A man sprang up the timber and through the door.

Thrusting at him with the dirk, Logan got home to Powert's upper arm, and the man cried out and grappled with him. Before he could slash Powert again, Jackman was up, and poked the little pistol Meg right into Logan's face. "Gallant, Logan, very gallant; but drop that." Logan flung down the dirk. Mary MacAskival was struggling in Anderson's arms. "A pleasant morning, eh, Logan?" Jackman said. "You'll not see another."

CHAPTER 13

They took Hugh Logan and Mary MacAskival out of the Pict's House. Anderson tied Logan's wrists together, behind his back, with a length of heavy cord, pulling the knots savagely tight. Jackman held the girl by the arm meanwhile; and when Anderson had finished with Logan, under Jackman's instructions he tied a cord to Mary's right wrist, and retained the other end of the cord in his hand while Jackman removed Powert's jacket and bandaged the flesh-wound with a strip torn from the tail of Powert's shirt. This done, Jackman had Anderson tie the other end of Mary's cord to Jackman's own left wrist.

"There!" Jackman said, contentedly, "a brisk morning's run, and no harm done. Anderson, Powert and I will take this charming couple to the Old House while you trot down the brae and call back Ferd and Niven; I think they should be near the shieling this side of Cailleach."

Anderson glowered at Logan. "Ye said I wud hae the thrashin' o' that clot, Doctor."

"That you shall, Anderson, my man, that you shall — once we're at the Old House. I do believe Anderson will learn all we need to know from you, Logan, in short order. Our treatment of you, Miss MacAskival, will need to be rather more laborious: the washing of the brain, as our Chinese friends say. But it will all come out in the wash, won't it? And Powert, too, will be given his fair turn at you, Logan: fair shares for all, eh?" Jackman ran his tongue over his thin lips. "In one thing, at least, you seem to have told me the truth, Logan: you've no people in

Carnglass, for you'd not have been cowering in that ruin if there were any. There's Carruthers to be accounted for; but I suppose he may have missed his footing in the dark and have gone over the cliffs. I must confess that my estimate of your abilities has diminished, Logan. Whatever possessed you to light that fire here by the chapel? You might have eluded us four or five hours longer if you hadn't done that. Well, drive him along, Powert."

With his unwounded arm, Powert gave Logan a fierce shove in the back, setting him stumbling in the direction of the Old House, and Jackman tugged on Mary's cord, pulling her with him behind Logan and Powert. The girl's face was quite drained of color, but very haughty. "My dear," Jackman said to her, casually, "how changed you are going to be within a few days! How very changed!"

Then, from somewhere below in the nearer valley, there came to them the crack of a rifle-shot. It was answered by another, apparently from a different gun. Next was a burst of firing, and then a faint cry.

Jackman's satisfied smile altered horribly; he was Rumpelstiltskin again. "Logan," he muttered, "is there a man of yours in Carnglass, after all? Or is that only Niven's or Caggia's nerves playing them tricks? Anderson, you and I must go down to see. Powert, we'll leave you with Logan; he can't do you harm. The girl will come with me. We'll send back a man to help you get Logan to the Old House, Powert."

Powert most obviously did not relish the plan. "Coom, Dr. Jackman, I've a bad arm, and this cove's a queer one."

"Nonsense," Jackman said, "we'll bind his feet, too, until we send Anderson or someone else for you." Away below, there was only silence, but Jackman ran his hand across his forehead uneasily. "Here: we'll put him inside the chapel with you, and you can watch the door, with your back to the wall: that's safe enough." Powert scowled, but shoved Logan toward the door of St. Merin's Chapel. Jackman herded the four of them inside.

Now that the dawn came through the broken tracery of the chapel's pointed windows, Logan could see that the single room contained seven or eight tombs raised above the floor, some of them very old; and a number of the flagstones, deeply incised by some rude stonecarver, apparently covered other graves. "Wha' in hell's yon!" cried Anderson, abruptly, pointing.

Near the northeast corner of the room, one of the flagstones had been raised, and now was leant against the wall. Where it had lain, a little mound of earth, freshly dug, protruded above the floor; and in the earth was thrust a curiously primitive wooden spade. The mound was about six feet long. They all crowded close to it. An earthenware dish had been set atop the mound, and the dish was filled with, of all things, nails and what looked like salt. Across the dish lay a branch from a rowan tree. "That," Mary MacAskival said softly to Dr. Jackman, "is how the spirits of the newly dead are laid in these islands."

"Wha' fule's been diggin' graves?" Anderson growled, looking back over his shoulder toward the empty doorway.

Jackman stood rigid; then, "I think Carruthers must be under that clay. Anderson, take the spade and uncover him." Mary MacAskival shivered slightly.

Anderson cursed, but under Jackman's hard eye he began to shovel. The grave was very shallow. In a minute or two, a heavy shape could be made out, wrapped in a big piece of tarred canvas. "That will be the head at the far end," Jackman whispered. "Powert, draw the canvas from the face."

Mary had turned away, but Logan, dreadfully fascinated, saw clearly the smashed and fallen face of a man he never had looked upon before. And Jackman screamed: he screamed twice, and so terribly that his men shook, for the screams were worse than the ruined face in the grave. "Lagg! It's Lagg!"

Quivering, Anderson dropped the spade. "Aye," he said, "Tam Lagg, that we pit ower the cliff into the sea. For the love o' God, Powert, cover his mug."

Powert, his teeth chattering, let the canvas drop back over the corpse.

"Logan," shrieked Jackman, turning a frantic face on him, "Logan, what are you? What are you? Do you make dead men rise from the sea? Was it you that put this thing here?" He had the pistol in his hand, and thrust it against Logan's middle.

He will fire now, Logan thought, for he's quite out of his head. There was the sound of a shot. But I'm not hit, Logan realized; I feel nothing. Jackman sprang away and looked out the doorway; the shot, after all, had come from outside, though in his tension Logan had thought, for an instant, that Jackman had pulled the trigger. Yet surely a gun had gone off fairly close at hand.

"Anderson, watch this door," Jackman ordered; he had a measure of control over himself. "Powert, give me that rope." He forced Logan to sit, and tied his ankles together. "We'll return for you in a few minutes, Powert."

"Me? I'll not sit here by the dead man." Powert scarcely could hold his rifle.

Jackman sent him a deadly look from those glowering black eyes of his. "You'll be another dead man yourself, Powert, if I hear another word from you. Now, Anderson, we'll look into this. Miss MacAskival, if you cry out, I'll be forced to put a bullet through your head." He shoved her through the doorway.

"Hugh," Mary called back, reckless of Jackman, "Hugh, I love you!" Then she and Jackman and Anderson were out of sight.

Powert, left with Logan and the corpse, still shook; and he cursed Logan and Jackman and Carnglass while he made his preparations as if for siege. He pushed the helpless Logan roughly against Sir Alastair's tomb, facing away from the doorway, and parallel with the open grave and the awful thing under the canvas. Then he pulled shut the sagging door of the chapel, so that some force would be required to budge it; and he himself leaned against a tombstone that came up to his shoulders, with his face toward the door, and his rifle in his hands, the barrel resting upon the head of another tombstone. So situated, Powert could watch the door, keep an eye on Logan and the sheeted thing, and have the comforting feel of stone at his back.

Logan himself, after the repeated shocks of that fair morning, was in little better state than Powert. Silent, he lay motionless against the tomb of Sir Alastair MacAskival, his brain dull, dull, dull. There were no more shots outside: only the rustle of a breeze in the rowan trees. The stillness was a trying thing. Powert was mumbling to himself: obscenities, blasphemies, scraps of nearly-forgotten prayer. The sunlight was pouring into the chapel through the unglazed Gothic windows. Five or six minutes passed thus.

Then a faint sound came. Was something stirring in the high graveyard grass, just outside the closed door? Did the door itself creak, as if very gently tried? "Anderson," Powert cried out, choking, "is it you, man? Dr. Jackman?" Nothing answered. Did the door creak again, ever so slightly, or was it the breeze? "Sing out," Powert shouted, glaring wild-eyed at the flimsy door, "or I'll shoot!"

High in the wall behind Powert was one of the pointed windows, its stone tracery for the most part broken away. It must be at least eight feet above the level of the graveyard. Though Logan could see this window, Powert, intent on the doorway, could not. And as something rose cautiously above the windowsill, from outside, Logan bit his lips to keep back a cry.

It was a man's head that cut off the morning light: a lean man, keen-eyed; and there was a long white beard on his chin; and there was a little black knife between his teeth. His eyes took in the room. Steadying himself by clutching the broken tracery with his left hand, stealthily he rose until his shoulders came above the window-ledge. In his brown right hand he held a large stone.

As if someone had thrust tentatively against it, the rotten door creaked shrilly. "Damn you," Powert was crying, "speak up, or I'll shoot." The white-bearded man outside the window drew back his arm and flung the stone with great force, as if letting fly at a rabbit. The rock caught Powert at the back of his head; he fell to his knees, the rifle clattering on the flagstones. At that the door burst open, and two men tumbled into the room, and were upon Powert before he could recover. A boy followed them, and kneeling by Logan, looked shyly into his face. These were the two men and the boy, MacAskivals from Daldour, that Logan had seen in Loch Boisdale, four days before.

Then there strode through the doorway a very tall old man, erect and vigorous and bearded to his chest, with a shotgun in his hand. He was worth looking at; but another man, hard on his heels, was still stranger. This was a burly broad-shouldered fellow, with a heavy, jolly face, and mild eyes that were exceedingly odd, though it would have been difficult to say why. Something in the look of his face was queer enough. Yet it was his clothing that made him conspicuous. The other men wore the caps and canvas cloaks and rough homespun tweeds of the crofters and fishermen in the remoter Isles. This burly man, in strong contrast, was dressed in what seemed to be the garments of a laird or prosperous farmer: green tweed jacket, green corduroy breeches and long stockings, good heavy shoes. Under the open jacket was a soiled yellow waistcoat; and on his head was a battered porkpie hat. These clothes were in wretched repair, with dark stains here and there upon them. The breeches, seemingly split at the seams, were held together by pins. One sleeve of the jacket was ripped open from shoulder to wrist. And although the clothes had been got on, they did not fit the man who wore them.

Resting a hand on the boy's shoulder, the tall old man bent over Logan and spoke in Gaelic. Logan shook his head: "I know only English." Frowning, the old man muttered through his splendid beard to the boy beside him.

The boy stammered a little, as if overwhelmed with shyness; but there was no fear in him. He spoke to Logan in good, if careful, English. "Malcolm Mor MacAskival of Daldour asks what is your name, and what do you do in Carnglass." The pirate-like old man looked hard at Logan.

These, then, were Mary MacAskival's people! She had not been woolgathering when she spoke of them. How she had summoned them, Hugh Logan did not know; but the five of them — two had gagged Powert, and were sitting on the man — were staring at Logan intently. This was no time for long explanations. "Untie me," Logan said. "I'm Hugh Logan, and I am to marry Miss Mary MacAskival."

There was a murmur from the men, and all five MacAskivals of Daldour took off their caps deferentially, and then put them back on again. With a fisherman's deftness, old Malcolm Mor undid the cords about Logan's wrists and ankles, and the two men who looked like twins promptly bound Powert with them. As he released Logan, Malcolm Mor said, in decent English, "Then I am your man, sir, and so are my sons and my grandson, and my nephew Angus, and my nephew Kenneth who is not here. We saw the man with the third eye lead the lady away. Will we after her?" Malcolm Mor tapped his shotgun. Malcolm Mor's two sons had old rifles; the boy and Angus, the queer burly man in the queerer clothes, were unarmed. One of the sons, almost bowing, handed Powert's rifle to Logan as he stood up and tried to get the blood to circulate in his tingling wrists and ankles.

Hugh Logan surveyed his little army. "Yes, we will," he said, "if they don't come after us first. Just now they're down in the valley hunting someone; but some of them will come back to the chapel." These men, he thought, would be good shots; and to live in Daldour, they must be hardy and probably courageous, though he doubted whether they had much experience at man-killing.

"It is my nephew Kenneth that they are hunting," Malcolm Mor observed. "I sent him to watch them from the bracken. It was Kenneth who shot his gun to lead them away from the chapel. They will not find him. We have watched them for a week, but we did not understand what they did, and there was no gentleman to lead us. We would have shot the man with the third eye when he took the lady away but we were afraid that she might be hurt. Is it so that they are robbers and murderers?"

"That they are," Logan said, emphatically.

"Then," Malcolm Mor went on, in the slow, gentle Island English, "it would be lawful for us to hunt them?" Logan suspected that the people of Daldour were extremely shy of the law.

"It would," Logan told him. "I am a lawyer, and I give you my authority."

Malcolm Mor MacAskival's old eyes lit up, and he smiled as some Norse rover might have smiled. "Then, sir," he said, "we will go after the lady, and take the Old House of Fear." He seemed to have no doubt whatsoever of the success of this undertaking by five or six men and a boy. "There are three more able-bodied men in Daldour, but we have no time to fetch them. Kenneth, my nephew, will come to us soon. Will we go down into the valley now, Mr. Logan?"

"Let's have a look about," Logan said. The men followed him through the chapel doorway. When Logan had thrown his rucksack on the fire, he had stuffed his binoculars into a trouser-pocket; and now he pulled them out and stared through them in the direction of the Old House, but, what with hills, rocks, and clumps of trees and thickets of bracken, he could see no one moving.

Then, a hundred yards away, and ascending toward the chapel, Anderson came into view. Logan dropped the binoculars and snatched up his rifle, but Anderson had seen them before he could get the gun to his shoulder. For a second, Anderson stared aghast; then, flinging himself around, he leaped downhill, vanishing into bracken, reappearing on a knoll, slipping, almost rolling down a talus slope, merging with the blur of gray rock and purple heather and green bracken. Logan fired twice, but could not have hit him. At that, Malcolm Mor and his two sons brought up their guns and fired also. They did not really take aim, and Logan thought they meant to frighten, rather than to wound; but also he thought that they could be brought to shoot to kill if they must.

"We can catch him," Malcolm Mor said, like a dog eager for the word from his master. "He is a town man, and we are faster."

"No," Logan decided, shaking his head, "no, there'll be three others down there, and they have Miss MacAskival with them, on a rope. We'll go down and after them, but together; and no one must shoot if the lady might be hurt." This deliberation was agony to Logan himself, but he had been an officer, and he knew something of tactics.

The MacAskivals nodded. "My nephew Kenneth will be watching them from the bracken," Malcolm Mor said. "We will go down, and he will join us; and if they take the lady to the Old House, then we will follow them into the house."

Malcolm Mor's nephew Angus, the burly man in the dirty yellow waistcoat, was nodding and smiling at every word his old uncle uttered. "Do you have a gun?" Logan said to him. The man opened his mouth, but words did not come out: only mouthed grunts, rather horrid. Malcolm Mor seemed somewhat embarrassed.

"He cannot speak," the boy — Malcolm Gille was his name — said apologetically. "He is called" — here the boy seemed to seek the English equivalent of a Gaelic term, and emerged triumphantly — "he is called Dumb Angus." Dumb Angus nodded enthusiastically at the mention of his name. "And," the boy went on, "he is simple. Dumb Angus is simple, and does not have a gun, but he is very strong, and he is honest, and he makes many jokes." Dumb Angus bowed and smiled, and tapped himself on the head to prove that he knew he was simple. "He cannot speak," the boy said, "but he makes jokes in other ways."

Logan checked Powert's rifle, and reloaded; one of Malcolm's sons — their names, it turned out, were John and Robert — brought him a cartridge-pouch that Powert had worn. What ought they to do with Powert? Malcolm Mor, now assured that the majesty of the law sheltered the persecuted sept of MacAskival, speculatively fingered the little black knife in his belt. "No," said Logan, "we'll bring them all to trial, if we can."

"There is one already taken and locked away," Malcom Mor offered. "His name, I think, is Carruthers. We took him the night before last night, and carried him to Daldour, and locked him in a byre, and he is afraid, for he thinks that we will eat him. Dumb Angus made him think so; that is one of the jokes of Dumb Angus. It is pleasant to have Dumb Angus in Daldour. We could carry this man too, to Daldour, but there is not time."

Dumb Angus was gesturing and beckoning, and pointing upward. At the east end of the chapel, behind the altar, ran a kind of low loft or gallery, of wood, probably built when the chapel was re-roofed by Sir Alastair MacAskival. "Yes," said Logan, "that will do. Put Powert there, at the back, and no one is likely to notice him until we need him." The sons of Malcolm carried Powert up the short flight of wooden steps, and tightened the cords and his gag. Dumb Angus might be simple, but he had eyes in his head.

And now they could start in pursuit of Jackman, for Mary MacAskival's sake. Anderson probably would have warned Jackman and the others by this time; but the warning might do no mischief, for those four guns going off at his heels must have sounded to Anderson as if half the constabulary of Scotland were after him. They could not catch Jackman and the rest before they reached the Old House, the odds were, nor would it have been safe to fire at the retreating gang with Mary MacAskival in their midst. But by night, Logan was resolved, he and the Daldour people would make their try. "Well, gentlemen," he said to Malcolm Mor and the others, "if you're ready, I am." And they started down the brae.

As they trotted and scrambled toward the valley, the boy running by Logan's side, Logan said to Malcolm Gille, "Why does Dumb Angus wear such clothes?"

"Those clothes were not his." The boy smiled broadly. "It is one of the jokes of Dumb Angus. They are the clothes of Mr. Lagg, the factor, that we found broken below the cliffs and buried in the chapel of St. Merin. For Dumb Angus, it is always Hallowe'en."

The humor of Daldour, Logan took it, had its grisly side. Dumb Angus it must have been that Rab had encountered two nights before. If even the simpletons of Daldour — and the whole band of Daldour MacAskivals was a remarkably odd-looking lot — were this resourceful, it might be just possible for Logan to get Mary alive out of the Old House.

CHAPTER 14

O n the flank of Cailleach, a little ferret-like man rose out of the
heather to join Logan and the MacAskivals: Kenneth MacAskival.
Like the rest of his family, he really understood English, when he chose,
and could speak it tolerably well when he had to. On learning from
Malcolm Mor that this gentleman was the betrothed of The MacAskival,
Kenneth gave Logan his report.

After firing twice that morning to draw Jackman away from the chapel, Kenneth MacAskival had contented himself with creeping through
the bracken and spying on the retreating party. The lady, Kenneth said,
never spoke, so far as he could hear; though the men thrust her roughly
along when, led on a cord as she was, she stumbled. They would be at
the Old House within a few minutes, the man with the third eye and the
rest, and could not be intercepted.

Logan and his men did not move toward the Old House so fast as
they could have. For Jackman might have laid an ambush, which had to
be watched for among the rocks and dens of rugged Carnglass. Once,
through his binoculars, Logan caught a glimpse of a hurrying figure,
very close to the Old House; then it was hidden again by a low interven-
ing ridge.

Either of two courses he might take, Logan thought. He might send
the MacAskivals in their lobster boat to Loch Boisdale or whatever other
port they could reach that had a police station, and ask for prompt help.
But this would take hours, many hours, and meanwhile Jackman would

have Mary MacAskival in the Old House. And Jackman would be thinking of the ruin of his scheme, and of the gelignite in the cellars. Besides,
would any police constable believe such a story, from such a crew as the
MacAskivals, without telegraphing to Glasgow or Edinburgh for orders,
which would mean delays? No, that plan wouldn't do.

So there remained to Logan only the storming of the Old House.
Briefly, he thought of trying to enter through the passage in the rock by
which Mary and he had escaped; but that was no go, since one of
Jackman's riflemen at the cistern-mouth could kill anyone who tried to
ascend. They would have to rush the place from outside.

The thing could not be tried until evening, for Jackman had more
men within the Old House than Logan had without, and Jackman's men
were desperate, well armed, and probably experienced in killing. By day,
it would have been mad. The oldest tower, with its little windows and
iron bars, would have been impossible to take even if defended by only
one or two riflemen, unless the attackers had mortars. The Renaissance
block was nearly as strong. But the Victorian addition was another matter. The gate was stout, and the ground-floor windows were small, covered by iron grilles, and shuttered within. The plate-glass windows of
the first floor, however, were immense and undefended, and could be
reached with a long ladder — after dark. Even supposing Logan and his
men got inside the Old House, they still would be outnumbered. Their
hope was that before they should make their rush, they might be able to
demolish the morale of Jackman's people, already badly shaken.

To help Mary, Logan would have taken any risk: if getting himself
shot would have saved her, he would have rushed the Old House that
hour. But the best chance for saving her, it seemed to him, lay in keeping
Jackman's people very much on edge, and busy — and in praying that
Jackman himself might not go mad altogether. And this meant that
some eight hours, eight intolerable hours for Logan, must pass before he
could act.

But meanwhile he could prepare. Giving the Old House a wide
berth, he led the MacAskivals to the farm steading nearest the castle. Before the troubles had begun, Simmons had kept the steading in some order, though there were only two animals about the place: two shaggy
and ill-tempered little Barra horses, grazing in a small field. Having
caught the horses, the MacAskivals harnessed them to a farm cart. This
they loaded with straw, and with what loose lumber they could find;

also they put two gallon tins of paraffin, discovered in the farmhouse, into the cart. In a shed they came upon a long ladder, which they piled atop straw and lumber. Then, keeping out of range of fire from the Old House, Dumb Angus and Malcolm Gille took the horses and cart circuitously round to the wooded policies of the New House, which was as close to the Victorian wing of the Old House as they could get without being fired upon.

While this operation was going forward, Logan sent Kenneth and John MacAskival to the rocky and bracken-covered hillsides that were barely within extreme firing range of the Old House. And there the two veteran poachers commenced a desultory fire against the windows of the Old House. Logan gave Powert's rifle to Kenneth, as the best weapon available, taking Kenneth's shotgun for himself. Concealed as they were by dense bracken, and shifting position after every shot, there was little danger of the MacAskivals being hit by retaliatory fire from the Old House. For their part, the MacAskivals were instructed not really to attempt to hit anyone, but to spend their time shattering panes and nerves. The windows of Mary's room in the old tower they left untouched. Lady MacAskival's room was on the seaward side of the Old House, and so safe. For that matter, the whole garrison of the Old House could retreat to the seaward rooms and temporary security, except for what luckless sentinels Dr. Jackman might leave to guard against a sudden rush. By early afternoon, every pane on the eastern side of the Old House had been shattered, except those in Mary MacAskival's windows.

For the first hour of this, three or four marksmen replied from the Old House. But they could have seen almost nothing to shoot at, and their risk of being struck by flying windowglass, if not by bullets, was considerable. The return fire slackened perceptibly in the second hour, and after that there came only infrequent shots from a single rifle on the second floor, as if to demonstrate that the defenders were still awake. Another rifleman on the roof of the old tower was driven below early in the game. What all this did to the nerves of Jackman's men — this sniping by an unknown body of enemies, who had not even made a formal demand for the surrender of the Old House — Logan could only surmise. The loss of Powert, too, coming on the heels of Carruthers' disappearance and the discovery of Lagg's body, must have made an impression.

Logan sent Robert MacAskival round to keep an eye on the back of the old tower, to make sure no one slipped out by the garden gate; the man hid himself behind an outcrop of rock and bided his time, leaving the shooting to the others. Accompanied by Malcolm Mor, Logan himself watched the main entrance from the plantation that stretched from the New House nearly to the rock of the Old House. And from Malcolm Mor, as they lay on their bellies under cover, that warm and fatal spring day, Logan pieced together a good deal more of the history of the recent troubles in Carnglass.

Poaching in Carnglass the shy twilight folk of Daldour took for a natural right. The older people of the Daldour MacAskivals, like Malcolm Mor, had been born in Carnglass and looked upon it as Eden; several of them, from time to time, right down to the coming of Dr. Jackman as Lady MacAskival's guest and master, had been servants at the Old House or on the two farms. Life in that windswept peatbog Daldour was precarious at best, and the dwindling race of the MacAskival crofters and fisherfolk had considered the killing of a sheep or a deer in Carnglass as no more than getting back a bit of their lost patrimony. That the sheep and the deer nominally belonged to old Lady MacAskival was little to them: she was a mere Lowlander, a MacAskival only by marriage — a bad marriage at that — and their enemy.

So whenever they dared — especially in the early morning or the evening, when the gamekeepers might be in their cottages — the Daldour men, for years, had landed in Carnglass under cover of darkness or fog, most commonly mooring their lobster boats in a great cave under the headland on which St. Merin's Chapel stood. The cave was known to very few; and though the ascent was precarious even for MacAskivals, still the descent was so risky as to daunt even the boldest hired gamekeeper, most of the time.

And it seemed that the taking ways of the Daldour MacAskivals, in recent years, had been winked at by The MacAskival herself, Miss Mary. For she had been a little girl on a barren island croft, and knew the rigors of the Daldour life. Besides, she was adored by, and adored, old Malcolm Mor, the chief man in Daldour, who for some years turned from fishing and poaching to being the gardener at the Old House, until Lagg gave him the sack. Malcolm Mor told her tales of the vanished glories of the MacAskivals, and of the witcheries of Carnglass, and showed the schoolgirl, during her Carnglass summers, the secrets of the Old House and of the Carnglass caves. What Malcolm Mor's kith and kin did, Mary MacAskival overlooked when overlooking was discreet. Now and again, on lonely rambles to the further reaches of the deserted island, Mary would meet with the furtive deer-stalkers and sheep-stealers from Daldour, who blended with gorse and heather and bracken when anyone else showed his face; and they would tip their caps, and offer the girl strange things washed up from the sea, such as "Mary's Nut," a Molucca bean, come by the Gulf Stream all the way from the Caribbean — for it brought good fortune, if worn on a chain round the neck.

As for Malcolm Mor, even after canny and tight-fisted Tam Lagg discharged the old pirate, Mary MacAskival kept in touch with him by a sepulchral line of communications. Their system was this: on her walks, Mary would slip a note into the receptacle in Sir Alastair's tomb at the chapel, and Malcolm would pick it up when next he climbed over the cliff-head from his boat moored in the cave far below. Malcolm Mor, though he was ashamed of the accomplishment as a decadent concession to modern civilization, could write a primitive English, and he would scrawl in his crabbed hand brief and respectful replies to The MacAskival's communications, giving news of his family to the lonely girl, and of how the fishing had gone. So long as she was permitted to ramble at will in Carnglass, Mary MacAskival could send letters to the outer world through this tomb postbox, for old Malcolm would post them in Loch Boisdale on the few occasions when the lobster boat crossed the rough waters to South Uist. Thus she had contrived to send her last message, the unsigned note, crumpled and water-stained, which reached Duncan MacAskival in Michigan. After that she had been too closely watched by Jackman and his men to make the attempt, and toward the end she had not been able to leave the Old House at all.

Before the coming of Jackman, and while Lady MacAskival retained some vigor and Lagg had the management of the island in his hands, two or three reasonably zealous gamekeepers made the poaching by the Daldour men a career of danger and daring, which they dared not attempt more than once a month, at best. The keepers' shotguns had wounded two or three of old Malcolm's sons and grandsons, and once the keepers almost had seized the boat moored in the cave.

But after Jackman's men replaced the old servants, the people at the

Old House scarcely visited the hinterland of Carnglass. Donley, nominally the new keeper, ordinarily stuck fairly close to his cottage near the Old House, and the regions round Dalcruach and St. Merin's Chapel, especially, became safe ground for the poachers. More and more of the queer, long-legged, long-necked, soft-fleeced sheep of Carnglass, and now and then a deer, were borne off triumphantly in the lobster boat to hungry Daldour.

Only one aspect of the new regime in Carnglass troubled the Daldour MacAskivals: Dr. Jackman and his ways. They spied upon him from the bracken, and sometimes crept close enough to perceive the curious spot in his forehead — which, among these misty folk who told legends over their peat fires and never saw the penny press and never heard a wireless, was at once recognized as the supernatural Third Eye of a Carnglass warlock. They saw the crew of town toughs he had gathered round him, too, and their suspicions grew. And Mary MacAskival rarely came forth from the Old House; at last she did not come at all, though they could glimpse her sometimes at the summit of the tower or in the little walled garden. For the people of Daldour, Miss Mary MacAskival was the symbol of their identity, and the hope of their salvation: for she had told old Malcolm, more than once that, when she was mistress in the island, she would bring back the MacAskivals to the farms and the crofts from which her aunt had expelled the last of them in 1914. The man with the third eye, they told one another, meant Mary MacAskival no good. They continued to watch. None of them were cowards, but they were shy of the law, for the law had expelled them from Carnglass; and besides, they were poachers, and in Daldour secret distillers of whiskey on which they paid no duty.

There were not many of them in Daldour, and few of the men were young. Of the men who should have been in their thirties, several had died during the war as naval or merchant seamen; and nearly all the rest, acquiring new tastes during their military service or unable to find places for themselves in the island, had gone off to Glasgow or America. The old and middle-aged MacAskival men in Daldour, for lack of young blood, withdrew more and more from the modern world, so far as modernity ever had touched them at all. They were shy of the law, shy of people from the mainland, shy of townsfolk, shy even of crofters and fishermen from the other islands.

A week ago, four MacAskivals, Malcolm Mor leading them, had put out in their boat, cloaked by fog and the setting of the sun, to land again at the foot of the cliffs below St. Merin's Chapel. Only the MacAskivals of Daldour could sail those treacherous waters in such weather. As they had been about to moor the boat in the cave under the cliff, Dumb Angus had taken Malcolm by the shoulder and pointed excitedly. Caught between two rocks near the cave's mouth, and awash in the ebbing tide, was the body of a man. They drew the corpse into their boat. It was Tam Lagg, who had been factor of Carnglass, and his corpse was terribly battered; he must have fallen from the cliffs. His hat they found a little later, lodged in a clump of ferns a few yards up the cliff.

"The sea casts its dead upon Carnglass," a proverb of the Island runs. Many men have drowned on the reefs in those waters, or have been caught in the currents and hurled against the cliffs in their boats; but it is a strange truth that the whirlpools and eddies in that merciless sea seem to bring up drowned men from miles round, and lodge what is left of them among the rocks or on the narrow beaches of the island called the Heap of Stones. The four men in the Daldour lobster boat had looked often upon drowned corpses; and they never failed to give those derelicts decent burial, that they themselves might one day need in their turn. The graveyard round the chapel in Carnglass, and the smaller graveyard by the bare beach in Daldour, were dotted with little wooden crosses marking the graves of seamen and soldiers from torpedoed transports that had gone down between Uist and Carnglass.

Bury Tam Lagg, then, the MacAskivals must. But they were afraid of the man with the third eye, at the Old House of Fear, who might lay the blame of this strange death upon them, since they had enjoyed an old vendetta with the factor of Carnglass; so they made no attempt to report the discovery of the body to the people in the Old House. They thought it best not to bury Lagg in Daldour, lest the body be found by strangers there and the MacAskivals be accused of foul play. So they wrapped Lagg in an old piece of canvas and, with great difficulty, got the body to the top of the cliffs, where they buried it in St. Merin's Chapel. On the grave they left a saucer of salt and nails, with a rowan twig atop it, to keep Lagg's wraith from wandering, should it be restless; for they thought it strange that a man so long familiar with Carnglass should fall to his death.

They were not sorry that Lagg was dead: they had detested him. And Dumb Angus, who dug the grave, took Lagg's clothes by way of compensation, and put them on, so that he looked for all the world like a stout scarecrow in those torn and stained garments. Malcolm Mor feared that this act might bring ill luck, but did not interfere, for they were accustomed to let poor Angus have his way in all reasonable things. And besides, Angus looked wonderfully comic in Lagg's clothes, and made the MacAskivals laugh, and so was happy. Many of the jokes of Dumb Angus were no stranger than this.

Logan learned these matters from Malcolm Mor there on the edge of the New House plantation of firs and aspens, while every ten minutes or so a rifle went off on the landward side of the Old House: Kenneth and John firing at the windows. Logan's men had no great supply of ammunition, but it was necessary to keep Jackman's people in constant uneasiness, so that the final rush on the Old House might have some chance for success. As Logan and Malcolm lay talking, Dumb Angus crawled up to join them, having finished his work of loading the farm cart and getting it into the New House plantations.

"Dumb Angus is simple," Malcolm Mor said, smiling at the burly man, "but also he is clever. He made the joke better by a doing all his own. Show Mr. Logan what it was you made, Angus."

Very cheerfully, Angus took off the injured green porkpie hat he had inherited from Thomas Lagg. Then he reached into a little leather bag that hung suspended from one of his shoulders, and drew out a thing seemingly shapeless. He pulled the thing all the way over his head, as if it had been a rubber mask, and clapped his hat back on. Then, gobbling unintelligibly, he looked Logan full in the face.

The effect was the more horrid because at first Logan could not recognize the origin of this dreadful mask Dumb Angus had assumed. It was not human, and yet had a semblance of humanity. It hung loosely on the head. It had nostrils, but no true nose, and a drooping dreadful mouth, and holes where its eye-sockets should be, with Dumb Angus's eyes glowing behind them. Angus wriggled with happiness at the effect he produced upon Logan. It was the face of one of the peculiar sheep of Carnglass, painstakingly skinned from the whole skull of the beast and made a loathsome mask by Angus MacAskival.

If this was what Rab had seen in the gloaming, with the dead Lagg's clothing on the heavy body below it, it was no wonder that dull-witted Rab had gone frantic with dread. "Poor Angus makes this on every Hallowe'en," Malcolm Mor was saying, "but this time he made it in the spring, because he had taken Mr. Lagg's clothes, and wished to make us laugh."

On the same evening that the MacAskivals buried Lagg, they had caught a glimpse of Donley skulking among boulders near Dalcruach, and they had hurried back to their boat and returned to Daldour, thinking that Donley might have seen them as well. But they had found they could not restrain their curiosity, and so sailed to Carnglass early the following morning, and from the bracken had seen Donley pursued by men from the Old House. They had debated among themselves whether they ought to reveal themselves to Donley and carry him off safely to Daldour; but they did not know the right and wrong of the feud between Donley and his pursuers, and also they had an ancient grudge against all gamekeepers; so they let the chase continue, only watching it from a fairly safe distance. Two or three times both Donley and the men from the Old House seemed to suspect that they were being tracked and watched, and to be correspondingly nervous. This tickled the fancy of the MacAskivals, especially Dumb Angus, and, without showing themselves distinctly, they dogged the Carnglass men like bogles.

These MacAskivals had seen Donley and Logan together on the shore, the night Donley had taken the dinghy. They had watched Logan for a part of the way as he followed the line of cliffs to the Old House. They had lingered near the searching parties that went out of the Old House in pursuit of Donley while Logan had been inside. And on one of these occasions, three of the MacAskivals — Robert, John, and Dumb Angus — had been imprudent. Carruthers and Rab, cautiously poking through the bracken near the ruined farmhouse where Lagg had been caught, had stumbled upon the Daldour men. Carruthers, in the lead a few yards, had found himself right in the midst of the three MacAskivals, and had shouted in astonishment to Rab. Instantly, Malcolm's two sons had dragged him down and begun to bind him, snatching away his gun; they were old hands at such fights with keepers. Rab had come running up, and Dumb Angus, wearing his sheep-mask and Lagg's clothes, had risen out of the bracken to confront him. Turning tail, the shocked and screaming Rab had run all the way back to the Old House, now and then firing into the bracken, but never hitting the delighted Angus, who had followed at a prudent distance. Logan knew the rest.

By this time, Malcolm Mor had become convinced that something was gravely wrong at the Old House, and was bent on helping Mary MacAskival if only he could determine what to do. He and the others took Carruthers back to Daldour in their boat, at the risk of a prosecution for kidnapping, and locked him in a byre, where they fed him well and asked him questions quite civilly; but the man was so terror-stricken that they could get nothing sensible from him. The day after the capture, the MacAskivals spent in Daldour asking these fruitless questions of their prisoner. Three hours before dawn on the present day, they had sailed once more toward Carnglass, with the intention of going straight up to the Old House, if necessary, and demanding to see Miss MacAskival.

Then, when almost under the northern headland of Carnglass, the MacAskivals had seen flaming against the night sky the fire which Logan and the girl had kindled. That beacon must be close by St. Merin's Chapel; and at the chapel Malcolm Mor had collected Mary Mac-Askival's letters, and the Cross of Carnglass had been the point of rendezvous when Malcolm, now and then, had met with the girl face to face. The odds were that this fire was a sign from Mary herself. Mooring the boat, the MacAskivals went warily up the cliff, reaching the summit just after dawn.

All the time, then, Logan realized, the girl must have entertained hope of the MacAskivals' coming. Why she had given him only hints, never speaking out, he could not say. In part, perhaps, she had hesitated to speak because she feared that, after all, nothing would come of this. And in part, likely enough, her pride as The MacAskival had prompted her to make the decision herself, without consulting even the man she loved. But most of all, Logan suspected, a certain lingering schoolgirl love of secrets had been at work. From the time Carruthers was missed and Rab ran shrieking into the Old House, Mary MacAskival must have been sure that the MacAskivals of Daldour were in the island. Her only chance of finding them hurriedly if they were in the island the next night, or of attracting their attention away in Daldour or out at sea, was to light the beacon, whatever the risk of attracting Jackman's notice. That act had saved Logan, but not yet Mary herself.

Well, Malcolm Mor and the others had got their heads over the summit of the sea-cliff just as Logan had been fighting with Jackman and his men at the door of the broch. The men of Daldour had crouched behind the tumbling drystone wall at the brink of the cliff, unnoticed by

Jackman's gang during the scuffle. In that moment, Malcolm had sent his nephew Kenneth scurrying stealthily round the kirkyard wall and down the brae, to create a diversion. And Kenneth, seeing two more of Jackman's men in the valley below, had fired on them to draw Jackman's party off at the time Logan and Mary MacAskival were held prisoners in the graveyard and the chapel. When Malcolm had watched the girl led away on a rope, he was ready to fight, law or no law. So he and the others had surrounded St. Merin's Chapel, stunned Powert, and discovered, to their astonishment, the betrothed of Mary MacAskival.

"Mr. Logan," said old Malcolm Mor, apparently quite confident of the issue of the fight that was coming, "when Carnglass is the lady's and yours to do with as you will, Dumb Angus would be a good gardener for you. It is a keeper that I myself would rather be. Dumb Angus is wise with animals and plants" — here he patted Angus approvingly on a burly shoulder — "and he would keep you always laughing."

Dumb Angus had put the animal-mask back into his bag. He also had slung over his shoulder, on a strap, the wooden spade that Logan had seen thrust into the earth in the chapel; Angus had forgotten it there when he dug Lagg's grave, but now had retrieved it as the only weapon ready to his hand. The wearing of such masks, Malcolm had remarked, was common among the few remaining MacAskival children, in Daldour and formerly in Carnglass, about Hallowe'en. Covered by that dead animal face, Angus had looked mightily like the picture of the Firgower on the ceiling of Jackman's study in the old tower. Whether this custom was some dim survival of a practice older than the Christian rites at the Cross of Carnglass, Logan could not tell. It might have been that the dead Pictish chiefs of Carnglass had worn such masks in heathen times, at ceremonies in the chamber within the rock beneath the Old House, or by the great broch on the cliff, the Pict's House. Be this as it might, the horrid false face that was Angus's delight, like so much else in Carnglass and Daldour, came as the last faint echo of an old Gaelic song.

All that long afternoon Logan lay in wait hidden by the fir trees, outwardly calm to hearten the MacAskivals, inwardly in torment at Mary MacAskival's danger within the Old House. As the sun began to set, he dispatched the boy to Kenneth and John, still sniping on the landward side of the Old House, with the word that they were to join him under the trees close to the gate of the Victorian block, the moment it was fairly dark.

When the light was almost gone, Malcolm and Angus harnessed the Barra horses — which had been tethered behind the New House — to the straw-loaded farm cart. The long ladder was carried to the edge of the plantation; the run with it to the first-story windows of the Victorian wing would be very risky, even if Logan's whole plan went smoothly, but the thing was possible. Climbing up the straw, the boy poured the tins of paraffin over the loaded cart. Angus crept under the cart, to urge on the horses so far as they dared use them. Kenneth, John, and Robert were to be stationed behind the cart. When the cart had been drawn to the edge of the trees, the horses must be cut out of their harness, and the men, keeping their heads down, must push the cart the remaining distance across naked rock to the gate of the Old House.

Malcolm Mor, Malcolm Gille, and Logan himself took position at the edge of the trees, prone, with guns ready to fire into the windows above the gate. These movements seem to have attracted attention from whomever was on duty at those windows, for one shot was fired from the Old House. But Logan's men did not reply, and as the dark descended, the great gray bulk of the castle of the MacAskivals lay still and ominous, with not one light showing. Now, Mary, Hugh Logan thought, I'll go to you. The MacAskivals beside him knew what they had to do, and none of them had shown much sign of fear.

The cart would be set afire against the gate, and Logan and the two Malcolms would blaze away at the adjacent windows, as if the assault were to come there. That was, after all, a venerable Highland and Island military device, especially beloved by Rob Roy; and though if the cart burned well it might char through the gate, there was no danger of the great house, which was all stone, catching fire. But Logan did not intend really to rush the gate. The true attack would be on the flank, around the corner: while the attention of the defenders was concentrated on the gate, Logan and his men would carry the ladder to the windows of the landward side and break in, if they could. And then, presumably, there would be shooting within the house; and the odds were not in Logan's favor. But this was the best he could do. It was all he could do for Mary MacAskival, and it might be too late.

Now the cart had been pulled by the horses to the edge of the trees. Someone inside the house must have heard the jingle of harness and the whinnying of horses, for a shot fired at a venture passed through the branches above their heads. "Now, Kenneth MacAskival, Angus!" Logan said. They cut the horses out of the harness, and four men commenced, shoving with all their strength, to run with the cart across the little plateau of rock to the door of the Old House. As yet, the straw was not alight, for they would need the advantage of darkness so long as they could keep it.

Into the quiet night came a hoarse shout of alarm from the house: Royall's voice, Logan thought in that instant. Two rifles fired at the cart, and then a third. Logan and his companions fired as fast as they could into the windows above the gate, and Logan heard a man scream. Still the cart ran on, and then crashed into the gate itself. The riflemen in the house were firing straight down into the cart now, and three of the MacAskivals ran out from behind it, leaping and rolling for the shelter of the trees; Logan and the Malcolms covered them with the best barrage they could contrive. That left Dumb Angus under the cart. Logan had given Angus careful instructions, through Malcolm Mor. Angus had been handed a length of charred rope, and a supply of matches. Crouching under the cart, he was to light the frayed rope, throw it into the straw, and run for it. For Angus was very quick of body. Now Logan saw a tiny flame spring up beneath the cart; it grew; still Angus lingered. Next a flaming coil was flung upon the dry straw, which caught. Two or three minutes passed, the firing from the house — were there only two rifles now? — sporadic. Then a mass of flame roared up from the cart, kindling the lumber among the straw also, and the light from it shown fiercely across the empty windows of the façade. Angus scooted from under the cart and down across the rock, Logan and the others firing to cover him; but there was no answer from the windows by the gate.

Now for the worst part. John MacAskival was useless, shot in one arm, and dazed with shock; Logan flung his gun to the boy, telling him to fire at will, for three minutes, into the windows by the gate; the boy was utterly delighted. The rest of them, seizing the ladder, swung out of the plantation toward the right, veered round the corner of the Victorian block, and set the ladder against a first-story window, Angus holding it firm at the bottom. Someone fired a shot from above them, but no one seemed to be hit.

Logan leaped up, the others behind him, and in two seconds was smashing out of the window-frame the shattered remnants of the plate glass, using his gun-butt, and expecting any moment to get a bullet in his chest. But the room within was silent. He flung himself into that room, and the four MacAskivals were at his heels. And now, indeed, there were gunshots; but they came from deep within the house, and no one opposed Logan as they burst into the corridor.

CHAPTER 15

Someone yelled in the corridor as Logan entered. But it was only a little paper-white man, dragging a rifle feebly as if it were a ball and chain: Tompkins. At sight of Logan, the butler dropped the rifle altogether, falling to his knees, and cried, "O Gawd! Mr. Logan, sir, don't 'urt me, don't! I'm your slaive, Mr. Logan! O Gawd, Jackman's mad, and they're murderin' heach hother below stairs."

Clutching at Logan's legs, Tompkins babbled on as to how he was only an honest butler and part-time burglar, unaccustomed to killing. Logan jerked him to his feet and forced him in the direction of the gunfire within the house. "In the billiard room, Mr. Logan, sir!"

Urging Tompkins before them, Logan and the MacAskivals ran to the end of the passage, rounded the corner to the left, and came to the door of the billiard room. Dead or dying, Royall lay face down across the threshold. Reckless, Logan strode over him. The big room, with its long windows looking toward the harbor, had three more men in it. One was Anderson, shot through the belly, writhing with his back against a leg of the billiard table. One was Rab, sprawled in the middle of the red Victorian carpet, a bullet hole between his eyes. The third was a man Logan had not seen before, lying on a sofa, his eyes bandaged, sightless, moaning in fear — Till, of course, the burned boatman. Where was Jackman? Two or three more shots, in quick succession, sounded within the house, somewhere below.

"Tompkins, tell me where Jackman's gone, or I'll finish you," Logan

188

said. The butler, stammering and choking, could only point toward the cellars below. Malcolm Mor ran in.

"In the room above the gate," Malcolm said — he slipped here into Gaelic, and with difficulty found his English again — "there is a man with long hair, like a gypsy, and he has been shot through the shoulder, and can do no harm." That would be Niven; and that left Jackman and Simmons and Ferd Caggia. And Mary, Mary.

"Tompkins," Logan said, taking the man by the throat, "show me where the crypt with the explosives is." The butler reeled in Logan's grip along the passage, and down a flight of stairs, and then pointed to an open doorway, from which stone steps led into shadows. Angus was behind Logan; the other MacAskivals were poking into the rooms.

Releasing Tompkins, Logan went down those steps to a little landing, and started to turn to the remaining flight that would take him to the crypt. A rifle cracked, and the bullet ricocheted from the wall. Logan flung himself back, nearly upsetting Angus.

"Jackman," Logan called down, "drop your gun and come up, and I'll promise you a trial. Otherwise we'll promise nothing."

But it was not Jackman that answered from the crypt. "Ah! Meester Logan, that is you?" The voice was rather faint.

"Who's there?"

"Fernando Caggia, your fren'. Meester Logan, you owe me a pardon for what I do."

"Drop your gun, Caggia, and come up."

A rifle was flung to the foot of the stairs. "Meester Logan, I cannot come up, for Dr. Jackman, he shoot me twice. But I save you."

Logan leaped down those stairs. A barricade of boxes and chairs stood before a little iron door, and between door and barricade lay Caggia, covered with blood. "In this room," Caggia said, trying to grin, "is the gelignite. Dr. Jackman, he try to reach it, but I, Fernando Caggia, do not let him. He shoot, I shoot, he shoot. I hit him once."

"Where is he?"

Caggia gave a weak shrug. "One minute ago, he runs."

Leaving Angus to watch the iron door, Logan dashed back up the stairs, and at the top Malcolm met him. "We cannot find that man," Malcolm said. "Will he be in the old tower?"

"Mary?"

"The door of the room of Lady MacAskival is locked, but there are people inside."

Now the boy had joined them, and as they ran into the Renaissance building, Kenneth and Robert came out of a passage and followed. They were at the door of the room which was hung with Spanish leather. Logan tried the knob fiercely; it would not turn. He smashed at the door with his rifle-butt, using all the strength that was in him, and it burst inward. Someone leaped for him. "Hugh, Hugh!" before them all, Mary MacAskival covered him with kisses.

Later, from Mary and Tompkins and Till, Logan got an understanding of what had passed within the Old House since morning. Wild with fury and bewilderment, Jackman had dragged her back to the Old House from the chapel, the three men with him as much afraid of their master as of the shadowy armed men whom Anderson had seen before the chapel. According to Anderson, there were twelve or fifteen of them, armed to the teeth. At the moment of his triumph, of his taking of Logan, suddenly Jackman had been undone. There was no way out.

Like a man in the grip of a nightmare, Jackman scarcely could speak. For a few moments, just after they had got back within the shelter of the Old House, a flash of his old power returned to him. Seeing Jackman bemused, Anderson and Rab and Caggia and Simmons made for the girl: they would beat out of her the truth about those armed men by the chapel. But turning on them, "like Rumpelstiltskin again," Jackman broke that mutiny, and hurried Mary MacAskival through the passages to her aunt's room. Thrusting her inside, he gave her a long look. "Well," Jackman said, passing his hand across his forehead, "I wish I had known you long ago. Now you are going to die. We all are about to die." He went out, locking the door behind him.

All that day, Mary knelt praying in the room hung with Spanish leather. Lady MacAskival, wasted beyond belief, lay motionless in her big bed, not seeming to hear the bullets striking the walls in the rooms across the gallery. Old Agnes sobbed in a corner. From the windows of this room, Mary could see only the harbor, with the burned yacht, and the empty sea beyond. And she prayed for Hugh Logan and for Carnglass.

It was Tompkins who told Logan much of what followed. Jackman, uncertain in movements and speech, as if half paralyzed, stationed Anderson, Rab, and Caggia in rooms on the landward side of the Old House, to reply to the sniping from the bracken. Simmons he put into the study, guarding the door of the old tower. He ordered Niven and Tompkins to duty in the rooms above the gate. For a time he went himself to the roof of the old tower and fired at the riflemen slinking among the distant rocks and heather and bracken; but all this was done as if he were sleep-walking. Then he went down to the billiard room, which was safe from gunfire, and sat at a table with his head in his hands. Royall tried to talk with him, but Jackman would not reply. Thereafter Royall conducted the defense, so far as there was any organized resistance.

Caggia, who had gone below stairs to get the men food, did not reappear. Rab and Anderson, driven from the landward rooms by the sniping, got at the rum. They drank it in the billiard room where Jackman sat, and cursed at Jackman, and Jackman did not answer. And the hours passed.

Royall, left alone in the landward rooms, had his cheek laid open by a splinter of glass, but he kept on firing. When the sniping ceased on that side, he went to the billiard room and again tried to rouse Jackman. At gun-point, Royall ordered Rab up to the room over the gate, to reinforce Niven and Tompkins. Anderson went below stairs, and Tompkins heard him crying defiantly to Royall — something about explosives.

When the attack on the gate came, and the cart was burning under the windows, Niven was hit by a bullet. In panic, Rab fled to the billiard room, screaming out, "The hoose! They're burnin' a' the hoose!" Royall and Anderson hurried in. This was told to Logan by the blinded boatman Till, who had lain helpless during the billiard-room fight.

"O aye, we're done!" Anderson roared. "Gie it ower, Jackman, we've had it!"

Then Jackman rose from his chair. "Royall," Jackman said, "keep the men here."

"Gude God," Till heard Anderson say, "the auld de'il's for the explosives! Jackman, damn ye, dinna open that door."

"Rab," cried Royall, "drop your gun." Shooting began then, Till cowering on the sofa. There must have been four or five shots, and after them running steps. Till could hear Anderson groaning and cursing. After that, Logan and his men came.

Edmund Jackman had made for the cellars and the gelignite. Down there, Ferd Caggia crouched behind a little barricade in front of the iron door; for Ferd had remembered Logan's words about Jackman's madness, and he, cat-like, had been watching Jackman. "Dr. Jackman," Caggia had said, "you don' blow me to hell." Jackman had fired at him promptly, and had hit him, but Caggia had fired back. After a minute's exchange of shots, the Maltese, wounded, still gripped his rifle behind the boxes and chairs. Jackman had leaped back up the stairs and was gone through the passages. Even his try for annihilation had failed.

❧

Simmons they found still in the study in the old tower, and took him without difficulty. But Dr. Edmund Jackman they did not find. The door to the garden was open, and Simmons said that from the window he had seen Jackman go over the garden wall, favoring one side as if he were slightly wounded.

"I think, Mr. Logan," Malcolm Mor said, "that because he is a clever man, he will have gone to look for our boat below the chapel."

Yes, he would have, Logan thought. In the course of the fight, Jackman must have recognized some of the attackers, perhaps old Malcolm; and, having seen them that morning near the chapel, he would guess that the boat was below those cliffs. That the wounded man could find his way down, Logan doubted. Yet so long as Jackman was at large, no one in Carnglass could be safe. The hound had become the fox now.

"Mary," Hugh Logan said, "I must be after him." She had an arm around him.

"I know the island best," she told him, "and from this night I am going to stay with you always, Hugh."

He looked down at her. "And who would guard the Old House, then, and do something for the men who've been shot, and put out the embers at the gate, and give the MacAskivals something to eat?"

Knowing that this was no moment for argument if Jackman were bound for the boat, Mary MacAskival looked proudly into Logan's eyes. "Then take Malcolm Mor," she said, "for he will know where to search, and I will send other men so soon as I can." The MacAskivals, having locked Simmons and Tompkins in a cellar, crowded round her deferentially for instructions. "Dr. Jackman shot my dog, Hugh, to hurt me. But do you come back to me, forever."

One last kiss, and then he left her in her strength and beauty, as the tears were starting down her cheeks. "Before sunrise, Mary girl, I'll be with you." Logan and Malcolm Mor went through the garden — for the great gate still was a charred and smoking hulk — and over the garden dyke below the old tower, the way that Jackman had gone, and they strode toward St. Merin's Chapel. Now and then Logan stumbled: he had been without sleep for twenty-four hours.

"If he can go down the cliffs," Malcolm Mor panted, "then the man with the third eye is more than man." Malcolm was a wonder: he had been on his feet nearly as long as Logan, and he was past seventy.

Beyond Cailleach, they flung themselves down for a brief rest. Their rifles seemed immensely heavy. Carnglass, in its nocturnal beauty, was at peace. The bleating of sheep, disturbed by the men, echoed from the heights where the chapel stood. "Malcolm Mor," Logan said, "I believe you think Jackman really is something not human."

"It would be well to have silver bullets for our guns." The old man muttered something in Gaelic. "But devil or not, he will have climbed up there." Malcolm Mor gestured toward the headland. They took up their guns again, and in less than an hour made out the shape of St. Merin's Chapel, and of the Pict's House, the Firgower's House, beyond it.

"If he has tried the path here," Malcolm said very low, "he will not reach the shore alive, not knowing the way, and having a bullet in him." Both Logan and Malcolm Mor moved slowly now; Logan doubted whether even Malcolm, while so weary, could descend this precipice, and he was certain that he himself could not. They climbed over the ruinous drystone wall close by the broch; from the dyke to the crumbling cliff-edge was less than a yard. A thousand feet and more below, the ocean heaved northward to the pole.

Then something rose from behind the dyke. Malcolm Mor tried to bring up his rifle, but a bullet struck the stock and sent the gun spinning from his hand. Logan had his rifle over his shoulder. He pulled at it desperately. And Jackman shot Hugh Logan.

Logan fell backward, and his head struck nothing at all, for he lay right on the cliff's edge, with only infinite space at the back of his head. There was a fierce pain in his right thigh, where the bullet from the little pistol had caught him. Edmund Jackman stepped over the broken dyke and stood only seven or eight feet distant from them, his left arm pressed hard against his side. The moonlight was full on Jackman's face, and the eyes were slits, and the face was that of a man lost in a nightmare, Malcolm Mor stood fixed by the spot where Logan lay.

"Young Askival and Old Askival," Jackman said. "I have the two of you." He pointed the pistol at Malcolm. "Put him over the edge, Old Askival."

Malcolm Mor bent slowly over Logan. He took Logan by the shoulders, and drew him back from that terrible cliff-lip, and propped him against a stone fallen from the dyke. Silent, Malcolm stared at Jackman. I am done, Logan thought, but if I can catch his ankle, Jackman may go over the edge with me, and Mary will be safe.

"Both of you at once, then," Jackman said dismally. "Old Askival and Young Askival." He took aim at Malcolm. Hugh Logan tried to hurl himself forward, but his smashed thighbone failed him.

There came, at that instant, a kind of gurgling cry, and a sound of running, of something hurrying right along the cliff's edge, at Jackman's back. Edmund Jackman turned his head. Malcolm and Logan and Jackman saw all at once the thing that was coming.

It was a burly man in tattered corduroy breeches, a long green jacket, and a yellow waistcoat, with a porkpie hat on his head, his arms flapping as he ran. He mouthed as he came, but what noise he uttered was not speech. And his face was a dead mask, and not human. The thing made straight for Jackman.

Mary had sent Angus after Logan. And, with the heroism of children and simpletons, Angus sought to put his body between Logan and his enemy.

But what Edmund Jackman saw in that dreadful masked figure, Logan knew: the shape of his victim, and the face of his nightmare horror. With a moan, Jackman turned to run. He took one bound in that high place, and upon the brink the heather gave beneath him; and where Lagg had gone down, there Jackman fell.

Though they say that the ocean yields up all its dead upon the skerries of Carnglass, no man found Jackman after. As from the cliff-head at Gadara, the unclean spirit was cast into the sea. And Logan, with Malcolm Mor kneeling beside him and Dumb Angus shivering with fright against the dyke, heard no sound from below but the suck of the tide upon the weary stones.